3099

D1308123

DOGGONE IT

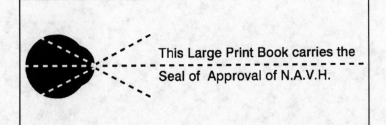

This Large Print Book carries the
Seal of Approval of N.A.V.H.

A DREAMWALKER MYSTERY

DOGGONE IT

MAGGIE TOUSSAINT

THORNDIKE PRESS
A part of Gale, Cengage Learning

GALE
CENGAGE Learning·

Farmington Hills, Mich • San Francisco • New York • Waterville, Maine
Meriden, Conn • Mason, Ohio • Chicago

GALE
CENGAGE Learning®

LIBRARY OF CONGRESS CATALOGING-IN-PUBLICATION DATA

Names: Toussaint, Maggie, author.
Title: Doggone it / by Maggie Toussaint.
Description: Large print edition. | Waterville, Maine : Thorndike Press, 2016. | Series: A dreamwalker mystery ; #3 | Series: Thorndike Press large print clean reads
Identifiers: LCCN 2016043851| ISBN 9781410496287 (hardcover) | ISBN 1410496287 (hardcover)
Subjects: LCSH: Women private investigators—Fiction. | Murder—Investigation—Fiction. | Psychic ability—Fiction. | Psychics—Fiction. | Large type books. | Paranormal fiction. | GSAFD: Mystery fiction.
Classification: LCC PS3620.O89 D64 2016b | DDC 813/.6—dc23
LC record available at https://lccn.loc.gov/2016043851

Published in 2017 by arrangement with Maggie Toussaint

Printed in Mexico
1 2 3 4 5 6 7 21 20 19 18 17

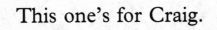

This one's for Craig.

ACKNOWLEDGMENTS

Critique partner Polly Iyer helped sharpen this manuscript. A tip of the hat to my awesome Five Star team of Deni Dietz, Alice Duncan, and Tiffany Schofield. Thanks for all you do to make my books shine. Thanks also to Deborah Holt, a patron of the Wetumpka, Alabama, Public Library, who won the right to a character name in this story.

CHAPTER 1

Spending twilight at June's Folly was nuts. This swamp was bad news to folks like me. I wanted my friend to turn her car around and get the heck out of here. Instead, I steeled my nerves for the coming ordeal.

Charlotte stopped the car, her high beams illuminating a two-story house in dire need of painting. Windows were broken. The door gaped open. A rocking chair lay on its side on the porch. Some wooden chairs had been busted up.

"Wow. Someone's torn this place up. Is that damage new or has it been like this?"

"I don't know about the house, but the holes in the yard look freshly dug," Charlotte said. "It looks like the pirate treasure vandals have struck again."

"I hate this." And I did. I hated being out here. I hated that such a beautiful house was going to ruin. I hated that vandals were digging up half the county hoping to strike it rich.

"Those movie people ought to be strung up by their heels."

My stomach churned with anxiety. I just wanted Charlotte to do her reporter thing so that we could leave this place. Air huffed out of my lungs. "Like that's going to happen. Everyone thinks Ford Morrison and his crew walk on water with all the money they're spending in the county."

"Boosting the economy is one thing, but all this hype about our alleged missing pirate treasure has folks all stirred up. My boss won't let me write about the vandalized lawns anymore because we've had over thirty yards documented with holes like this. What a shame."

Charlotte was in a tight race with another reporter to be top dog at our weekly paper. She was better than the other guy, but the competition had the boss's ear. Unless we had another big case, my friend would be stuck covering her regular beat.

Fortunately, she'd thought up this cool ghost story series to keep her name on the front page. "Not even the spooky legends about this place were enough to keep it off the vandals' radar. I wonder what Horace June was thinking, building his home way out here in the swamp."

"Must've been a loner. No, that's not right. I read he had a family."

"Maybe his in-laws tried to snatch his kid."

Charlotte made a tsking sound. "Don't go projecting your troubles on Mr. June. I'm sure he had plenty of troubles of his own."

"Speaking of troubles, we should phone this in."

"Not yet! We're here to find ghosts, and those clowns who work for the sheriff might scare them away. We need to stay focused. I saved June's Folly for last because of all the ghost stories. I'm sure this place is haunted." Charlotte glanced my way. "Are you sensing something already, Baxley? You look like you've seen a ghost."

I wasn't sensing anything. I'd shielded my extra senses as soon as we turned down the driveway. "I haven't set foot on this swampland since the time we snuck out here in high school, and I got so sick my father had to come get me."

Charlotte let go of the steering wheel and turned to face me. "I remember. You said you had a stomach bug."

"I wasn't sick, at least not in the usual way." I managed a half smile at her reproachful look. "Something out here short-circuited my senses. My father warned me the same thing would happen if I came out to this place again."

Charlotte shook her head. "I don't get you, Baxley Powell. If this place is toxic to dreamwalkers, why'd you come with me tonight?"

"Because."

Charlotte snickered. "Because what?"

I stared at the fluid headlight beams and motley sand piles. Charlotte couldn't begin to understand the things I'd seen, the beings I'd encountered. "Because I'm a grown-up. Because I've learned how to be a dreamwalker, and I have the streak of white hair to prove it. And because I won't let fear defeat me."

"That's my girl."

I faced her, serious as a heart attack. "I wouldn't do this for just anybody."

Her expression grew pensive in the faint dash lights. "Surely you don't believe the scary rumors about this place? Somebody made them up."

"No doubt, but there's often a little truth behind a legend."

Charlotte turned off the engine, cut off the lights, and the yard plunged into darkness. "That's why I asked you to come along. You've got an *in* with the spirit world.

Help me figure out the real story of June's Folly. That's what my readers are longing for — the truth."

My reporter friend was on the last column of her haunted house series for *The Marion Observer.* She'd recounted every ghost story ever told about Sinclair County and gotten positive feedback from the community. There was even talk from the tourism people of them asking Charlotte to run a weekend ghost tour, complete with minibus, loudspeakers, and a nifty headset microphone.

"I'm the wrong kind of detector for the information you need. I talk to dead people who've crossed over. Earthbound spirits are different critters altogether. You need a medium for that."

"I don't have a medium." Charlotte opened her door and started gathering her gear from the back seat. "I've got a best friend who talks to dead people. Just change your frequency or something. I need the lowdown on the ghost out here."

The warm, muggy air from outside quickly overpowered the cooler air from the car. With reluctance, I unsnapped my seat belt. "If only it were so easy. I would have dialed in normal years ago."

"Come on, be a sport. Let me know which

ghost rumor is correct. Is the ghost of June's Folly a French-speaking giant with a pet alligator or a boatload of drowned slaves shaking their chains of death?"

Charlotte made it sound so easy. Run a little extrasensory recon, chat up the ghost, and then go home under my own power. "I'm accompanying you because you are my best friend, but I don't speak ghost. Sometimes I can make contact with a spirit by touching an item that belonged to a dead person. Most times spirits come to me in my dreams. I'm not planning on napping out here in swamp world." I clicked on my flashlight and stared into the darkness. "I hope I don't break my ankle."

She joined me in front of the warm car. She'd slung a camera around her neck, tucked a pad of paper under her arm, stashed a pen behind her ear, and carried a jumbo flashlight. "Quit bellyaching. I have to turn this story in tomorrow. You feeling anything yet?"

"I'm feeling stupid for agreeing to play ghost detective with you, but I didn't want you out here alone at night."

"Thanks. I appreciate the moral support."

We picked our way through the obstacle course of dirt piles and holes, navigating toward the sagging house. The family that owned June's Folly hadn't resided in Sinclair County for forty years. Consequently, the stick-built cypress house had seen better days. The historical society had tried to get it donated to the county, but the present-day heirs were adamant. The house wasn't for sale or donation.

I stopped and peered in a dirt hole. "Do you think they found anything?"

"No way." Charlotte's breath came out in little huffs, whether from the humidity, her plus-size weight, or the lure of a good yarn, I couldn't tell. "People have been combing this property with metal detectors for years. Trust me. If a pirate's horde of gold were buried here, it would have been discovered long ago."

As someone who lived from paycheck to paycheck, the likelihood of finding buried treasure seemed smaller than winning the Georgia lottery. "I can't imagine a pirate leaving behind his gold."

My friend shrugged. "He couldn't stash it in the bank."

"Good point." The bottom board was torn off the steps, and another hole excavated at the foot of the stairs. This disregard for private property upset me. "I have to call the cops."

"Not until we're finished. Unless . . ."

Charlotte glanced around furtively. "Unless you think the diggers are still here, and we're in danger."

"No need to whisper. If someone's here, they would've heard the car. And if they somehow missed that, they would've heard us talking."

"Gotcha. We scared them off. Or the ghost did. I wonder if they planned to rip up the floorboards and dig under the house."

I stared at her, alarmed. "We're going in the house? Count me out. I didn't sign on for breaking and entering. I can't do that. I'll lose my job as a police consultant."

Charlotte shone her light on the weathered facade. "No breaking required. The front door is open."

I added my beam to hers. Sure enough, the paneled door with the centrally located doorknob gaped on its hinges. "Dang. You're right. Still, this place belongs to someone. We don't have the right to stroll inside. We'll be trespassing."

"Just a peek inside. If the ghost is here, it should repel us at the door, or so goes the legend. Speaking of ghosts, is anyone talking to you? Maybe shaking some chains or speaking in French?"

"All I'm hearing is a desperate reporter." Cautiously, I touched the banister to see if

16

it was secure. It was. I used the railing for support as I carefully trod the rotten, squeaking steps. Drifts of thickened air stirred my hair and sighed through the pines.

Charlotte halted. "You hear that?"

Her voice sounded too high. "The wind?"

"Chains clanking. And a sad, mournful song in another language."

"Truly?" I heard nothing of the sort. Was Charlotte's imagination getting away from her? Was there a ghost?

Charlotte sank to the porch decking, her gear clunking as she landed heavily on her rear. "I, uh, need a minute."

"Okay." I sat on the top step beside her. Other than feeling dread and a shiver against the elements, I seemed normal with no sign of sensory overload. I marveled that I was still functioning. A little maturity and a little extrasensory training and I had a whole new perspective on this place.

"Don't you feel it?" My friend's teeth chattered. "I'm freezing."

I estimated it was nearly eighty degrees and humid enough for spiders to dance on the air. Puzzled, I touched Charlotte's arm. Her skin felt cold to the touch. Ordinarily, Charlotte would be griping about the heat and the humidity. Something was crossing her wires.

"Look at you! Working those earlier ghost sites must have unleashed a latent talent." I gazed at her with frank admiration. "You're the ghost detector tonight, Char. I'm not picking up anything."

"Are you looking?"

She had me there. "Nope. I don't want to have to call my father to come get me again. That would be embarrassing."

"I thought you were doing this to prove yourself as a bad-ass dreamwalker."

"My main thought is that you have your answer to the ghost question. Chains and mournful singing support the drowned slave legend. Time to go home."

"There's more to this, I know it," she insisted. "Help me prove it. You can handle whatever it is I'm feeling. I haven't passed out or anything."

Like that would reassure me. But there was a certain logic to her claim. I was being a wimp by keeping my senses and my body shielded.

Charlotte had called me out. Worse, she was right. Just because I never heard ghosts before was no reason not to listen for this one.

My talents and my shielding abilities were much more finely tuned now. I'd been talking to the dead for months. I didn't have to let childhood fears dictate my actions. And, the sooner I gave Charlotte what she wanted, the sooner we could go home.

With that, I closed my eyes and opened my senses to the night. Immediately, I plunged into a freezing fog bank.

CHAPTER 2

"Baxley! Wake up! You better not be dead, you hear me?"

Charlotte's insistent demands added to the din inside my head. Wind roared. Fog boiled like a kettle on the stove. A crowd of people were talking. Most of the conversation I couldn't make out, but it sounded like a dozen radio stations were coming through on the same channel.

Simultaneously, every hair on my body electrified. I felt the steady pressure of something otherworldly on my jeans. Chilled skin, bones, and joints rendered me immobile. Cold. I was so cold.

"Baxley!" Charlotte yelled, shining her flashlight in my face. "I know you're in there. Your eyes are moving back and forth, and you're freaking me out. Whatever it is you are seeing or sensing, snap out of it. I didn't mean for this to happen. Fight back, darn you. Fight back."

Her words jabbed through my iced thoughts, needle sharp, but I couldn't speak, couldn't do anything.

Something with red eyes advanced through the fog. It was hip high, as tall as a child. Not low enough to be an alligator. Or a small dog. But it might be a large dog. A mastiff or a Great Dane. It loomed over me, striking terror in my gut.

"Go away," I shouted into the fog. "Begone!"

The eyes remained. Watching. I tried to transition through this inhospitable corridor to the next world, but couldn't. I tried to wake up. Couldn't.

"I renounce you, evil spirit," I shouted. "You have no power over me."

The beady red eyes glowed brighter.

Would it pounce on me?

I needed to get out of here. What was this foggy place? What held me fast?

Strangers shouted in my head. Maddening. I wished I could clamp my hands over my ears. I couldn't take much more of this chaos. I needed help. "Charlotte!" I tried to thrash, to pinch myself, but my hands went right through my body.

Not a good sign.

I couldn't stand the chill of this place. The longer I stayed in this temporal zone, the less I was myself.

I needed help. My father and daughter were connected to me in the spirit world. "Daddy! Larissa! Can you hear me? I'm in trouble. Get Mom. I need your help."

The fog thickened like day-old grits. Something bumped against me, knocking me down.

I needed immediate help. Someone who could kick spirit butt. Rose. But Rose didn't do anything for nothing. Was I desperate enough to contact a demon?

"The rose tattoo on your hand is glowing," Charlotte yelped. "It's possessed or something. What's going on in your head? Wake up, Baxley. There's no way I can carry you to the car. To hell with the ghost feature for the paper. I don't want to be here anymore."

My tattoo. I bore the mark of an entity from the spirit realm. Hope flared. "Rose?" I whirled in the murk, unable to get my bearings, knowing this wasn't what I saw during my dreamwalks. I was trapped in limbo. "Rose, are you here?"

Rose wavered before me, tall and thin with red eyes. Her wings weren't visible, so she was still working undercover in demon mode.

"You should not be here," Rose said.

Her words were as clear as if we were having a conversation in my kitchen. Must be a direct link between us. "I'm stuck between worlds. Can you help me?"

"We're connected in both worlds and everywhere in between."

Her admission added to the confusion in my head. "I didn't realize, but I'm glad to see you. How did you find me?"

"You made a pact with me. You're mine now, Baxley Powell."

"What are you going to do with me?" I wished I could retract my question as soon as I uttered it. Ignorance was bliss in my case. It was scary enough knowing that angels could pretend to be demons. It was super scary finding out that angels could hurt people.

"Your fate is already sealed, have no doubt of that."

Cryptic words when I needed reassurance. "Am I dying? If so, I'm not ready to go yet. I've got a daughter to raise."

"An earthbound spirit is tormenting you. I believe you humans call this void hell on earth."

"Can you get me out of here?"

"What's it worth to you?" There was always a cost. Rose wasn't a friend. She had all kinds of powers, and she was looking for a foothold in our world. I needed to be sharp, or I could be in big trouble. "I can't grant you an open favor. My father warned me about the consequences of that."

"Did he? How unfortunate. Hmm. How about an hour of your life instead?"

I recoiled at her suggestion. "What other options do I have?"

"You could grant me permission to take an hour of a loved one's life."

"Never."

"Then you're stuck. Make up your mind. I've got places to go, spirits to terrorize, souls to steal."

The idea of being totally out of control of my actions scared me. "There has to be another way. What if you remove this earth-bound spirit?"

"You'd commit an unknown spirit to my eternal dominion?"

That didn't sound right either. "Yes. I mean no. Let's revisit the favor option."

"It's off the table. An hour of your life in exchange for the secret to break free of this earthbound spirit."

"When will you take the hour? Will my friends and family know? Will you embarrass me? Would you hurt someone, and I'd be blamed?"

24

"I don't answer questions. Deal or no deal?"

Rose started fading. I panicked. "I'll do it. You may have an hour of my life."

She glowed. "Excellent."

My skin burned. I found it difficult to breathe. Rose thinned before my eyes. "Wait. You didn't tell me how to get out of here."

"The ghost dog's name is Oliver."

With that, Rose vanished.

Charlotte slapped my face, hard, and I gasped in a gulp of the dense fog. It burned all the way down. My vision blurred.

A dog did this to me? I tried to gather my wits, but all I could think of was jumping back into my skin. I called the dog's name. The red eyes appeared again.

It was a dog. And being a petsitter, I knew a thing or two about dogs. I tapped my metaphorical leg and called the dog again. The glowing eyes edged a little closer, but not near enough for me to grab. I heard the sound of a chain rattling.

Encouraged, I squatted down and called the dog again, this time in the voice I reserved for small children. It trotted over, a jet black Great Dane dragging a heavy chain from its collar.

I held my hand out, and the dog sniffed

it. The fog lessened. I tentatively petted the beast. His cold fur warmed under my touch. He made little noises of comfort as I scratched under his chin and ears. He lay down and rolled over, exposing his belly for me to rub.

"You're a good dog, Oliver. Such a good dog." As I scratched him and he made pleased doggie moans, I realized his neck was all torn up. I carefully undid the wire holding the heavy chain around his neck.

Oliver rolled to his feet and shook, his tongue laving my hands and face. "That's a good boy."

The fog thinned to nothing. I saw Charlotte staring down at me. The world twisted and bent, and then I opened my eyes to my reality.

"Don't you ever do that to me again," Charlotte said, panning her flashlight over my length. "You scared me to within an inch of my life."

I'd made it back to the land of the living. I struggled to sit up, but my limbs felt like they were being poked with pins and needles. "You owe me big for this."

"Thank God you're all right."

"God had nothing to do with it. A friend from the Other Side helped me get back.

26

Otherwise, I'd still be stuck in the frigid void."

"Glad you're okay, but I'm dying to know. Did a pirate ghost grab you?"

I snorted and drooled a bit. Tried to wipe it away from my chin. Couldn't. "Why'd I let you talk me into this?"

"The suspense is killing me. Dish."

"You're not concerned for my health and well-being?"

"Nope. The chill is gone from the air, and I no longer feel like I'm going to vomit. You did something to the ghost. I hope you didn't banish it permanently."

Now that I'd made friends with Oliver, I doubted he was going anywhere. "The ghost isn't a cursing Frenchman, an angry giant, a marauding alligator, or a horde of suicidal slaves."

Charlotte's hopeful expression fled. "We have a different ghost? How come nobody got it right?"

"The ghost I encountered is a dog."

"A dog? How's that possible?"

I tried to sit up again and was successful this time. I massaged the cold from my joints, but I couldn't stop trembling inside. "Animals have spirits too."

"Not saying they don't, but why would an animal haunt this place?"

"He didn't say because he can't speak. He's a dog, Char."

"You must be making this up. To protect me or something. I'm not buying it."

I managed a small shrug. "You wanted the truth."

"I wanted something to entice people out here. To boost tourism. How's a ghost dog gonna do that?"

"Until this yard gets straightened out, nobody should venture out here. I need to call the cops."

"Don't bother. I tried already. Cell phone wouldn't work."

"Try again."

She pulled her phone from her pocket, the lighted display brightening the air around her hand. "Huh. How'd that happen?"

"I guess the ghost dog generated so much energy it blocked the cell signal."

"I never heard of such a thing."

"Doesn't make it impossible." Speaking of signals, I needed to amend the telepathic one I'd sent to my father and daughter. I quickly sent out a mental pulse to my family. *I'm okay.* Since neither of them could do more than receive a telepathic message, I didn't expect an answer.

Instead, I fumbled in my pocket for my

phone and called the sheriff. "Gotta problem out at June's Folly. Looks like vandalism and B&E."

"No corpses? I'm shocked," the sheriff said.

"Even so, Virg and Ronnie should investigate the incident, and the property owners should be notified of the damage."

"You're sounding mighty feisty this evening. Maybe I'll head out there instead."

"We agreed to knock off the innuendoes."

"A tiger can't change his stripes."

"Not interested, and get over yourself. You going to tend to this, Wayne, or should I appeal to a higher power?"

He snickered. "I'm the boss. You can't go over my head."

"I have your wife on speed dial."

The line went dead for a long moment. "Don't move. I'll send Virg and Ronnie right out there."

CHAPTER 3

The sheriff's go-to guys were not my favorite people. A few months ago, Virg knocked me out with a Taser. The jolt short-circuited everything, sending me on a terrifying out-of-control dreamwalk. Since then the deputy and I were on high alert in each other's company. He seemed to think I'd zap him with my mad woo-woo powers, while I was never sure if he'd whip out his Taser.

While we waited for the deputies to arrive, we used pages from Charlotte's notebook to write up our statements. I'd learned a thing or two about police work since I'd hired on as a police consultant.

The deputies rolled up, lights flashing but sirens off. I opened the door of Charlotte's shoebox-sized sedan and filled them in.

"Looka there," Virg said from the safety of his vehicle. A drip of cocktail sauce dotted the front of his tan Class A uniform. "Somebody's done crawled all over this place and ruint it."

"It's those movie people," Ronnie added with a glower. His fierce expression was at odds with his rounded face and genial personality. "They brung this down on us. Nobody cared about lost pirate treasure until Ford Morrison's film crew made such a big deal out of it. Now half the county looks like this. It ain't right."

"I hear ya," I said, somewhat startled to share his opinion. "We need to stop these outsiders from digging everywhere."

"Only way to do that is to find the treasure," Virg said, emerging from his cruiser. He shone his flashlight across the lawn. "Looks like it ain't here."

Charlotte joined me. "Vandalism is bad for tourism. Can't you catch the clowns who do this?"

"Take a gander," Ronnie said, a wad of tobacco bulging from his lip. "They's nobody here. I can't catch 'em if I don't know what they look like. We'll write this up, but it'll be a cold case from the start. We got no leads. I'll bet you ladies already disturbed my crime scene."

My gaze went to the Taser, just in case Mister Itchy Trigger Finger decided to make an example of us.

"We walked in a straight line from here to

31

the porch and back," Charlotte said, hands on her hips. "Can't you find a shoe print or something?"

"You got us confused with TV show cops," Virg said. "We don't print shoes. We do fingers. That's it."

The joys of life in the sticks. We had no crime lab, and samples we sent out for analyses cost the department big money and took weeks, if we were lucky, to get results.

"Right. Well, there might be fingerprints on the doorknob. We didn't touch it."

"The doorknob. On the front door." Ronnie backpedaled toward the police cruiser, horror etched on his face. "Nobody's been able to step foot inside that place for decades. Everybody knows a ghost guards that door."

"Don't be a wuss. Baxley says the ghost is a dog." Charlotte clamped her hand over her mouth. "Oops. So much for breaking the news in the paper."

"Then Baxley can carry herself up there and look for prints. I ain't stepping foot on that porch until daylight comes."

In my down time as a police consultant, I'd been learning techniques like lifting fingerprints off surfaces. But I wasn't feeling at all charitable toward Virg and Ronnie. They were getting paid good money as deputies, and they were supposed to collect evidence. My cross-training was for staff shortages. Clearly, sheriff's personnel were on the job. I was not here in an official capacity.

"Do your job," I grumbled. Bone-deep weariness had settled in, sharpening my tongue and fraying my patience. "I've had enough swamp for one night. I'm outta here."

"Can't leave yet." Virg shot me an ugly smile. "Need your signed statements."

I grabbed the papers from the dash. "Ahead of you. All the *i*'s dotted and *t*'s crossed."

"Wouldja look at that," Ronnie said, fingering the one-page statements with a joyous smile. "All we gotta do now is tape this place off and snap a few pictures. Then we can get back to patrolling."

Charlotte and I hopped into her Jetta and left. "Those guys wouldn't know evidence if it socked them between the eyes," Charlotte said once we reached the highway.

My mood brightened with each tire revolution away from that swamp. I'd had my run-ins with the boys, but I felt a smidge of loyalty toward the sheriff's department. Thanks to them, I still had a roof over my head. "They're not so bad. They came promptly, and they are trained to follow procedure."

"You surprise me, Bax. Thought you had little use for frip and frap."

"Sometimes I surprise myself."

Lights blazed from my parents' place deep in the woods. Unlike June's Folly, these woods were high ground and smelled like home. Wind chimes tinkled, and the drone of the Weather Channel blotted out any conversations taking place inside.

"You want to join us for dinner?" I asked. My mom always had a soup pot simmering, and my dad's homemade bread bordered on legendary.

"Sure, but I can't stay long. I've gotta write up a story about the ghostly hound of June's Folly."

Before I opened my door, Larissa, Mom, and Dad spilled out of the house. My daughter raced around the side of the car and hugged the daylights out of me. "You're okay," she said.

I nuzzled her soft hair. "I'm okay."

"We were worried," Mom said, her brow furrowed. "Larissa and Tab sensed your distress, but you made it back safe and sound before we could figure out where you were."

34

"You could say that," I wrapped my arms around my daughter and held her close. She smelled delightfully woodsy with undertones of fresh paint and cookies. "Things didn't go as planned, but when was the last time that happened?"

"I have dinner ready," Mom said. "You girls can tell us all about it."

"Not much to tell," I said, moving cautiously toward the house with Larissa standing on my feet. She got clingy sometimes, so we pretended to slow dance until she felt at ease. Having only one parent was hard on a kid. Especially when the other parent was missing and presumed dead.

I braced for the certain firestorm of parental disapproval. "We went out to June's Folly to finish up Charlotte's haunted house series."

Dad's mouth gaped. He shook his head, his gaze clouding. "It isn't safe there."

"The house is falling down, and the yard's an accident waiting to happen, but we made it out in one piece. Two pieces, because there were two of us."

"I wish you hadn't gone out there," Dad said. "Swamps are dead zones for people like us. You're lucky to walk out of there on your own power, Baxley. What gives? How many times have I told you to avoid

35

June's Folly?"

I didn't appreciate his chiding tone, but I'd earned his censure by going out there. "Charlotte asked me to go with her on a newspaper assignment. She didn't trust anybody else to come along."

Charlotte cleared her throat. "I didn't mean for anything to happen. Baxley didn't tell me the real reason she'd had to call you all those years ago when we went out there. I am so sorry."

My mom patted Charlotte's rounded shoulder. "You're fine, dear. Don't fret."

"Where'd you go, Mom? One minute I felt you in my head, and the next you were gone," Larissa said.

The tattoo on my hand heated, and I hid it under the table, ashamed of my painted skin. My father had been the dreamwalker for most of my life, and he didn't sport a single tattoo. He'd never colored outside the lines. I couldn't mention my deal with Rose to anyone. I couldn't reveal the price I'd paid to return to the real world.

But I owed my daughter an answer. "Like Pap says, the energy deficit out there throws people like us for a loop. I checked out for a bit, but I'm back and glad to be with my family. And I'm very sorry to have worried you."

"Looks like you could do with a pick-me-up." Mom handed me a fistful of fresh crystals. The moldavites and amethysts hummed in my palm, and the rose tattoo cooled down.

My fingers closed around them, and I felt a profound sense of peace. Tension ebbed from my shoulders. "Thanks. You always know how to help."

The kitchen table was set for five, with steaming soup bowls set all around. Another tip of the hat to Mom. She claimed she wasn't psychic, but she had her ways of knowing things. The phone rang, and Mom shrugged. "They'll call back."

And because it was her house and because she chose not to answer the phone, none of us made a move toward it. That's how things rolled in the Nesbitt household. Larissa and I lived a few miles down the road, in a place I'd inherited from my maternal grandmother, but my parents' place had a special healing quality. Not just for me. People from all over the county came to my mom for her tea and soup.

As far as I knew, crystal recharging was something she did only for me and my father. It struck me that there might be a lot I didn't know about my mother. Not that she hid things from me, more that she

37

focused her entire being on helping family and friends.

"Your soup smells divine," Charlotte said as she found her place at the table.

Anxious to change the subject, I accepted the gambit. "Smells great and I know it will taste even better. Thanks for including us."

That earned me a sharp look from mom. "Of course I included you. Did you think I'd turn you away like a stray? No one's ever been turned away from my door or my table."

My daughter cocked her head, mischief dancing in her emerald green eyes. "No one? What if an entire army showed up? Would you feed everybody?"

"I would feed them."

"What about two armies?"

"I'd feed them too."

"How?" Larissa spooned up another bite of vegetable barley soup.

"With my two hands. That's how. If I couldn't meet the challenge, I'd ask a friend for help."

Everything seemed cut and dried in my mother's daily life. She didn't get stuck between worlds or have to pay a high price for her bad decisions. She didn't have an outstanding IOU with a demon. She didn't harbor any fear about when or how that debt would be paid.

"Baxley?" Mom asked. "You all right?"

I jolted out of my musings. "Fine, why?"

"Your dad just said he met the movie star man today. Ford Morrison? Aren't you impressed?"

I glanced over, and my father grinned like a kid with a pocket full of change. I could take the high road and keep my concerns to myself, but bitterness crept into my tone. "They got to you?"

Dad sobered. "Not sure what you mean by that. Reed Tyler from the Tourism Office brought him by my office. Reed and Ford were completing each other's sentences like they'd known each other forever."

"Those movie people are riling folks up," I said. It was Reed's job to befriend people who brought employment opportunities and spending to the county, but I didn't have to suck up to the outsiders. "Tell 'em, Char."

Charlotte's chunky rhinestone-faced watch caught the light and nearly blinded me as she gestured with her hands. "The newspaper doesn't cover the police scanner calls anymore for dug-up yards, but we keep a running tally for each newspaper edition. There've been eight calls already this week, and June's Folly will make nine. This is the highest activity ever."

"This Ford fella, he's all apologetic about the mess," my father said. "Swears his guys had nothing to do with it."

My aging-hippie parents were so trusting and gullible. If I told them gold would rain from the sky at midnight, would they believe me? "He can deny it all he wants, but we didn't have these vandalism problems until Ford Morrison got the brilliant idea to make a movie about our pirate treasure legend. Now every Tomasina, Dixie, and Henrietta with a shovel are running around and digging up the county. I wish the movie crowd would fixate on a new town with another legend. I wish they'd pack up and head home."

Dad leaned back in his chair and gave me a considering look. "That's unfortunate."

The blaze in my power-whitened hair tingled at the roots. I absently massaged my scalp, dead-certain I wouldn't like what was coming next. "Oh?"

"Because he made me promise to introduce him to you."

CHAPTER 4

Later that night after my daughter went to sleep, I stared at the ceiling above my bed. Shadows veiled the walls, the darkness broken by shafts of moonlight angling through the blinds. Try as I might to doze off, my eyelids kept opening. I scrunched them tight and tried to shut down my brain, but thoughts raced through my mind.

Would Rose the demon take an hour of my life while I lay defenseless in my sleep? What would she make me do? Would I know if she took more time than our agreement? And what was that place where I got trapped? I wanted to talk to my father about it, but I couldn't broach the topic during dinner with Larissa hanging on me.

Larissa, age ten going on twenty-five. All kid, but with a wisdom well beyond her tender years. I'd hoped she'd be normal like her father, but she inherited my Nesbitt ability to see the dead and shared my love of animals.

Tomorrow I would drive her to Jacksonville. Her grandparents had insisted she visit them this summer, and now that school was out, the time was upon us. Larissa kept saying she didn't want to go, but these were Roland's parents. My daughter needed to spend time with the Colonel and Elizabeth, to get to know them. That was only fair.

While she was gone, I'd be alone for the first time since my husband went missing from his special military assignment. I dreaded the week away from my daughter.

Maybe I could use the time to identify my watcher. I'd become aware of the stranger in the woods about six months ago, when I'd been investigating a love-triangle homicide. He'd subdued a large man, hogtied him, and left him as a present for me to find.

A quick pulse of my senses, and I realized he was out there now, communing with mosquitoes, flies, and chiggers. Poor fella.

I yawned and counted stuff in the room. Four corners where the walls met the ceiling. Six items on my dresser. One worn-out wingback chair beside the bed. Three pillows. I yawned. I missed some numbers. Two and five. Two glowing eyes on the purring cat nestled beside me. Five. What were there five of?

Fingers and toes came to mind. I hadn't lost any of those yet, and I hoped I never did. I was fond of my digits. My eyes fluttered, and my breathing deepened. Finally.

I drifted along in a bumpy dreamscape, drifting in and out of REM sleep, until I landed in a vision. Two people were toweling dry after a shower. The woman had her back to me, but the man's profile was fully visible. I didn't know him from a hole in the ground, but his tanned, buff physique would be the envy of any middle-aged male. The woman had curves in all the right places, though her tan was more of the farmer-tan variety.

"You're all right, Hollywood," the woman murmured in an appreciative tone. She wrapped the white towel around her torso and secured it. "That was wonderful."

"Hang with me, Bea-u-tiful, and you could be famous," Hollywood said, preening in the lightly fogged mirror.

She swatted his bare behind. "Not interested in changing careers, but I'm noticing how good we are together."

"Babe, we're better than good." He enfolded her in an embrace. "We're dynamite."

She laughed, deep and husky, and cuddled closer. "Careful, you're bordering on being a cliché. Friends with benefits, remember?"

"Can't help it. You do something to me. That perfume. It's addictive."

"Not wearing any perfume, silly."

"Even better." He nuzzled her neck playfully, and she shrieked. "Thinking about another round. You game?"

"You bet." She let the white towel drop and twitched her hips. "Give me everything you've got. Run *wide open.*"

The dream faded to black, and I roused. Dawn was beginning to break. Who were these people? Why did I dream of them? Other than the fact they were a heterosexual couple who enjoyed intimate relations, the dream fragment gave me nothing useful. No landmarks. No real names.

One thing was for certain. I only dreamed of dead people, and so far my sleeping dreams originated from persons with a violent or sudden death. Which left me wondering if this was a murder-suicide or if one lover did the other in.

I yawned and stretched, earning the stink-eye from Sulay, the Maine coon cat who shared my bed. Sulay was a temporary boarder until Bonnie Chapman could leave rehab, but Bonnie's health seemed to be in a downward spiral. Sulay ruled our roost, bossing around Elvis, the Chihuahua I'd rescued from the snake-handling church, and Muffin, a Shih Poo rescue.

The upshot was that we'd become a three-pet family. With Larissa headed to her grandparents for a week, the dogs would soon join me and Sulay in my bed. Bound to be interesting.

CHAPTER 5

"I don't want to go anywhere," Larissa said as my truck rolled toward the Georgia–Florida line. "I want to spend the summer with you and Mama Lacey and Pap and my dogs. And Sulay. I don't want to be cooped up in stuffy old Jacksonville."

"Your father's parents want to spend time with you." I eased my truck around an older RV. "They've taken his death hard."

"He's not dead, Mom."

"You and I believe that, but we don't know why he's missing, and we shouldn't offer his parents false hope. The Colonel and Elizabeth may seem like forces of nature, but they're people with feelings just like everyone else. They adore you and want to be part of your life."

"It's going to be boring. I won't see you or my friends. I'll be at their mercy."

While I shared her trepidation about parting, my fears were born out of what the

Colonel and Elizabeth would do if I didn't grant them access to Larissa. They'd been making noises for over a year that they wanted custody of their granddaughter. The argument they'd given was that they could provide for Larissa in the style in which a Powell should be raised.

My finances had improved with each passing month, but we weren't affluent and lived on a budget. Elizabeth Powell spent money like she was made of the stuff.

"I'm sure they'll go out of their way to make sure you have a good time. Give them a chance. They love you as much as Mama Lacey and Pap."

Larissa snorted. Her pert little nose tilted up. "No way they'd let me paint an animal mural on the outside of their house."

"You're right, but they'll offer you the equivalent in their world. I can promise you that much."

"Why?"

"Because they can."

Larissa's golden ponytail waggled, and her earnest expression fell. "But I don't want to be like them. I want to be like you."

"Be yourself. That's what growing up is all about. Spending time with your Powell grandparents is an opportunity to explore new things, to expand your horizons. The world is bigger than Sinclair County, Georgia. In eight more years, you'll be heading off to college, a career, and a family of your own. If you take advantage of opportunities as they come along, you'll have a better handle on who you are. Trust me, some people spend their entire lives searching for their identity."

"I already know who I am and what I want to be. I want to be a dreamwalker, like you."

I winced. "You will be a dreamwalker one day, and quite possibly something else as well. All of that's in the future. For this visit, the Powells don't need to know how different you are from them."

"You want me to lie to them?"

My fingers tightened on the steering wheel. "No. I would never ask that of you. But this is a tricky subject. The Powells place a higher value on their lifestyle choices."

"They must've hated living in Sinclair County all those years ago."

I stopped myself from nodding. Be accepting, I told myself. Encourage inclusivity. "I don't know about that, dear, but they truly enjoy Jacksonville. They're looking forward to spending time with you and showing you the big city."

"I'm a country girl."

"You can be whatever and whoever you want to be. If you learn nothing else this summer, I hope that truth sticks with you."

After the flurry of hugs, the Colonel collected Larissa's suitcase and escorted her into a house larger than most third-world countries. I was stuck with Elizabeth in the cavernous foyer.

"What have you done with yourself, Baxley? What happened to your hair?" Elizabeth demanded. My mother-in-law looked like she'd stepped off the runway of a fashion show. Not a gray hair was out of place. Her designer clothing fit and flattered her trim figure, as did the modest heels she wore.

Trying out a new look sounded lame. Telling her it was a tangible sign of my dream-walking power wouldn't fly. "My hair has a mind of its own these days," I offered.

"Really, dear. It ages you terribly. My hairdresser could fix that this afternoon. I'd be happy to make the call."

No hairdresser could fix my hair. God knows, I'd tried everything. The white forelock wouldn't take dye and my head ached when I tried to hide the offending lock under a ball cap. "Maybe next time." I gave a tremulous smile. "I'll pick up Larissa next Saturday."

"We offered to keep her for the entire summer," Elizabeth countered, her patrician features frosting.

"A week is what we agreed on over the phone."

"What's that?" Elizabeth reached for my hand. Her mouth dropped, and she stared at me as if I'd grown two more heads. "A tattoo? What sort of home environment are you providing for my granddaughter?"

"A safe, nurturing environment. You and I are different people, and if we focus on our differences, we'll only see division. Both of us love Larissa and want her to be happy. Let's keep that in the forefront of our thoughts."

Larissa darted down the winding stairs, shiny tennis racket in hand. "Mom! Look what I got!"

"How nice." I didn't miss the superior smile Elizabeth shot me.

"The club pro has agreed to give Larissa private lessons while she's here," Elizabeth said. "There's a youth tennis clinic that runs next week. We thought she might enjoy meeting some young people down here."

"I'm sure she'll have a fantastic time with her grandparents." I glanced over at my daughter. "One last hug."

After hugs and goodbyes, I drove home on autopilot. My intuition told me the Powells were up to something, and it took every bit of common courtesy I had to leave my daughter with them. *It's only a week,* I reminded myself. In the span of a lifetime, that's not very long.

Seven days, 168 hours, 10,080 minutes; not that I was counting.

I'd just crossed the state line and was thinking about lunch when the sheriff called. "We've got a missing persons case. Come to the office immediately for a briefing."

CHAPTER 6

"Who's missing?" I settled into the upright chair across from Sheriff Wayne Thompson's desk. Other than the stacks of folders on one corner of his desk, Wayne's office was neat and tidy. A trace of his brisk aftershave perfumed the air. I'd known the sheriff since high school, and it still irked him that I'd resisted his tall, dark, and handsome play for my favors.

"One of the movie people," the sheriff said.

"Couldn't take the slower pace of life in Sinclair County?" I asked.

His brown eyes narrowed. "Not funny. Ford Morrison came in here and filed a missing persons report, but he wants it quiet in case the guy took an unplanned vacation. Only a few people know he's missing, and if it winds up in the paper, I'll know you blabbed to Charlotte."

I worked to release the tension in my jaw.

"I can keep my mouth closed. You should know that by now."

"Charlotte breaks a lot of police stories."

"She doesn't get the information from me. She figures it out. Charlotte should be a detective."

"The Atlantic Ocean will ice over before I hire Charlotte Ambrose in my department. She's a loose cannon."

I shrugged because he was right. Charlotte had been the instigator of most of our childhood adventures. Better get this conversation back on track. "So, who's missing?"

"Marv Kildeer. He's Ford's right-hand man on location. He's the advance guy who scouted out locations for filming a few months back. He's been with Ford for a dozen years, and Ford says it's highly unusual for Marv to vanish like this."

"What do we know about Marv?"

The sheriff handed me a thin manila folder. "He's married, though he and his wife maintain separate residences. Originally from Chicago, he headed to Los Angeles nearly twenty years ago in hopes of breaking into the movies. Did some scenes as a stunt man on Ford's first movie, and they hit it off. Went to work for Ford after that."

I scrolled down the page. High school

education. A year of community college. Lots of local theater credits. Waiter. Step-and-fetch-it guy. Not much career ladder climbing to Marv Kildeer's life accomplishments. "What's he look like? How will we know where to look?"

The sheriff turned his computer monitor to me. "Tamika is printing this image out for me. This photo's two years old, but Ford says this is how Marv looks. I had hopes you could touch his toothbrush and find him."

The punch of steely blue eyes on the screen took my breath away. "Damn."

The sheriff stilled. "Is that a good damn or the bad kind?"

"It's an I've-seen-that-guy-before damn."

"Recently?"

"Yep."

"Do tell."

"Working on it." I wracked my brain to place this tanned, ripped guy. Calling him an Adonis would be an understatement; guys would kill to look this handsome. His straight teeth were blindingly white, his hair thick and peppered with a hint of gray. But his smile didn't quite reach all the way to his eyes.

Something was off.

It seemed like he had plenty of secrets.

Like fooling around with another woman. The pieces of the puzzle clicked in my mind. "Oh yeah, I've seen him." I met the sheriff's penetrating stare. "In my dreams."

Wayne scowled. "Is he dead?"

"Can't be certain, but I don't get live people in my dreams. Wrong frequency."

He sat back in his chair, a considering expression on his face. "What can you tell me about him?"

"His ego may be the size of Texas. His body is a woman's wet dream. And the woman he's having a torrid affair with is probably not his wife."

"That's not much to go on. What else you got?"

"They were naked. Well, there were towels at first."

His cheek twitched. "You watched them have sex?"

"I can't change the channel. My dreams are rarely peaceful. Usually something bad is happening, so, yeah, I watched."

He beamed a knowing, self-satisfied grin my way. "You're blushing. You didn't want me to know about your X-rated dreams?"

"Let's get back to the missing man."

"Is it like watching porn? Did you get all horny and everything? Do you become one of the lovers?"

"No. No. And hell no. Sometimes I experience a vignette through the eyes of the victim. But not this time. This time I was shown the scene."

He waggled his eyebrows. "Pick up any new tips?"

"Wayne. This conversation is inappropriate. How are we going to find Marv Kildeer? You mentioned a toothbrush."

"I'm thinking we'd be better off grabbing a pair of his dirty boxers instead."

I shuddered. "Gross."

"Hmm. The boxers might be a good idea. We might find him and the woman he was bopping."

"Where was he staying?"

"At the bed and breakfast on the city square."

"Have you already checked his place for evidence?"

"Did that first thing this morning. No sign of a struggle. It's like he went out for the day and didn't return. He missed breakfast today and yesterday."

"So he's been missing more than twenty-four hours."

"Yes. But I haven't entered him into the Missing Persons Database yet. Discretion."

"Those movie people bring in lots of money, don't they?"

He nodded. "They do. Over a million dollars added to our local economy so far. We need that infusion of cash. Let's do what we can to keep them happy. Like finding this guy."

"I'm willing to be your people detector, but I can't guarantee anything."

"We'll take my car."

"No way. I'll follow you. Last time I rode with you, I ended up stuck at a crime scene for hours."

CHAPTER 7

Sinclair Manor at one time had been the home of a lusty sea captain. His wife and eight daughters lived in this grand house while he plied the sea. But the big, drafty place was a money pit and a heating and cooling nightmare, so it changed hands many times through the years. Now it earned its keep as a bed and breakfast.

The two-story Victorian exuded Southern charm with the deep, wraparound front porch and cozy padded rockers. A fat gray tabby perched on the nearest rocking chair and eyed me with frank interest as I marched right past. He leapt down and followed me inside.

I listened while Wayne conferred with the owner, Johnny Lee Hudson, about searching Marv's room. Johnny Lee had only lived in the county for about six years. Imports like him didn't necessarily know about dreamwalkers or what we could do, though this was the first time I'd tried to find an allegedly living person who was missing. Usually the dead in my dreams made me work to learn their true identities.

But I could be putting the speedboat ahead of the trailer hitch. We had no proof Marv was dead. Only a fragment of a dream, and that wouldn't stand up in court, or anywhere else for that matter.

"You're a psychic?" Johnny Lee asked.

The blended scent of cinnamon and cloves wafting from the innkeeper's clothing made my mouth water. "Sometimes I'm able to point the way to finding people."

His eyes lit up. "Can you do readings? I'd love to have you do a show for our guests. At your convenience, of course."

"I don't do readings or shows. I consult in police investigations. My full-time job is a pet and plant caretaker."

"Pets? You know cats?" I nodded and he continued, warming to the subject. "Two days ago, Alfred Hitchcock stalked out to the porch and refused to come in this house. This from a fat cat who used to spend all day on the parlor sofa. Now he followed you inside. Are you a pet psychic perchance?"

I turned to study the plump kitty who regarded me steadily. Acting on a whim, I knelt. "Here, kitty, kitty."

The cat sauntered over and sniffed me. I scratched between his ears and heard his purring response. I stood. "Your cat seems all right now."

"He scratched the tar out of me yesterday when I tried to bring him inside for the night. My partner said he's turned into a psycho watch cat. You want to take him home with you?"

I was aware of the sheriff's shifting stance and of him glancing at his watch twice. "He belongs here at Sinclair Manor. Maybe he has a new girlfriend nearby."

"Alfred Hitchcock was a rescue, and he lost his boy parts before we got him. If he doesn't chill out, we can't have him here. Too much liability."

The cat twined itself around my feet and strapped its tail on my jeans. "He seems calm to me. He's behaving like a normal cat would act. It's possible that something was bothering him, but now he's fine. I'll be glad to work with you and your partner and Alfred Hitchcock after we examine Marv's room."

"Thanks." He jerked a thumb in the direction of the grand staircase. "Marv booked the Highlander Suite for two months. Third door on the right upstairs."

Johnny Lee bustled into the kitchen and began clattering pots and pans. An innkeeper's day never ended.

The sheriff took the lead up the creaky steps. The rich patina of the stained wood brought to mind decadent chocolate caramels. This place had me jonesing for sweets.

"Awful chatty with the inn keep," Wayne observed. "You know he bats for the other team."

My back teeth clenched automatically. I worked them apart. Far be it for me to criticize anyone's lifestyle choices. "He's a pet owner concerned about his cat."

"You a pet psychic now?"

"I'm a dreamwalker. Big difference."

Wayne snorted. "Ta-may-toe, ta-mah-toe."

I ignored his comment and focused on Sinclair Manor. There was a lot of history in this house, many energy trails laid down by people coming and going. The result was like walking through a minefield of energy bursts. Something, then nothing, and so on. I girded my senses, preferring to use them on Marv's room instead of trolling through the stairs and halls.

The sheriff opened the door to Marv's room. Fingerprint powder dotted the bureau, nightstands, table, and desk, indicating they'd already dusted for prints. Clothes were tossed on the dresser, dotted the floor, dangled from hangers, and littered the bed.

"I know what my grandmother would say about this guy," I ventured from the doorway. "No home training."

"Living out of a suitcase for a couple of months isn't easy," Wayne said. "You've never let the laundry pile up?"

"There's a method to this?"

"Sure. He's probably getting several wearings out of his slacks. My guess is his button down shirt and power suit are at the mid-county dry cleaners. His swimsuit and workout gear are probably on the bathroom floor, right where he dropped them after working out."

I stared at Wayne. "Are you claiming to be psychic?"

"Nah. I'm a guy. I know how he thinks when it comes to clothes. In his job, he has to dress a certain way, but he's a slob at heart. If I didn't have Dottie riding me about picking my stuff up, our entire house would look like this."

"Thank goodness for your wife." Wow. Never thought I'd say that.

Wayne caught my eye and grinned as if he'd read my mind. "Okay, Madame Dreamwalker. What do you want to touch? Looks like just about everything in here is well used by him."

"Close the door. I don't want a distraction from the other guests. I want to look around a bit first. You see any evidence of a woman staying here with him?"

He shooed the cat out and shut the door. The cat in the hallway howled once then quieted. His paw reached under the door. "His wife's in California — oh, I see. Check the bathroom."

The bathroom door was open, so I threaded my way through Marv's mess to survey the area. Toothpaste globs dotted the sink. One toothbrush rested on the counter. Manly hygiene products, bar soap, and body wash sat in the shower caddy.

Nothing pink or floral-scented here. No thongs or lacy bras. No negligee.

From the look of the chaos, only a guy lived here. If a woman had passed through these doors, she'd been careful not to leave a trace of her presence.

I glanced in the trashcan. "Empty. That's odd."

"You think a guy who doesn't pick up after himself would throw something away?"

"Yeah. There'd be used tissues —"

"Bet you anything this guy used toilet paper for any sniffles he may have had."

Roland used to do that. Hmm. Wayne had

a point. "What about the beer bottles, chip bags, and soda cans? Where are the empty cartons of takeout food?"

Wayne pulled out a notepad. "Questions for Johnny Lee. You got enough ambiance yet?"

I glanced around searching for something out of place, other than the general untidiness. "No watch, billfold, phone, computer, tablet, or keys."

"You think an old place like this has wifi?"

"I do. Marv is from the generation that expects Internet connections everywhere they go. Any leads on his rental car?"

"We have an APB out on it. Are you done trying to do my job? How about you tune into channel woo-woo and get me something I don't know?" He grabbed a pair of rumpled jeans off the floor and shoved them at me. "Start with these."

He was right. Time to quit stalling and do my job. I opened my senses and grabbed the jeans. The light flickered. I plunged into darkness with a soundless scream. Terror welled in my throat, blocking the air. Something was wrong. This wasn't how this part of the process felt. The transition to my dreamscape seemed to take forever, as if I were traveling in slow motion.

I blocked the fear and focused on arriving

in the land of the dead. I whirled and tumbled through a freezing cold space where I dared not breathe. *Come on, Marv. Show me something. Get me out of here.*

With a thud, I hit bottom. I blinked at the gray twilight. Finally, something that looked familiar. I'd made it, but the trip had been a doozy. I scrambled to my feet but froze when something quite close to me moved. My metaphysical heart leaped in my throat.

"What the hell is this?" the sheriff asked from the ground beside me.

CHAPTER 8

"Wayne." I gave him a hand up, steadied his spiritual body in the gloom. "What are you doing here?"

"You tell me."

"I've never experienced this before. My transition to the dream plane was terrible, as if something was dialed in wrong. It took too long to breach the gap, but I guess that was because I was transporting both of us. Are you sure you're not psychic?"

His arms windmilled. His eyes rounded. "Hell, no. Get me out of here. Take me back to solid ground. I can't see a damn thing in this murk."

I wasn't buying his story. For him to travel out here, even accidentally, meant Wayne had some untapped powers. This was neither the time nor the place to get into that discussion with him. "Be glad you can't see. It's creepy in here. I'm not sure how you tagged along, but I'm looking for Marv before I try to get us home. I need time to catch my breath. That transition was brutal."

Spirits drifted by, their voices disjointed, their forms transparent.

Wayne edged closer to me as I flinched. "Where am I?"

"This is where I seek answers among the dead. Marv's jeans brought us here. He should be nearby, or else we made a wrong turn, in which case we've got bigger problems. At this point, I'm hoping for Marv. Come on."

"Wait. Am I . . . dead?"

"You're temporarily in two places at once. You'll be fine. I do this all the time." I tugged on his arm. "Let's go."

His posture stiffened. "How will we find this portal again in the darkness? Don't we need to pinpoint this location so we can get home?"

"Don't worry. I can get home from any place out here. Well, most anywhere. I've hit a few trouble spots."

"Is that how you ended up with the tat?"

"Yes. Stay close. You need me to get home. Your job is to not get separated from me, or you'll be wandering out here in spirit form for all eternity."

He clamped a hand on my arm, the grip

manacle strong. "No problem. I won't let go."

I marched straight ahead as if I knew where I was going. I didn't, but I wasn't about to look dumb in front of my boss. A group of bad-boy spirits approached with catcalls and jeers.

"Bug off," I said. "Be gone, I command you."

"I can help you find someone," one of them said. "I know everybody up here."

The group's spokesman coalesced into a human-looking composite of a street-smart urban thug. Lots of attitude, messy hair, and baggy pants. Not exactly the tour-guide type, but I wasn't about to consider his offer. "I wasn't born yesterday. Get lost. I will not be party to your mischief."

"Who are you talking to?" Wayne asked.

"A newb!" the thug ghost exclaimed. "She brought us a human sacrifice. Dibs."

"No one is touching my companion. Leave us alone or suffer the consequences." I flashed my tat at them.

They shrunk away, cursing. As if on an unseen cue, they thinned as one to spirit fog and moaned off.

I shivered and trudged on through the murk. *Come on, Marv. Show yourself. Come out from where you're hiding.*

"Who was that? A welcoming committee?" Wayne asked.

"No. Do me a favor and don't talk to anyone up here. Especially if you start to see something. Do not look in their eyes."

"I don't like this place."

"You get used to it."

"Babe, you need to get a new sideline. This is crazy sauce."

"Welcome to my life. It's chock full of crazy." I stopped at a mental crossroads. "Don't take this the wrong way, but zip it. I need to focus on finding Marv."

"Gotcha."

A tableau slowly unfolded in my mind. Phone in hand, Marv, aka Hollywood, ran out of a restaurant to a sedan as a jean-clad man in white rubber shrimp boots tossed a bucket of water through the open window. "You can't do that!" Marv shouted.

"I did it, and I'll do more if you and your kind don't pack up and get the hell out of here."

Marv sighed as if he'd faced this level of animosity before. He punched a few buttons on his phone, looked up to face the shadowed man. "Free country, buddy."

The wiry, bearded man brought his fisted hands up in fighting position. "I'm not your anything, except your enemy. We don't want you in Sinclair County. Go home."

Marv raised his hands in surrender and backpedaled toward the restaurant. "I won't press charges about the car if you tell me what will make this right. Can we make a donation to your favorite charity? Is there a political candidate you want to help?"

"You cain't buy me. This is my county, and we rednecks like it just the way it is. We don't need high and mighty movie people coming in here and flashing a lot of green."

"I understand you're upset. Why don't we get together in the morning and talk this out with clearer heads?"

"You saying I'm drunk? I'll have you know, I've never been to one of them meetings. I chug a six-pack for breakfast and function just fine."

"Whatever," Marv said. "I'm authorized to negotiate with you, and I'd like for us to reach an agreement."

"You're all a pack of liars. Actors fib for a living. I don't trust a word coming out of your movie-star mouth."

"Cap'n Bee trusts me."

"You leave her out of this."

"Cap'n Bee is working with us on identifying possible shooting locales. In return, we agreed to fund the food pantry for a year."

The light shifted, and I saw that the

vandal was missing a digit on his index finger. I wished I could see his face.

"Lies," the vandal yelled. "Bee oughta know better than to trust a scalawag like you."

"We've already made the donation. I'm a man of my word. Ask around."

"I will, but you stay the hell away from her. She's good people."

"Exactly."

The scene faded. "Wait!" I called out.

Marv looked up at me, his eyes defeated. "I tried."

As the spirit wavered before me, I felt a fresh wave of panic. "Please don't go. I need more information. Who killed you?"

"I tried to do the right thing, and it got all messed up. Tell Ford I'm sorry."

"About what?"

"Everything. This was to be his breakout role, the blockbuster to end all blockbusters. This will bust his chops."

"This is about your boss?"

"My whole life was about him. He called. I jumped."

"Where are you? We can't find your body."

Marv faded to a wisp and drifted away. His "on the set" was nearly inaudible.

"Done," I said triumphantly to Wayne. "We can go home now."

71

"I didn't hear or see anything," he said, "but I'm beyond ready to leave this fruitcake factory."

"Me, too. Hang on with both hands. The ride will be as bumpy as before. Here we go." I pictured Marv's room at Sinclair Manor and the jeans that the sheriff and I both held. The bottom fell out from under us, and we tossed, turned, and whirled in the near-darkness until I wished I was dead.

Wayne was counting on me to get him home. He hadn't asked for a taste of the afterlife, but he'd gotten it anyway. I had to make this right.

Faces flashed before my eyes. My daughter. My parents. My husband. Sliding and bouncing like a rubber ball tethered to a wooden paddle. *Focus, Baxley. You can do this. You can end this freefall if you sharpen your focus.*

I needed to break through to my reality, but having Wayne piggybacking on the transition was holding me back. I didn't have enough juice to get us home. *You could ditch him,* my subconscious nagged. *You've soloed through here a hundred times or more. Wayne is the problem.*

I tightened my mental grip on the sheriff. He was extra baggage, but he didn't ask to take this dreamwalk. He was my responsibility, and I had to see this through.

Except the sector in my thoughts occupied by Wayne's spirit was ice cold.

Not good.

If I didn't get us out of here soon, we'd both wake up dead. Worse, we'd spend eternity out here, tumbling through nothingness, forever stuck in a spiritual washing machine.

I pictured every aspect of the room where our bodies resided. Nothing. I summoned up the texture of Marv's denim jeans as a remote anchor. No help there.

On the horizon, a hint of a light beckoned like a faraway oasis.

Instinctively, I shied away from it. Light didn't belong out here. I'd never seen light during any of my other transitions. Light couldn't be good. It might even be death.

The whispers started anew.

Save yourself.

Live for your daughter.

Your family needs you.

Sinclair County needs you.

Release your burden and live.

Give him to us.

"No." My voice came out as a whisper, so I said it again. "No. I'm not abandoning anyone. We're getting through this together or not at all."

The whispers faded and there, underneath the melee, was the most welcome voice of all. *Mom?*

"Baxley, hear me. Dial in my voice."

Mom? Where are you? Where am I?

"Time is short. Go to the light. Follow it home."

Not the light. I'm not ready to die.

I drifted and tumbled. The light stayed on the horizon. My mom had guided me home once before, when a deputy tased me. I knew I could trust her, but what if something out here was tricking me?

CHAPTER 9

We would die if I did nothing. I knew that. Following mom's advice to go to the light wouldn't make me any deader than inaction, and I couldn't get home on my own. Bottom line, I had nothing to lose.

The glow of the light seemed dimmer. How far had I drifted from it?

I couldn't feel Wayne at all now, but I hadn't consciously released him. He had to still be with me. It was the cold, I told myself. I was numb, too. With Herculean effort, I crossed the shadowed void.

Mom's voice looped through the same soundtrack over and over again, and as I approached the light, I heard her more clearly. The familiar sound made me move faster. I wanted to be home, to feel my parents' loving arms around me.

My surroundings became more and more illuminated, but the only thing I saw was brightness. There were no people, no houses or trees, only light. The beacon of my mother's voice drew me further into the glare.

"Baxley, hear me," Mom repeated in my head. "Dial in my voice. Time is short. Go to the light. Follow it home."

I was going home.

Home.

I blinked against the flaring light as it revved with rocket-launch intensity. Too much. I would be blind. And yet I kept plodding further into the glow, trusting in my mother's voice.

Another blink and blurred shapes appeared. Orbs. Squares. Rectangles. Faces. A white ceiling. A sunny window. Marv's room at the B&B. My hand twitched, and warm fingers squeezed my numb digits. I squeezed back.

"You did it," Mom said in a hoarse voice. "You came through the void. And you brought Wayne with you."

"That's my girl," my father said, pride ringing in his voice.

I glanced around the old-fashioned bedroom. Evangelist Bubba Paxton of Pax Out church beamed at me. Running Bear and Gentle Dove, my parents' Native American friends, also sent smiles my way. I tried to speak, but my tongue felt too big, my mouth parched. Mom put a straw in my mouth. I sipped the water and nodded when I had enough.

"Y'all having a party?" I managed as warmth seeped into my icy limbs. I was on a cot of some sort. White sheets. Cozy blankets atop.

"Something like that," Gentle Dove said, compassion easing her lined face. "How do you feel?"

"Tired, but okay. How's Wayne?"

"He's resting easier now. He should wake up in a few minutes," Mom said. "You had us worried."

"Bax, you proved your chops when we rescued your dad a few months ago, but this is amazing," Bubba Paxton said, his face bright with wonder. "How did you take a nonsensitive with you to the Other Side?"

"I have no idea. I wasn't even ready to dreamwalk and suddenly Wayne and I both were hurtling through the curtain of life." I shuddered. "I never want to do that again."

Mom tucked warm blankets around me. "Are you warm enough?"

"Getting there. How long was I out?"

"A while," she answered.

I tried to guess, but the light seemed bright for late afternoon. "A few hours?"

77

Bubba Paxton snickered. "More like all night."

How was that possible? "What? How?"

"Your father realized what happened right away. He called me, and then we pulled in our friends to help guide you home."

I nodded to my dad. "Thank you. I was truly lost out there. I don't know how Wayne accompanied me. Certainly it wasn't a deliberate effort on my part. The transition going out was horrible, the one back impossible. Without your help, we'd be trapped in the void forever."

Running Bear and Gentle Dove sobered, as did Mom, Dad, and Pax. They knew only too well what I'd faced. Soon as I rested, I'd figure it out because I definitely didn't want to make this mistake again. God, I was tired.

A new worry throbbed in my head. "Larissa? Did she call?"

"We haven't heard from her," Mom said. "Should I call her for you?"

"No, thanks. I'll check in with her later when I can speak privately." Other responsibilities came to mind. "What about my dogs and Sulay? Have they been locked inside my house all this time?"

"They're fine. We asked your neighbor, Mr. Luther, to take care of them until you were able to go home. I gave him a key. Hope that was all right."

"Thanks." The need to close my eyes and sleep rode me hard, but I couldn't conk out, not until I shared my findings with the sheriff. At a movement in my peripheral vision, I turned to see the sheriff stirring. His normally hearty coloring looked two shades from death. Hard as this had been on me, he'd suffered too. What had gone wrong?

"Where am I?" Wayne asked. "Why am I so thirsty? Why can't I get up?"

Mom and Gentle Dove went to his side. "You're at the B&B. Marv's room," Mom said. "You were conducting a missing person's investigation. And you can't move yet because every part of you is waking up."

"What do you mean?" Wayne's voice was laced with suspicion. "What have you people done to me?"

"Your spirit went into the void with Baxley and then y'all got stuck there," Mom said.

"That sounds like science fiction. Last thing I remember is handing her Marv's blue jeans. Now I wake up feeling like I'm coming off a three-week bender. Is there something you aren't telling me? Did I have an accident?"

"Whether it was an accident or intervention, we can't say. In our collective memory, this has never happened before, but you're living proof it can occur. Both of you weren't wholly present when we arrived. Just your relaxed bodies. You went on a dreamwalk, Sheriff."

"I don't believe it."

"Believe, brother," Bubba Paxton said in a sing-song evangelical voice. "Baxley's the bomb."

"What time is it? How long have I been here?" the sheriff asked.

"Y'all have been out overnight. It's Sunday. Nearly noon," my father said.

"My wife's going to kill me. No way can I explain this."

Dottie would kill him. I cleared my throat. "I hope someone called and explained his absence."

Mom nodded at my dad. "Tab instructed the dispatch gal to phone her and tell her he'd been summoned out of the county overnight on official police business."

I laughed and managed to sit up, swinging my legs over the side of the cot. The room shifted, then slid into place. "That's the truth!"

"Not funny," the sheriff grumped. He tried to sit up and collapsed in Marv's bed. "This is a nightmare."

"This is life," I said, unable to keep

disdain out of my tone. "If not for every person in this room, both of us would be dead. Think on that before you complain too loudly. I, for one, am very grateful to be alive."

Wayne groaned and muttered under his breath. "Tell me it was worthwhile. Tell me I didn't risk a divorce and death over nothing. What did you learn?"

I wasn't ready to test my legs just yet. I was tired beyond exhaustion. And something else, something I couldn't quite put my finger on. "Marv is definitely dead. He showed me a conversation he had with a disgruntled county resident, a scrappy guy wearing shrimp boots. I didn't catch the man's name but he was wiry and ornery. Oh, and part of his index finger was missing. Anybody know who he is?"

"I may have an idea," the sheriff said. "Did this guy kill Marv?"

"I don't know."

"Where's the body?" Wayne asked.

"That I do know. Marv said he was on the movie set."

White-faced, Wayne groaned again and forced his torso up from the bed, bracing his arms on his legs for support. "They filed for permits to film in a dozen places

throughout the county. He could be anywhere."

CHAPTER 10

With Wayne's entire police force checking movie filming locations in the county for a body, and with Larissa safe with her Powell grandparents in Jacksonville, I fell into my bed fully clothed, sunlight streaming through the windows. Sulay and both dogs jumped up beside me, and I was glad for the company.

If I dreamed, I didn't remember any of it, but my windows were dark when I awakened. I glanced at my watch and saw I'd slept five hours. The big Maine coon cat was tucked close to my side, her eyes intent on my face.

"What?" I asked.

The cat stared.

At the sound of my voice, the sleeping dogs roused to walk over my body and lick my face. Sulay rose, arched her back, and hissed. Her tail swished back and forth.

This cat never exerted any extra effort.

Her behavior alarmed me on multiple levels. I opened my senses to see if anyone was near my house, but nothing happened. There was no winging of thoughts outward, no inner eye giving me unexplained visions of places beyond this room.

The absence of ability disoriented me. Was I . . . broken?

I tried again, with the same result. My breath caught in my throat. All my life I'd been the girl who was different. Now it seemed the very thing that had set me apart was missing.

A chill swept through me.

Sulay hissed again, still walking around on her tiptoes.

Something was very wrong here, with me and the cat. At a noise downstairs, I bolted off the bed, heart pounding. The dogs barked and jumped down, ready for this new game I was playing, only it was no game. An intruder was in my house.

Gun.

I needed a gun.

The rifle was in the hall closet, the Glock in the kitchen drawer, and the Beretta in my truck. I bent and grabbed Roland's baseball bat from under the bed. Darkness cloaked me, but I was used to walking in places with low light.

My breath came in short bursts, my ears pounded. I blinked the sleep from my eyes and crept toward the closed bedroom door.

Wait a minute. I wasn't thinking straight. I should call the cops. Where was my phone? I glanced around, realizing I'd dropped the phone and my keys on the kitchen counter when I'd come home this afternoon.

I cursed my bad luck. The only good thing about this situation was that Larissa was safely in Jacksonville. I placed my ear on the door and listened. Water running, cabinets opening. Had my parents come by with dinner? Was I making something out of nothing?

Regardless, I was going downstairs to check it out. I turned and motioned for the dogs to sit. "Stay," I said in a stage whisper.

Elvis whined.

"Hush," I whispered. "It isn't safe down there. I'll be right back."

Treading oh-so-carefully, I eased the door open and slipped through. Sulay darted past, lightning quick. Did she have a death wish? "Come back here," I whispered. The cat charged down the stairs and turned to watch me. I could see her because light spilled into the hallway.

From the kitchen came the sound of mixing, then the electric can opener whirred.

Sulay took off like a shot. Even I knew that sound meant dinner.

Not many intruders would bother to feed my pets. "Hello?" I called when the can opener stopped. "Who's there?"

"I am," a thin voice answered.

I recognized the voice as belonging to my nearest neighbor, Mr. Luther. He'd come to feed my animals. Relief washed over me like a summer shower. I continued into the kitchen.

"Hi, Mr. Luther," I said, catching sight of the trim elderly man. One would think someone in his eighties wouldn't notice much, but his clear eyes were as sharp as his mind. "Thank you for your help."

"Glad to do it, dear one. Feeding your pets is the least I can do for someone in community service like you." He turned and saw the bat in my hand. "Hope you're not planning to cosh me with that."

Heat rose to my face. "Sorry. I heard someone down here and thought I'd better defend myself."

"Bats are fine weapons, but guns are better."

"I've got guns, but none are in my bedroom."

"Remedy that. A beautiful gal like you

86

should have protection where you need it most."

"I'll take your advice under consideration. How'd you get in?"

"Your mom gave me a key."

That's right. I remembered Mom telling me about the key. "And I want you to keep that key. I'm thankful for your help. Can I fix you dinner?"

He nodded to the crock pot and basket of bread. "Dinner's ready to go."

"You cooked?"

"Not me. Looks like Lacey and Tab's handiwork. They's mighty worried about you."

"With good reason. I had a dreamwalk go sideways yesterday. Never had that happen before."

He shrugged and settled into a chair. "There are some hiccups in any new job. That soup smells delicious. I'll take you up on dinner, if you don't mind."

I moved forward to get bowls and plates. "Of course I don't mind. I'm glad for the company because my daughter is away."

"Off to see the Powells in Florida?"

"Yes. They've been wanting her to visit for a long time." I didn't want our conversation to be only about my family. Mr. Luther had remarried after his first wife died. His only

87

son had been born when Mr. Luther was in his late fifties. The wife didn't stick, but the kid did. "How's your son? What do you hear from him?"

His eyes flared with alarm before he hastily spooned in another bite of the thick chicken and corn chowder. If I hadn't been watching, I'd have missed the whole thing. What was that about?

"Morley's traveling every which-a-where with his unit. He bought me some newfangled gadget that's a phone and movie camera to talk to him with, but it didn't suit me. Told him he could call me on the regular phone like a good son should or mail me a real letter. You'd a-thought a zombie passed over his grave. These youngsters today think they've invented communication. Everything else seems stone aged to them."

I needed a gadget like that to keep up with Larissa. God, I missed her. Was she getting enough to eat? Was she remembering to use sunscreen?

"Baxley?" Mr. Luther asked.

"Sorry, wool gathering. My thoughts veered off to my daughter's welfare once you mentioned communication with Morley. I'm remembering how much he liked the outdoors. How old is he now? Does he have a family?"

"No family. He's twenty-four. Been a soldier for six years and still standing, so he must be good at it by now."

"Where's he stationed?"

"Benning, last I heard, but his unit moves around a lot."

Fort Benning was in Columbus, Georgia, so he was only three hours away. "You're lucky he's so close. Seemed like Roland spent most of his tours of duty overseas."

"You get your benefits yet from the army?"

Nothing was private in a small town. "No."

"They should be coming along any day now."

I glanced up. "Why do you think that?"

"It's time."

How odd, but he didn't elaborate. The rest of the meal passed with talk about the warmer weather and bugs, both of which were plentiful in summer. Before long, Mr. Luther was driving home in his car, and I was alone with my pets.

I did the dishes, called and thanked my parents for the meal, started a load of laundry, and puttered around the house. I hadn't heard anything from the sheriff, so I assumed his deputies hadn't found Marv's body yet. I wished spirits would be more forthcoming about the cause of their demise, but it seemed like they all had a story to tell.

Elvis and Muffin barked and alerted me to a car pulling in my drive. The visitor parked by my truck and trotted up the back steps. It was nearly eight at night. Who would drop by this late without calling first? I stood in the hallway shadows feeling alone and vulnerable. What should I grab, the bat or a gun?

The knock at the door was instantaneous and urgent. An unfamiliar face pressed against the glass panel in the door. "Dream-walker lady. You in there? I gotta speak to you somepin' turrible."

CHAPTER 11

A dreamwalking client. Not a killer. I drew in a normal breath and opened the back door. "May I help you?"

A balding black man bounded into my house. The dogs kept barking. From atop the refrigerator, the cat gave him the stink eye as the intruder circled my kitchen table. His body twitched and shook. "You gotta fix me. I done got the whammy laid on me."

I shushed the dogs. "Please sit down and tell me what happened. My name's Baxley. What's yours?"

"People call me Stinger, and I can't sit down." Stinger danced around like he had fire ants in his boxers. "I'm too wired. I gotta have them excommunicated."

It took all I had not to snicker. Since I had no priestly powers, I supposed he meant exorcised. I didn't have those kinds of powers either. I leaned up against the dishwasher and stayed out of his way.

"What's going on?"

"Dead people. That's what."

Was he talking about Marv? "Do you have information on a police matter?"

"I don't know nuttin' about the po-po. I gotta get these dead folk outta my head."

Hmm. I barred my arms and stared at him. "How'd they get in there?"

"Do ya think I know?" his voice rose into falsetto range. He gestured wildly with his hands, jangling the keys he held. "Get 'em out. I don't want 'em yammerin' at me all the time."

Whatever was going on, Stinger was convinced it was real. I wasn't so sure, since the alcohol fumes coming off of him were nearly one hundred proof, and his pupils nearly eclipsed his eyes. Despite my skepticism, I was intrigued. "When did you first notice the voices?"

"This morning. I tried to drink them away, but they won't leave me alone. Then I downed a bunch of pills, but they's still talking up a blue streak. Somebody said you could help. Please. You gotta get them out."

"Are they saying anything in particular?"

Stinger grabbed his head and moaned. "Noooo."

The guy was in real distress. I needed to do something to ease his mind. "Put your keys on the table."

"Why? How will that help my head?"

"Sometimes I can tell things from an object a person has touched."

Without looking up, he hurled his keys in my direction. My hand went up reflexively and I snagged them before they hit the window behind me. "I'm not sure how long this will take, maybe ten to thirty minutes."

"Anything, so long as I can think straight again."

I opened my senses, expecting to have a rushing sensation, followed by a momentary disorientation. I got nothing. No flash of light. No distortion. No vision.

Huh. My pulse skittered out of control.

I tried again.

Same negative result. White-hot disbelief seared me. This wasn't right. I should've recharged during that nap.

Stinger had bent over the center island, holding his head. I walked over to him and placed my hand on his shoulder. Nothing. Not a jolt. Not a buzz. Flat-out zippo. I pulled my hand away and shook it.

Were my dreamwalking abilities damaged? How was that possible? This guy needed help, and I was out of gas. What would my father do in a circumstance like this? Easy. He'd look to my mom for help. She'd make the person a cup of hot tea.

I bustled over to the sink, filled the tea kettle, and turned the stove on. The busy-work hid my distress, but it couldn't stop the question hammering in my head. Was my talent gone? "Change of plan. Sit down, please."

"What?"

He seemed to be in a daze. I guided him over to a chair and sat him down. I noted his hand had moved to his right ear. "I need you to sit down for a few minutes."

Almost immediately, Elvis, our rescue Chihuahua, ran up Stinger's leg and began licking his face and hand.

"Elvis? Dat you, buddy?" Stinger asked.

I got down mugs and the tea. "Sure is. You know this dog?"

Stinger petted Elvis, and for the first time since he arrived, a smile broke out on his face. "I do. He belonged to my buddy. Before he went off to jail, that is. I'd heard Elvis found a new home, and he seems to be fat and happy."

"I see."

Stinger made cooing noises, and Elvis waggled all over. Clearly these two were old friends.

"Cooley could make this dog turn in circles, dance on his back legs, beg, you name it, this little guy could do it."

"I've never seen him do those tricks."

"Cooley would bring him to the club in his shirt and all the ladies would go wild. This dog got him more action . . . Oh, excuse me, I should hush my mouth. I apologize."

The kettle whistled. I busied myself with the tea preparations, biting back a smile. When I turned around, the man was nuzzling the dog and darned near humming. "You seem to be doing a lot better now that you're holding Elvis. Are the voices gone?"

Stinger started, cocked his head to the side, and grinned. "All clear. You did it."

I wasn't so sure about that. Stinger needed help, and I had none to give. Only one solution explained his sudden improvement. "Elvis might be a therapy dog."

"How could you tell?"

"For starters, put him down and see if the voices come back."

Stinger set the dog on the table. Elvis promptly leapt back into his arms. "You notice anything different?" I asked.

"Nuttin'."

"He wasn't down long enough. Let me hold Elvis for a minute or so."

Stinger reared back in alarm. "I don't want the voices to come back."

"Neither do I, but if Elvis stops them, we need to know." I reached for the Chihuahua. Stinger reluctantly parted with the dog. "What do you take in your tea?"

"Coffee. I drink coffee."

"Of course you do. But tonight you're trying a cup of tea. What do you put in your coffee?"

"Whiskey."

I had some bourbon, but this guy didn't need more booze. One-handed, I squirted a little honey in both cups and then stirred the tea. Stinger took a cup from me, a worried look on his face.

"The voices are still gone, but what if they come back? Can Elvis come home with me tonight?"

At the sound of his name, Elvis vibrated with anticipation. He whined. "I'm sorry. Elvis is my daughter's dog now. She would be heartbroken if anything happened to her pet. You're welcome to hold him all you like this evening, and even come back tomorrow to hold him again, but I insist he stays here."

Stinger's expression fell. He stared into his steaming tea as if it held the mysteries of the universe. "Can I hold him again?"

My heart panged. The man wanted to hold the dog, the dog wanted to see the man, who was I to stand in their way?

"Sure, so long as you abide by my wishes. Elvis stays here. He's Larissa's dog now."

I handed him over, and Elvis went nuts over Stinger. "He remembers you all right."

"Me and Elvis is pals. I'd keep him for my buddy, while he was, uh, busy, and we had a good ole time."

My phone rang. Unless it was Larissa checking in, I'd let it go to voice mail. I plucked it from my pocket and stared at the display. The sheriff. Was there a break in the case? I nodded toward the other room. "Excuse me. I gotta take this call."

Stinger and Elvis didn't seem to notice I'd stepped into the hall. "Pets and Plants," I answered.

"Put your woo-woo hat on. We got two bodies."

I took another few steps away from the kitchen, careful to talk softly. "Two? I thought we were only looking for Marv. Is there a crime spree in Sinclair County?"

"Can't say, but these 'uns are sure as hell stiff. Tab will meet us at the scene. I'll pick you up in five minutes."

At the sound of the back door slamming and Muffin yapping, I whirled. Stinger was long gone. With Elvis.

CHAPTER 12

Out of courtesy to my peace of mind, the sheriff muted his siren, but the flashing lights painted the county-scape an eerie blue as we zoomed down back roads to the swamp. The sweet scent of honeysuckle filled the night air. "You didn't tell me we were going to June's Folly."

"Would it have mattered?"

I would've grabbed every one of my crystals and a toy for the ghost dog. "I guess not."

"You're not a very good liar. What's wrong?"

"Don't laugh. I'm a dognapping victim. Stinger came to my house tonight yammering about voices in his head, and he stole Larissa's dog. I have to get that dog back before Larissa comes home from Jacksonville."

"Stinger's been going through a rough patch since his wife died of cancer. He doesn't know what to do with himself."

"Getting tanked on booze and pills is a lousy idea, Wayne. Stealing a child's dog is lower than low."

The sheriff thought about that for longer than I liked as he cleared the four-way stop. "Sometimes a man numbs the pain so he doesn't do something stupid."

"Like what? What could be more stupid than stealing a child's dog?"

"Eating his gun. Holding up a bank. Ramming his truck into a pine tree."

My hand clamped over my mouth. "He's suicidal?"

"We've picked him up a few times this last month. He pointed a gun at Virgil."

Suicide by cop? "He's lucky Virg didn't light him up with the stun gun."

The sheriff said nothing. I arrived at the obvious conclusion. Virg had used his stun gun. "Not again. You can't let that man run around tasering everyone. He shoots that thing off at a moment's notice."

"Which is why I let him carry it. Virg may be trigger-happy, but no one is resisting arrest these days. They know he'll fire up the stun gun. That's worth its weight in Golden Isles as far as I'm concerned."

I muttered under my breath, not wanting to say this was another heavy-handed cop tactic. I liked this job, even if I did get calls at all hours of the day and night. I cleared my throat and changed the subject. "What about Dottie? She kick you out for not coming home last night?"

"Now that's the oddest thing. She was all smiles. I don't trust that woman when she's happy. Something's afoot."

I'd ducked Wayne's advances in high school and as an adult for a reason. He was a serial womanizer. His marital status and his kids didn't slow him down one bit. I had standards, which is why I'd chosen another boy from high school. Roland Powell seemed trustworthy, monogamous, and faithful. I'd been wrong about his values. Now he'd left me high and dry, so my instincts about men weren't the best.

As the silence dragged on, I realized I should say something. "God help you."

"What? Oh. Dottie. Yeah. Well. She'll figure out some new way to torture me and our bank account."

Time for a new subject. At the rate we were going, I'd run out of topics before we reached our dreaded destination. "You never said who the other victim was."

"A local. You know Belinda Donlin?"

"Doesn't ring a bell. Who is she?"

"A fishing boat captain. Maybe you've

100

heard of Cap'n Bee's Charters? Bee is short for Belinda."

I'd seen her ads in the newspaper and her business cards in the local restaurants. "Bee. That makes sense."

"What?"

"I had a dream earlier. Of Marv. Before I knew his name. He called the woman with him Beautiful, but the way he said it was bee-utiful."

"Ah. The sex dream. I remember you mentioning it." In the faint gleam of the dash lights, the sheriff waggled his dark eyebrows. "Tell me more."

"Not much to tell. They were intimate. And now they're both dead."

"I got that much. Seriously, no sex details?"

"Get over yourself. What's your theory? Did they die because of their liaison, or was it more of a case of one of them being a target and the other person being in the wrong place?"

"Don't have a theory yet. I've got something better."

At his knowing look, my curiosity spiked. I studied his profile, a dark silhouette on an even darker background. "What?"

"A police consultant with a victim hotline. Let's streamline the process this time. Dial

101

in the dead people at the scene, get the suspect's name, and I'll make an arrest tonight."

"Fat chance. It doesn't work that way. The odds of my getting answers tonight are lousy." Terrible in fact, since my extra senses weren't working. Not that I would admit my deficit to the sheriff. I cleared my throat. "How'd they die?"

"Exsanguinations."

Blood loss. It might be an accident if one person bled to death, but two? No way. We were looking at murder.

Wayne pulled up in the driveway beside two police cruisers, the sight of the torn-up yard causing the sheriff to swear. "Damn movie people and their commotion. I'll be happy when the entire crew pulls out of here."

"I thought you were all about progress and more money in the county's coffers."

"I don't call this," he said and paused to gesture at the vandalized lawn, "progress. These people need to take their monkey business and their alleged pirate treasure rumors elsewhere."

"I've heard similar rumblings around town."

He exited the vehicle, grabbed his gear bag, and leaned down to speak to me. "You coming?"

Last time I was at June's Folly I got stuck between worlds. I wasn't looking to blunder into the wrong place again. A sense of trepidation and global disaster taunted me. Distorted faces seemed to swirl in the mist drifting over from the swamp. I had to get a grip and unfreeze my limbs. "Give me a few minutes, okay?"

Just then, my dad parked the coroner's van beside the sheriff's Jeep. The men chatted briefly, then the sheriff hurried inside. Dad plunked down in the driver's seat beside me. It was a relief to see his familiar tie-dyed shirt and faded jeans. "Wayne said you needed a minute. What's going on?"

No one else was in sight, but even so, I lowered my voice. "I've got a huge problem."

CHAPTER 13

My father closed the Jeep's door, his parental concern blanketing me. "What's wrong?"

I looked out the dark window toward the cypress swamp bordering this old place. For some reason, my psychic block seemed magnified out here, as if the fate of the free world hung in balance. "You ever run out of gas?" I asked, dreading his answer.

"In my vehicle?"

"In your senses."

"Ah. I wondered about that." His eyes filled with understanding and empathy. "Carrying Wayne over the divide and back burned a lot of juice. You still feel like you want to sleep for a week?"

"Yes."

"Did you try sleeping with your extra crystals?"

My head bobbed. I stared at his craggy profile. He didn't seem to be exhausted. Somehow he'd recharged today. Not. Fair.

"Why would I do that?"

"It'll help. I'll loan you my crystal shirt, though I'm sorry you need it. What about food? Is your appetite okay?"

"Nothing's wrong with my eating, and if anything, I'm hungrier than before. But that could be stress. I've got a serious situation here. The sheriff expects me to go inside and tell him something useful about Marv and Belinda's killer. I got nothing extra, only the faces in the mist that the normals claim to see." I told him about my failure to help Stinger. "I'm wasting everyone's time by even being here, but I couldn't bring myself to tell Wayne I was broken. I couldn't take a chance that he'd fire me. I need this job."

My father nodded sagely. "To answer your question, yes, I ran out of gas a lot. Over the last year, I crashed every time I crossed over and back. If not for your mom and her crystal therapy, I wouldn't be walking around today. I'd be in the loony bin. With any luck, you're experiencing the same temporary effect from pulling too much power."

I heaved a sigh of relief. "Thank goodness."

"Don't get me wrong. This is serious, but fixable. Time is the best healer after shorting out your extrasensory circuits. And your mother's crystals."

The air inside the sheriff's Jeep felt safe. But out there, out in the misty swamp air, something unseen triggered my deepest fears. If it were up to me, I'd put this car in reverse and never return. "Every time I step foot on this property something happens to me."

"If you feel the dark pull of June's Folly, then your senses aren't totally fried. That's good news. The other good news is your mother insisted I bring extra crystals with me. I'll be right back."

I let out a shaky breath. It would be okay. If my dad had returned whole from this sensory void, so could I. And my mom, bless her, intuitively knew what we needed to survive.

Dad opened my door and handed me a fistful of crystals. My fingers tingled as they closed around the unexpected lifeline. A sense of calm and well-being came over me, with guilt riding hard on its coattails. "Don't you need to keep some for yourself?"

He grinned and patted the sides of his jeans. "Both my pants pockets are fully loaded. I wouldn't dream of coming out here without these fancy rocks."

I eased up and out of the vehicle. The

night sky didn't explode. The rough ground didn't rumble or split open. Snarling creatures didn't emerge from the swamp and invade my body. My fears had ramped all out of proportion to the situation, but I wouldn't let fear beat me. Not now. Not ever.

I pocketed the crystals. "Thanks, Dad. I couldn't do this job without you."

"We're all connected, honey. Don't ever forget that. My mother used to call it the web of life."

Bubba Paxton stepped out from behind the coroner's van with a gurney and a sheepish grin. "Feeling better?"

What was the former drug dealer turned evangelist doing here? I covered my surprise with good manners. "Hey, Bubba. You part of Daddy's coroner team?"

"Me and Tab been a team for awhile. He asked me to ride along tonight."

Because it was June's Folly. Dad had brought reinforcements, and whether it was for his benefit or mine, the result was the same. We were stronger because of our numbers. Lesson learned. "I'm glad to see you."

Bubba fiddled with what looked to be a body bag. "You get in a bind inside, and we've got your back, you hear? Sensitives

107

look out for each other."

"I'm getting the message loud and clear. Don't walk into a known danger zone alone."

"Let's grab these bodies and get the heck out of the swamp," Bubba said. "I hate this place."

Flashlights bobbed in the windows of the old house. I clicked on my light and started forward across the uneven ground. "My sentiments exactly."

We made it across the yard and up the steps before Bubba and my dad froze. "Something's got me," Bubba said, his voice trembling. "I feel the cold on my legs."

I smiled, even though I barely felt the chill. Instinctively, I touched my moldavite necklace. "Say hello to Oliver. He's a ghost dog." I softened my voice. "Good boy, Oliver. You're a good doggie."

"A dog?" Bubba said. "Why didn't you say so? Can you see him?"

"Not right now, but it's Oliver. I'm certain of that."

Bubba squatted on the porch and extended his hand. "I like dogs. Hullo, Oliver. Can we be friends?"

A large mutt materialized by Bubba's hand, tail wagging. "Looka there," Bubba said. "It is a beautiful dog. How'd you get stuck out here?"

I knelt beside Bubba, and Oliver lay down between us, his head on my lap. We took a moment to pet him, then at a noise from inside, Oliver faded from sight.

"The chill is gone." Bubba grinned from ear to ear as we rose to our feet. "You know the darnedest things."

That knowledge had come at a high price. I didn't want to think about when Rose the demon would collect on my debt. I raised my flashlight to eye level and crossed the threshold. Broken furniture populated the rooms visible from the foyer. My light didn't penetrate the depth of the gloom in here. Not a good sign. The less time I spent in this creepy house, the better.

Even with my senses blanked out, the scent and pall of death slowed my stride. Heaviness filled the house with edgy emotion, terror, and pain. Death smelled ripe and coppery. A lot of blood had been spilled in this house. The front door creaked open another inch, the raspy sound grating on my ragged nerves.

"Hello?" I called as I crept forward, noting that the police flashlights were farther inside the dwelling. It figured that one of the county's most famous haunted properties was a movie set locale. I wondered if they'd already filmed here, or if that was still on the schedule. Would they even finish the Ford Morrison movie now?

"This place is beyond creepy," Bubba said. "The darkness is wrong. It's too thick, and it sets my teeth on edge."

"We're here to do a job," Dad said in a tight voice. "We'll collect the bodies and leave."

"Watch the steps," Wayne instructed from above as a beam of light panned down the staircase to my right. "Keep to the outer edge."

I heard the rasp of a zipper as Bubba and Dad opened a body bag behind me. There were two corpses in this house. Marv's and Belinda's. I transferred the flashlight to my left hand and reached my right into my pocketful of crystals. I could do this. I was a police consultant, after all. I'd stared death in the face before.

The blood coating the stairs was mostly on one side. I hugged the opposite wall as the sheriff had suggested. So intent was I on my footing that I didn't glance up as I walked. When I reached the upper landing, the gruesome tableau stunned me. I lost my balance, staggered, and would've tumbled down the steps if not for Daddy and Bubba's hands steadying me.

Linked together by physical touch, we viewed the scene.

Two sets of lifeless eyes stared at us blankly. A naked man and a woman had been strung up, lashed to the railing by their bound feet. Their wrists were duct-taped together. A crimson slash at each neck bespoke the violent means of death, as did the river of dried blood cascading down the worn steps.

I'd never met Marv, so I focused on Cap'n Bee. Her body was unmarred, and except for the gruesome throat slash, her skin was alabaster pale. I couldn't miss her torso. Her full breasts and lush hips were the stuff of male fantasies. Who knew she had all of that going on under her baggy clothes?

For completeness, I scanned Marv's lifeless body. No bruises, no apparent signs of a fight. His skin tone was pale also. Guess losing all your blood would do that to you.

Blood splatter marred the wall across from the bodies. That, along with the river of blood dried on the steps, told the gruesome tale. No question in my mind, the double murder occurred here. I did the math. Marv was last seen Friday night. Charlotte had been out here in early evening. We nearly walked in on a murder. I shuddered at the close call.

"Your thoughts, Madam Consultant?" the sheriff asked.

"Someone had it in for these people," I began slowly, taking strength and solace from the physical connection to my father and his assistant. "They died here in this house, but how did two people who look to be in their primes allow this to happen? Why didn't they resist?"

"The autopsy will tell us if they were drugged. Tap into your woo-woo powers and get us a lead so I can close this case."

"It doesn't work like that. The dead choose when they talk to me. I'm not a psychic channel you can tap into at will." I'd been summoned to a few murder scenes now. I'd seen crimes of passion and crimes of opportunity. This looked like nothing I'd seen before. "This was planned out in advance. Your killer is making a statement."

"Yeah." Ronnie snickered from behind the sheriff. "He's saying you're dead."

"It's more than that, and you know it." My voice rose. "This place is private, so the killer wouldn't be disturbed. I'm surprised the railing held. Everything else in this place seems to be falling apart."

"He thought of that," Wayne said. "The railing is tied off to wall studs in two places and reinforced with two by sixes at the posts

112

and the rail."

"You think this killer's a guy?"

"A woman couldn't hang two adults upside down and slit their throats. This took brute strength and carpentry know-how."

"Point taken." I needed to say something to redeem myself. "Where are their clothes?"

Ronnie lowered his camera and pointed down the hall with his light. One door gaped wide. "In the nookie room."

CHAPTER 14

A stained double-sized mattress lay a-kilter on the floor. Not a sheet or pillow in sight. Clothes and shoes had been discarded carelessly. Empty beer bottles and potato chip bags added to the décor, if that word even applied to this untidy mess.

If I was at a hundred percent, all I'd need to do is make contact with something they'd touched to get a reading of what happened here. With my powers unavailable, that was out of the question. I had to rely on my regular senses.

The open window brought night sounds indoors and cleansed the air. Instinctively, I drew near the window and shone my light along the walls, ceiling, and floor, careful to keep my hands to myself. "No blood, but they definitely undressed in here. Somehow they were subdued after they began, uh, recreating."

"Recreating." Wayne's smug tone irritated

me. "I like that. Before tonight, I wasn't aware these people were acquainted, much less sleeping together. Far as I knew, Bee played the field, but jealousy's a powerful motive. I'll check into their personal and professional lives."

From the hallway came sounds of commotion and groaning. Guess they were cutting the bodies down. Wood creaked and moaned. Two heavy thuds sounded in succession, then relative quiet descended. I drew in another breath of moist swamp air and noted the frogs and insects were creating their night music.

I was about to mention leaving when I heard another muffled double thump and realized Wayne was standing in the doorway, shielding me from the bodies. For a guy who had a bad reputation as a skirt chaser, he had fairly decent protective instincts. I focused on drawing in deep cleansing breaths.

"You want to touch anything?" the sheriff asked over my shoulder, his aftershave blending with the fresh air.

I'd been so intent on breathing I hadn't realized he'd moved next to me. His body heat helped counteract the unearthly chill of the room. "Not tonight. I'm overwhelmed right now. June's Folly is a hot zone for sensitives, and I need to leave here as soon as possible."

He touched my shoulder. "It's okay, babe. This place has bad juju for everyone."

Anger flashed through me lightning-fast as I shrank away from his hand. "I'm not your babe." The need to leave intensified. "I'm done here. I'll wait for you outside."

He nodded, pleased, if the smirk on his face was any indication. My stomach sank as I realized he'd played me for my own benefit. Thanks to him, the fire in my belly would see me out the door and then some.

"You look like you've seen a ghost or two," Wayne said. "I'll have Virg run you home. He tossed his dinner and is outside in the squad car."

Virg? My least favorite deputy? "I'll do it as long as I get to hold his Taser gun."

"No." Wayne scowled. "Virg won't shoot you again. If he does, he's out of a job. You tell him I said so. If you don't want to ride with him, you can hitch a ride with your dad and the victims. Ronnie and I'll be here a few hours yet bagging evidence."

Not much choice, seeing as how I wanted to scratch off. "There's a lot I'd like to tell Virg, but he tunes me out."

"You'd understand if you had a wife like Virg's."

"Seriously, the man has a problem with women."

"Seriously, he shows up for work on time, does his job, and the only complaint I've ever heard about him has come from you."

"Humph." Wayne had an answer for everything. Mercifully he didn't press me for a killer's name. "I'll give Virg another chance."

"All right then. Good night."

I stepped around him, holding my flashlight in front of me like a shield. As I turned the corner to go down the stairs, I glanced at the spot where the bodies had been and then over at the spray on the opposite wall. Something seemed off, but stare as I might, I couldn't see anything worth mentioning. Since I didn't want to keep breathing this blood-scented air, I hoofed it down the steps, avoiding the blood trail.

I passed out of the house and across the yard without incident. My father, Bubba, and Ronnie broke apart as I approached. Expectation lit their faces; even my father looked hopeful and he knew of my spiritual outage.

"I got nothing. I'm a dreamwalker, not a magician," I said, watching their faces fall. "We'll catch this killer, just not tonight."

My father nodded. "We were making arrangements to fit you in my van. Bubba says he can stay with the cops and catch a ride back with one of them."

Bubba wanted to leave as much as I did, and if he stayed here, that left no one to help my dad unload the corpses at the morgue. I shook my head. "The sheriff said Virg would take me home."

Ronnie looked alarmed. "Virg isn't doing so hot."

The unmistakable sound of retching rent the air. "Maybe I'll drive Virg home."

"Against regulations," Ronnie said.

"It's a car. I can drive," I scoffed. "Trust me, Virg is past ready to leave June's Folly. I won't tell the sheriff if you won't."

"He doesn't like secrets."

I held out my hand. "Give me the car keys. If there's any fallout, you can say I took them from you."

Ronnie's face hardened, then his buddy retched again. Reluctantly he reached into his pocket, slipped a key off a fat wad. "All right. But I'm doing this for Virg. Any trouble, and you take all the heat."

"Deal." I took the key. Before I could walk away, my father touched my arm. "I have something else for you. Wait a second while I get it."

I followed him to the front of the van and took the heavy chambray shirt from his

118

hands. A sense of well-being immediately enfolded me.

"Put it on," Dad urged.

I stroked the fabric, torn between boy-do-I-want-to-take-this and I-couldn't-possibly-accept-a-gift-of-this-magnitude. "Your crystal shirt? Don't you need it?"

"Not tonight, I won't. It's a loaner for the night, but I want it returned tomorrow."

"Understood." I kissed his cheek. "Thanks for thinking of me. I'll put it on when I get home. I don't want anything to happen to it." Treasure in hand, I hurried to the squad car. Virg sat in the passenger seat, his legs out the door, his head supported by his hands. He moaned as I opened the driver's door and cranked the engine.

"Buckle up, Virg," I said. "I'm getting us out of here."

"I feel terrible." He slowly pivoted in his seat, his moon-shaped face puke green. His khaki-colored uniform with dark brown trim and snazzy gold accoutrements had several suspicious spots down the front.

For my sake as much as his, I opened the front windows and flipped the AC to max. Virg groaned and held his head as I backed the squad car up and eased down the grassy lane.

"Hang on. Just a few more miles and you

should be feeling better."

His eyes scrunched shut. "I want to die."

"Understood. Y'all got any ginger ale in here?"

"Nooooo."

The coroner's van followed me down the long dirt drive. I eased over the bumps in the road, trying not to jostle Virg. Even though I was mad at the big guy for Tasering me a few months back, I felt sympathy for his current distress. At last we hit the pavement, and the air started smelling less swampy. Virg hadn't thrown up since we left the driveway, which was good news for both of us.

He liked to groan, though, which was purely irritating.

"Can I get you anything?" I asked, remembering the twenty-four-hour mini-market out by the interstate. I could zip in there on the way home.

"Whiskey."

I was darned sure he wasn't supposed to drink on duty, plus I'd never heard of anyone drinking whiskey to stop throwing up. "Fresh out."

"Just as well. My wife would kill me if I drank a lick. I've been sober for three years now. But this. Tonight. God. It's terrible."

I agreed, but I didn't know how to console

him. What did one say to a 230-pound man who'd been so sick to his stomach he couldn't do his job? I'd seen this man at other homicide locations, and he'd never so much as belched. Why was this one different? Could he be a sensitive like me?

"Any chance you've got a bit of psychic in you?" I asked.

"I don't believe in that stuff." He shot me a furtive look and angled so he was facing me. He regarded me steadily for some time. "My aunt's a little like you. Not that she can talk to dead people, but she knows things somehow."

I wracked my brain thinking of Virg's people and came up blank. "What's your aunt's name?"

"Estelle. Estelle Hightower. She doesn't live in this county. She's up Richmond Hill way."

That explained why I didn't know her, but I'd bet a cup of coffee that my parents knew her. "Is that where you're from?"

"More or less. My parents lived here for a few years when I was a kid, then my dad got on at the mill, and we moved across the county line. But I always liked it best in Sinclair County. Until tonight. She didn't deserve this."

That caught my attention. "She? Who are

you talking about?"

"Bee. She was the sweetest, nicest person." He banged his coiled fist on the dashboard, causing the entire array of electronic gadgetry to shimmy.

"Easy there. We don't want to have to explain how the air bag deployed while you were driving me home."

"Can't help it. I want to punch something. And drink hard liquor. And I don't want to go home and have to tell my wife about this one."

"Why not?"

"Because Bee and I have a history. We were drinking buddies a few years back. She and my wife, they used to be close."

CHAPTER 15

The gruesome crime scene images were vivid in my mind the next morning. I'd hoped to dream about Marv and Bee, but I slept deeply and undisturbed in my father's crystal shirt. Did that mean my other senses were still on the fritz? I didn't want to know. I didn't even want to do any dreamwalking until I was a hundred percent again.

I carefully removed the crystals from the various pouches before hand-washing the garment and hanging it to dry in the shower. This morning I felt more pep in my step, more fizz in my biz.

Much better than yesterday, in fact. Hope sparkled, a glittering diamond of possibilities. Whatever normal was for me, I was darned close.

After rattling around in the empty house for half an hour and missing my daughter, I tried the Powells' number in Jacksonville. The housekeeper answered and said no one was home. She gave me Elizabeth's cell number, and I tried that one.

The call flipped to voice mail, and I left a message saying I missed Larissa and I loved her. After I hung up, doubt crept in. Did I come across as a desperate mother? I shouldn't have to justify why I'd called.

But last night reinforced something.

Life was short.

I didn't want Larissa to think she was out of sight and out of mind. The phone rang. The number displayed was Elizabeth's cell. I answered immediately.

"Mom, I'm busy," Larissa said in a hushed tone. "Besides. You. Didn't. Call."

I'd almost called a dozen times, but I didn't want to alarm my sensitive daughter with any of my news. I went for breezy. "You could've called me any time, you know that. Is everything okay?"

"I guess." Larissa sighed. "These people do everything on a strict schedule, even meals."

Maternal alarm flared from zero to sixty in the space of a single heartbeat. "Are you hungry? I can leave right now and be there in about ninety minutes."

"I'm fine. I figured it out on my own. I can't talk now because tennis camp is starting."

I was annoyed she didn't have time for me, but I'd expected the Powells would offer her everything money could buy. "All right then. It's great to hear your voice, and I'll see you on Saturday."

"Uh. Mom. I might want to stay longer. There's this boy . . ."

A boy? She was ten. I shook my head. She was growing up much too fast. "We'll talk about it later, when you have more time." A few I love yous later, and the call ended.

Before I drove Larissa to Jacksonville, I'd had every confidence she would cope in the different environment, but I'd also assumed she would be eager to come home afterward. Now I wasn't so sure. Could I handle her being away for more than a week?

My throat constricted, and I felt weak in the knees at the prospect of a longer separation. I sagged against the kitchen counter, flooded by longing and emptiness. I clutched my belly with both arms, blinking away the moisture in my eyes.

Sulay watched me with slitted eyes from her cat perch atop the refrigerator. Muffin whined at my ankles. I picked him up and petted his furry head. He licked my hands and face, helping me stay grounded in this moment.

Don't borrow trouble, my mom would say.

125

She was right. I'd done the right thing in allowing Larissa to visit her paternal grandparents. The child I'd raised wouldn't be seduced by luxury or a country-club lifestyle. But making a new friend might tip the scale. I shook my head to clear it. Larissa was fine, and I had work scheduled.

On my to-do list today were bringing Elvis home and making my monthly rounds of the snowbirds' houses to care for the landscaping. All of the properties had year-round lawn care contracts with local vendors, but most of the lawn guys didn't want to fool with trimming bushes. I did, and the word spread quickly through the migratory community. In April, I'd lined up two clients, who told two more, who told two more, so that I had ten homes on my roster, and a nice revenue stream for the entire growing season.

With determination, I released the dog from my arms and set about loading my clippers, trimmers, and rakes in the truck.

I hoped to postpone the visit to the sheriff's office until tomorrow. Wayne would want results, and I couldn't guarantee anything until I'd fully recovered my senses. But I wasn't out of the driveway before my phone rang.

"Get over here," the sheriff said.

126

"Good morning to you, too," I answered.

"I've got the entire press corps from *The Marion Observer,* along with stringers from the regional dailies in my lobby demanding answers, and we're circling the wagons. Do not talk to Charlotte before you get here. Come in the back door. And hurry."

The fact that my best friend in the whole wide world was a reporter was a problem. Worse, Charlotte could think circles around all of us. But this wasn't about Charlotte. This was about me doing my police consultant job.

It was a point of pride that I now had a key to the officer-only area of the station. I didn't have to be buzzed in through the lobby anymore. I was one of the guys. Sort of.

So much for my landscaping schedule. Ah, well, I could tend to those clients tomorrow. I patted my pocket full of crystals and mentally flipped over to my police consultant persona. "I'm on my way, but it's gonna cost you Stinger's name and address."

"What? Oh, right. Your stolen dog. We'll get to Stinger, but this murder investigation takes precedence."

"Gotcha." I sped down the road. One bonus of working with the cops was not having to worry about speeding tickets when

127

the sheriff summoned me like this. What could be so terrible that he wanted everyone involved at the station?

The miles flew by and I pulled into the back lot beside the coroner van. Three TV vans from elsewhere were parked in the other lot, and a knot of people milled on the lawn. The sheriff was right. This case was about to go nuclear.

CHAPTER 16

I darted up the sidewalk to the law enforcement building. A shout went up in the public lot, and I noticed large cameras pointing my way. Great. With my glaring white forelock and workman's clothes, I'd look quite the character on the TV news.

The door swung open, and I ducked under Virg's beefy arm into safe quarters. "You feeling better?"

Virg squared his husky shoulders. "Damn straight. Then the morning turned into a bona fide disaster."

"What's going on?"

"Someone leaked pictures of the crime scene to the Internet and the press ran parts of them. The sheriff wants that someone's head on a platter."

No way were those gruesome images fit for prime-time TV. "Ooooh. Very not good. What can I do?"

He gestured down the empty corridor.

"The sheriff called a meet. You're the last one to arrive on his list of attendees."

I was last to arrive because I wasn't already in town like everyone else who worked at the cop shop full time. I hurried to the distant conference room. On the phone, Wayne had sounded like he was in a foul mood, and I didn't want his ire leveled at me.

After I sat down, the sheriff convened the meeting. I glanced around the large table at the familiar faces. Daddy. Bubba Paxton. Virg. Ronnie. The sheriff. Even Dr. Sugar, the retired coroner, had been called in for the pow-wow.

"Last night we discovered the bodies of Marv Kildeer and Belinda Donlin out at June's Folly," the sheriff said. "According to the Medical Examiner, the time of death was approximated at midnight the night before. The state lab is putting a rush on the tox screen samples. I called this meeting because I don't want any of you saying more than 'no comment' to the media. The clock is ticking, folks. We must narrow the scope of the investigation and get a bead on this guy.

"Whoever killed these people showed no remorse and may kill again. Remain vigilant and carry a weapon at all times. That includes you, Baxley. We don't know if Marv or Bee were targeted individually or collectively. We'll sift through their phone and computer records and visit each of their places of residence. We have the signed warrants to proceed.

"After my official statement to the media, I'll take Baxley with me to visit Bee's place out on Winslow Creek. The rest of you will examine the stacks of records I've compiled, looking for anything out of the ordinary. Let me assure you, the world is watching. We don't want to come off as buffoons or illiterate rednecks. And we damn well want to catch this killer before he strikes again."

He paused to sweep the room with a steely gaze. "We will eat, sleep, and breathe this case. Any questions so far?"

A pin drop in the room would have been deafening, so absolute was the silence. I was afraid to blink lest I draw attention to myself. My cell phone vibrated in my pocket, which earned me a nasty glance, but I let the call roll to voice mail.

The sheriff rose, planted his palms on the table, and leaned forward. "If I find out one of you leaked those photos to the press, you're fired and you'll never work in this county again. I do not want outsiders breathing down my neck. The GBI and the

FBI called this morning and offered their help, but I've successfully got them on hold. This is a high-profile case. We work together, as a team, or it's all she wrote."

I didn't want state or federal investigators nosing around down here either. Dream-walkers needed to stay under the radar. I kept my gaze averted and hoped like anything the sheriff wasn't looking at me.

Wayne then addressed each person by name and asked if they'd leaked the photos. Each person offered a vehement no. Dr. Sugar said he wasn't even at June's Folly, which was a good point.

At my turn, a thought tumbled out of my mouth uncensored. "Of course not, but we weren't the only ones at the scene, Sheriff. The killer could've taken those pictures."

"Way ahead of you," the sheriff said. "We've got tech whizzes working on the origin of those pictures. People, you can take this to the bank. We'll catch the killer, and we'll track down the person who sent those pictures."

I wanted to ask where he got tech whizzes, but I kept that query to myself. My pocket buzzed again. Thankfully, we were dismissed.

Before he left the room, Wayne said. "Don't go anywhere. We're leaving soon as

I get this press announcement out of the way."

As people filed out, I snuck a look at my phone. A call and a text from Charlotte. The text read "what's going on?" I hoped our lifelong friendship was strong enough to withstand current events. I texted her back with the politically correct response of "no comment."

Pocketing the phone, I glanced up to see my father had lagged behind. "How're you doing?" he asked.

"Better. Don't know if I'm all the way back." I scoped out the room and hall. Deserted. Just to be safe, I lowered my voice. "I'm a little afraid to try anything."

"Got your crystals?"

I tapped my other pocket. "I do. I washed your shirt this morning, and I'll get it back to you as soon as it's dry. Mom's a genius to have thought of that."

"She's something else all right. Any word from Larissa?"

"We talked this morning. She's okay and asked to stay longer."

He placed a firm hand on my shoulder. "Tell her we miss her next time you speak to her."

Besides the comforting warmth emanating from his hand, I got a quick shared image of my mother crying. I reared back to search my father's face, needing an immediate explanation before I took another breath. "Is Mom all right?"

"You are recovering if you gleaned that from my touch." His smile didn't reach his eyes. "A friend of hers got some bad news."

Guilty relief washed through me. "Who?"

"Gentle Dove. The tiredness she's been feeling is more than aging. She's very ill. Cancer, she says, but she won't consider chemo or radiation. It's breaking your mother's heart."

"I'm so sorry. I'll come by the house after work today, sooner, if I can break away."

"Good."

The sheriff bustled into the room. "Ready to go?"

I blinked. "That was fast."

"I meant for it to be fast. No point letting them trap you with questions."

My phone buzzed again. Another text from Charlotte. I scanned the screen. "Bite me."

Wayne took the phone from me, scrolled up the message list, saw my approved response to Charlotte, and nodded. He handed my phone back. "She going to be a problem?"

"No more than usual."

CHAPTER 17

Belinda Donlin's creekside house looked like it had been built in the 1960s. The low-slung concrete block house had no fancy porch or architectural relief, no landscaping to soften the austere lines. It was a black-roofed squatty toad in need of powerwashing to remove the green tinge from the exterior walls.

Unlike June's Folly's disturbed landscape, Bee's lawn was lush, green, and intact. Wayne handed me a pair of gloves, which I put on while he wiggled into another pair. We'd already knocked, and no one answered the door.

"How're we going to get in?" I asked, thinking it might be entertaining to see the sheriff in action. I could easily see him kicking the door in or shooting the lock off. But the forces of law and order probably frowned on destruction of private property.

He pulled a set of keys from his pocket

and jangled them under my nose. "Hoping one of these will do the trick. Found these in her clothes."

I was hoping I didn't go cross-eyed from looking at those keys. "Sure. Go for it."

The second key he tried snicked in the lock, and the door swung open. Frigid air tinged with an ammonia smell spilled out of the house. Bee must like her air conditioning a lot. I crept in behind the sheriff, who made a quick circuit of the two-bedroom house to make sure no one was inside.

In one bedroom, a small ginger-colored cat mewed piteously. I picked it up, cuddled it close. "Easy, little one. You're all right. I've got you."

I stopped following Wayne and hurried to the kitchen to find food and water for the kitty. She ate ravenously, then turned her nose up at the overfull litter box in the bathroom. "I wouldn't use that either. Give me a sec, and I'll fix you right up."

The litter and scooper were beneath the sink, so I was able to clean the box quickly. Once I finished, the kitty relieved herself.

"You done playing with the cat?" the sheriff asked. "I could use some detecting help here."

I joined him in the blue and white kitchen where he was rummaging through drawers.

"What are you looking for?"

"Personal notes, letters, calendars, anything that might shed some light on her private life."

I glanced around at the furnishings. The furniture looked like it had been assembled from a thrift shop in that none of the overstuffed pieces matched, not that style mattered to me. On the wall was a nautical chart, several framed pictures of boats, and a photo of Bee and her brother in front of the fort down in St. Augustine.

The house was neat, though it was in need of a good dusting. The TV was on the small side, and books filled the end tables and a small bookcase. Another bookcase bulged with liquor bottles.

"Looks like she enjoyed reading and drinking. She lived alone. And there's the cat."

"Women and their cats."

Did he snort? "What's wrong with cats?"

He moved into the bedroom and thumbed through her clothes. "Come on. A single woman with a cat. That's a cliché if I ever heard one."

A blue and white quilt was tucked neatly under matching pillow shams on the queen-sized bed. Going by her home, Bee appeared to be an upstanding community member. "Cats are good company." I had a cat, and my cat was as good a companion as either of our dogs. Which reminded me I needed to track Stinger down and get Larissa's Chihuahua back.

He grunted and turned to face me. "You getting anything from your spidey senses?"

"No. I can't feel anything through these gloves."

He crossed to the dresser and opened drawers. "Seems like there should be sex toys or something."

Puzzled, I shook my head. "Why would you think that?"

"She liked sex enough to sneak around with Marv. Far as I know, she hadn't dated anyone steadily for awhile, so she might have had a backup plan. For, uh, personal relief."

"I do not want to be having this conversation with you."

"Then give me something else. Take the gloves off."

"What about fingerprints?"

"We'll exclude yours. This place doesn't have the look of being searched, so I doubt a raging killer came through here."

I rolled the gloves down my hands, tucking one used glove inside the other and stuffing the wad in my phone pocket. Glancing around the room, I contemplated lowering my guard, dreading what that might do to me and equally dreading if nothing happened. "Keep in mind that contact doesn't always generate results. My best leads come from dreams."

"Find me something. We need a lead."

"I didn't see a computer or phone."

"Phone was with her clothes. No computer though. How do you know she has one?"

"She's a living, breathing member of the twenty-first century."

"Maybe. She had social media apps on her phone. I could have the tech guys check her posts against her phone log. If she had a computer and it's missing, that would mean something."

The closet drew me. I edged closer, gritting my teeth together in anticipation. "Don't touch me if something happens. I don't want to accidentally drag you into the dream world again."

"Trust me on this. I won't come near you with a twenty-foot pole. Life is too short, and I want to live it to the fullest."

Tentatively, I touched the closet doorknob. A slight sensory jangle but no flash of insight. I studied the colorful hangers, the shoes lined up in soldier-straight rows. This woman had a tidy streak that intrigued and repelled me. Why would you keep everything so shipshape if you lived alone?

Her wardrobe consisted of a lot of khaki-colored slacks and white polos with her business logo of a navy blue marlin on it. A few nicer outfits, blazers and trousers, were in the back of her closet. Shoes ranged from flip-flops to boat shoes to work boots. A splash of color caught my eye. A pink robe, tucked between the work-a-day slacks and the good stuff.

I shoved the other hangers aside to study it. Roses embellished the collar. Unless I missed my guess, the thing was silk and tunic length. Just long enough to cover everything down below, unless you moved. A silk item would need special laundering care. Chances were high that Bee didn't take it to the dry cleaners every time she wore it.

"You got something?" Wayne asked from across the room. "You're awful quiet over there."

"A slinky, shorty robe. It's out of character when you consider how no-nonsense and functional the rest of her clothes are."

"My body fluid light's in the Jeep. I'll get it."

Gross. I didn't want to think about body

fluids, but given the woman had been consorting naked with a man at the time of her death, body fluids on a robe were more than possible.

I took a deep breath. *This is your job,* I reminded myself. *You want to use your abilities to help people, even if those people are dead. Especially if those people are dead.*

With that, I lowered my guard. Inside the closet was a background hiss of emotional static, which reassured me my senses were working to some extent. I felt nothing earth-shattering, nothing filled with bad vibes from a killer's touch, nothing I perceived as Bee being in great distress.

So far, so good.

Time to take the touch test. Out of the corner of my eye, I noted Wayne had drifted closer. "Keep your distance," I warned.

"Duly noted," he said, sarcasm thick in his voice.

I couldn't worry about his bruised ego. This was as important to me as it was to him, more maybe. I couldn't be the dream-walker if I went out of commission each time I crossed the divide.

Holding my breath and bracing my legs for whatever might come, I inched my hand forward and then closed my fingers around the shoulder of the sleek fabric. Time bent.

Light flickered. And I found myself in a dark hole.

CHAPTER 18

I scrambled to orient myself in the dark dreamscape. Instead of arriving in an illuminated scene, I'd landed in a confined warm space. With my fingers, I established the enclosure to be about the size of two people sandwiched upright. Perhaps a closet? But there were no knobs or clothes rods. Just me and the tight space.

Had I come to the wrong place? Was I broken? Panic flooded my thoughts. If I couldn't dreamwalk, was I trapped here? *Stop that. You had a clean transition. You're not broken. Pull yourself together and do your job. Think like an investigator.*

Why had I been brought here? With sight and touch being of no help, I focused on scent and sound. I sniffed and came up with nothing. No noise met my ears either. Wait. What was that? I listened harder.

Two voices. A man and a woman. I strained to make out the words, but they were garbled and muffled. I pushed harder, determined to learn something from my efforts. The voices ceased, then I heard a soft feminine murmur and an answering male rumble of satisfaction.

Great. I'd tumbled into a sexual encounter. I hoped the video track didn't dial in all of a sudden. It might be too much of a shock to my system.

I assumed the woman's voice belonged to Bee, and until I learned otherwise, the man's voice must be Marv's. The darkness didn't thin. Looked like I'd get my wish and only receive an audio transition during this dreamwalk.

"You're amazing," Bee said. "I wish we didn't have to sneak around."

"Better this way," he said. "There's someone in my life who's out to make me miserable."

Bee yawned, her voice turned soft and dreamy. "Why's that?"

"We began dating, and she got mad because she said Ford owned me, but she's wrong. He's my boss, not my slave master. I jump when he says jump because I have a good job and want to keep it."

"I understand. I do whatever it takes to please my charter customers. I want their repeat business."

This audio-only message had severe limitations. I didn't like being blind, but I desperately needed context and body language. Maybe that was the point. If I couldn't see the lovers, I'd hear other noises in the background.

In the darkness, I heard the sound of water lapping against a surface. Waves, maybe. And very faintly, a buoy bell. They were near water. Could be at Bee's place. No. You couldn't hear that buoy from the mainland. They must be on a boat. Bee's boat. That fit.

"This woman never understood the need for a job. She tried to control me, so I broke it off with her. But she won't let go. She follows me to our shoots and makes my life miserable. I wouldn't wish that on you."

Springs creaked. "Did you get a restraining order?" Bee asked in a crisper voice.

"I don't want to cause trouble for this person. I want to be done with her."

"What's her name, in case she comes around here? I have no qualms about filing a restraining order on a whack job."

"Her name's Cassie, and trust me, you don't want anything to do with this loony chick."

"Hmm. Maybe you say that to all your women, Hollywood. You got one stashed in

145

every port?"

Hollywood was the nickname Bee used for Marv in a previous dreamwalk. This was turning out better than I'd hoped. I'd dialed in both murder victims.

"Get real," Marv said, followed by a heavy sigh. "I'm married to my job. It's only chance moments like this that I can get away and relax. You're the exception, Bee-utiful. Sooner or later my boss will notice that I prefer to take a boat to scout shoot locations, and he'll shut us down."

"Ford seems like a good guy. I can't believe he would be so unfeeling as to limit your personal time."

"He doesn't suffer fools. There are easily two dozen qualified people who call him daily to ask about my job. I slip up, and I'm out. Over the years, I've gotten very good at not slipping up." Fabric rustled. "Where are you going? I've got the entire afternoon off."

"Maybe so, but the tide is ripping out of this creek. Unless you want to be stuck out here for the next six hours, we have to move the boat."

"Screw the tide. I wanna be with you."

"You are with me."

"I mean, really be with you. I could live like this, Bee."

Silence. "You'd quit your job?"

"I could. I have savings. I could find something else to do around here."

"That's sweet."

"You don't believe me?"

"I believe you believe it. Lord, Hollywood, men don't make grand gestures for me. I'm no starlet. Just an average Joe plying the sea."

"You're better than an actress, Bee-utiful. You're real."

The voices faded, and the darkness grayed. I vectored back to reality, to Bee's closet. My hand still gripped the silk robe. I blinked against the strong daylight and released the sleek fabric. Quickly, I did an inventory of my faculties. I could see and touch. I heard my slow, even breathing. Seemed like I was a hundred percent. Absently, I touched my moldavite pendant, and the gemstone centered me right away.

"Well?" Wayne asked. "Any luck?"

I turned slowly. His dark hair was framed by the bright sunshine outside the window. Not quite a halo or an orb, but close enough to make me want to snort with derision. No way was Wayne Thompson angelic.

"Yeah. Plenty. They were doing it again —"

"Lucky you."

"Afterward, they talked. Marv had a

stalker named Cassie. He was talking about giving up his coveted job to stay here with Bee, but Bee didn't seem too happy about it."

"You get a last name for this Cassie?"

"No. I wasn't able to interact with them. One of them must've wanted me to hear their conversation because that's what happened."

"Anything else?"

The rose tattoo on my hand stung. I rubbed it with my other hand until the pain subsided. "Uh. They were on Bee's boat, and she was worried about the tide going out."

"Not sure that's useful, but I'll make sure her vessel gets a onceover." He studied me. "Are you okay? You look a little pale today."

To my credit, I didn't squirm. "I'm fine." No way was I telling him about my earlier fear of going psi-blind. I glanced over his shoulder. The bed had been stripped. The dresser and end tables looked bare. "You've been busy."

"I got my UV light and bagged evidence while you did your thing. Body fluids covered the bed. I need that robe. It lit up like a Christmas tree."

"I'll bet it did." Those two seemed like they spent their time together with no clothes on. "Are we done here?"

"What's your rush?" He scowled. "Thought you'd screen the evidence from the scene and catch me a killer."

"One dreamwalk per day allows me time to recharge between events." And it would give me time to figure out if I'd missed anything in the vision.

His eyes narrowed, and my chin jutted out. Why did he doubt me? Did he think I was a slacker? I didn't have spirits on speed dial. Each visit I took to the spirit realm exacted an energy cost and more, which I was willing to pay, but I didn't know my limits.

"Don't want you to burn out," he conceded. "You did good, though. A stalker is a strong suspect, and a female stalker would've been jealous of Marv's relationship with Bee. I still say a woman couldn't have trussed up those bodies like that, but this Cassie woman could be an accomplice. Let's head over to Ford's place and see what the movie people have to say."

Crap. He wasn't letting me off the hook and he was my ride. "And then we'll hit the station?"

"Yep. That evidence can't wait. I need you to go through it today."

"I will." My pocket buzzed again.

149

"She's been texting you every ten minutes."

"You looked?"

His lips ghosted into a brief smile. "Didn't have to. I'm a highly skilled crime investigator. Charlotte's as tenacious as a Jack Russell terrier."

"I'll deal with Charlotte. Later. Let's get this done. And the cat's coming with us until you locate her next of kin."

"Keep the cat. Timmy Ray's a drifter. Last I heard, he was working on an oil rig in the Gulf, but that didn't pan out."

"He'll turn up. He always was the sort to sense a windfall, and Bee's place on the water is valuable real estate."

"Don't know how any siblings could be more different than Bee and Timmy Ray. She worked hard as two men, while he did everything he could to get out of working."

The word *motive* lit up in acid green in my head. "You know what that means."

"Timmy Ray profits from Bee's death. Gotcha. He's already on my suspect list."

CHAPTER 19

Though it was mid-morning, the two-story Victorian cottage beside the river had lights blazing in every room. Cars dotted the lawn, all of them nosed in under the wide-spreading oaks. Outsiders learned quickly about heat build-up in cars down here.

Best of all, the rabid press had been repelled at the gate to River House by the extra security Ford Morrison had hired. Who said money couldn't buy peace of mind?

Leaving Bee's ginger kitty in the Jeep with the air conditioning running, I followed Wayne up the steps, my work boots sounding heavy on the old wood. These days, faded grandeur had a new name, shabby chic, but I thought the house would look worlds better with a couple of coats of paint. The whimsical curlycue gingerbread trim always made me smile.

Long ago, I'd learned to protect myself

from unpleasant surprises. Though my strongest, clearest talent was dreamwalking, my other extra senses often blindsided me if I wasn't careful. Emotions radiated from people in constant waves, like a radio tower broadcast. Being near others was tolerable if I blocked that energy. Touching a person in the grip of strong emotions could and had blasted through my protective buffer occasionally. The same was true for objects that had been touched by people in the grip of strong emotions.

Consequently, I'd raised my sensory guard as soon as I awakened from the dreamwalk over at Bee's place, and I wouldn't let it down until I was safe at home.

And I had the extra protection of a pocket full of my mother's crystals. Which reminded me, I needed to stop by and console my mom about Gentle Dove as soon as I had a break in this busy day.

Marv's assistant met us at the door, clipboard in hand. Lou "LA" Alfredo looked like he'd never had a wardrobe malfunction. His white slacks were finely creased, his light blue dress shirt with the neatly rolled-up sleeves were starched to perfection. His coiffed brown hair would be the envy of half the females in the county, myself included.

"Sheriff. Ms. Powell. What can I do for you?" LA asked.

"I'm here to see Ford," the sheriff said. "Official business."

"Mr. Morrison is on the phone with his financial angel, explaining the production delay. He can't be interrupted. And he's waiting for three more important calls. This is not a good time to visit."

My breath hitched at the unmistakable slap of negative energy from the movie underling. Sheriff Wayne Thompson was not above throwing his weight around, especially in the line of duty. This insect was blocking the lawman from doing his job. Through my lashes, I saw Wayne lance the guy with his death glare.

"If he's not out here in five minutes, I'm pulling your permits until further notice," the sheriff said. "A member of your staff was murdered, in case you've forgotten."

LA's nose lifted. "Every person here feels Marv's loss. He was an integral part of the production. But that old adage is true. The show must go on. We have deadlines to meet or our funding goes away. May showers put us behind schedule. We literally can't afford to come to a screeching halt because Marv passed on."

"The man was murdered," Wayne said

153

through clenched teeth.

LA's earnest face and finely chiseled lips sagged a smidge. "I saw the pictures online. Gruesome stuff. Any leads?"

I sucked air in through my teeth, expecting Wayne to blow his top over those leaked photographs. He'd threatened to fire whoever had done it on his staff. Fortunately, the bloody stairs and the bodies hadn't been shown online — just the exterior of the house and the bloodstained wall by the stairs.

"No comment. This is an active police investigation," the sheriff said.

LA flicked his glance over to me. I waved him closer and whispered near his ear, "No comment."

The man gasped and jerked away from me.

Wayne's grin was feral. "You have two minutes to get your boss out here, or my deputies will haul every person in this house to my jail for obstruction of law enforcement personnel."

"Mr. Morrison will be right out." LA scurried away like a ghost crab on speed.

Wayne waited until the assistant was out of earshot. "You surprised me."

"LA rubbed me the wrong way. Too put together. Too full of himself. I didn't like his demeanor or his negative energy."

The sheriff nodded and spoke in a confidential tone. "Looks like he plans to fill Marv's shoes as Ford's right-hand man and all-around gopher. The man benefited from Marv's death. In my book, we call that motive."

"Definitely." At the rate we were going, we would fill the jail with suspects for these two homicides. My Nesbitt granny used to tell me not to look under rocks if I didn't want to see what crawled out. She made a good point.

Ford Morrison emerged from a room down the hallway. He looked exactly like he did in the movies, only shorter. I'd envisioned him to be six feet tall, but he was about my five-six in height, and definitely shorter than the sheriff. But the blockbuster movie star projected charisma in spades. Heads turned as the king of onscreen suspense strode our way.

The actor shook hands with the sheriff, nodded at me, and directed us to the front parlor. Two scrawny kids who looked to be college interns scrambled out of the room with their tablets and ear buds and stacks of papers. Ford invited us to sit.

The wooden rocking chair seemed the most innocuous, so I chose to sit in it.

Wayne commandeered the large leather chair, leaving Ford the entire sofa.

"Such terrible news about Marv," Ford said, his sorrowful expression worthy of an Academy Award.

I was struck by the revelation that it would be very hard to read an actor like Ford. He made his living pretending to be someone else. If he wasn't convincing, he would be out of a job. His facial expressions, his body language, even the nuances of his voice were the products of a lifetime of pretending. I was here as an observer, but my hands itched to touch this man, unshielded. I needed to know if he was a liar.

"Did Marv have a problem with anyone on the job?" the sheriff asked.

Ford blinked, drawing out the fragile moment as his jaw dropped. "You're kidding. You think . . . You think one of us hurt Marv? No way. No way in hell."

The sheriff knew a thing or two about theatrics. Anyone who lived with his wife Dottie had a finely honed BS meter. He gestured toward the room and Ford's staff. "And yet, it's business as usual around here. People are working. Marv's assistant told me you were too busy to see visitors. That doesn't sound like grief to me. That sounds like a person with an ulterior motive."

Ford lunged to his feet and he glared down at Wayne. "You don't understand. Until this movie is in the can, my funding can be yanked at any time. I have to reassure my backers that we're a go. But we aren't. You see us milling around at River House. We're not filming. We're reordering our lives so that we can go on without Marv." Ford's voice faltered. "I'm devastated. Marv is, *was,* my best friend. We've been together years, which is an eternity in the movie business. He's practically my brother."

Wayne let the emotional words fade from the air before he continued. "I heard Marv had a woman following him around. Cassie or something."

"The redhead?" Ford scoffed and eased back into the sofa. "She wanted to read for a part, but I have a thing against redheads. Best for me to avoid them altogether."

"What's her full name?"

"Cassie Korda. I told her she needed to change her name if she wanted to make it in show biz because it sounds too bouncy, but she was adamant about keeping her name. Some people, you know?"

"Got an address for Ms. Korda?"

"Marv has it." Ford's face fell, and genuine grief filled his eyes. He scrubbed his face and took a moment. "Sorry. Force of habit. LA's filling in the assistant role for now. See if LA can find her file. I know she sent us her package initially, but she could've sent it to the production company, to me, or to Marv."

"Is this woman dangerous?"

Ford's eyes rounded. In that moment, he looked like a cartoon of his famous face. "Her? She looks strong, but a gal couldn't lift Marv. He was no lightweight. And that fish camp woman, Beulah. She had some muscle to her frame as well. No way one gal could kill two healthy adults. Not unless she had help."

"The boat captain's name was Belinda," I piped in.

The sheriff shot me a quelling look. "You do background checks for the people on your staff?"

"Marv took care of hiring and firing. He had some arrangement worked out with film schools that brought us extra hands and feet each semester. He convinced me it was a great deal. We got inexpensive labor, and their people got experience on a set of a movie."

"He hired everyone on your staff, even the actors on your movie?"

"No, of course not. He vetted tryouts

based on my specs. I oftentimes asked him to recruit a certain type of acting professional, but I have final say in casting. I'm the producer as well as the star of the show."

"Even so, that put Marv in the position of gatekeeper for two personnel areas, your staff and your cast. I need to see the records of people he interacted with. We'll start with this project, but I'd like to see your employment records for the last twelve months."

"You're asking for a lot."

Invisible lightning flashed from the sheriff. "I'm just getting started. Two people are dead. My job is to make sure the killer is brought to justice."

Ford nodded and shouted for LA to come back in the room. After ordering the man to give the cops everything, Ford dismissed his gopher and turned back to face Wayne. His blockbuster face filled with cold speculation. "You ever do any acting? I could set up a screen test for you this afternoon."

Wayne stood, towering over the actor. "I'll pretend you didn't try to bribe me with fame and fortune while I'm investigating you and your staff. If there's a murderer in this crew, I'll find him. My men will be out this afternoon, and I expect them to have access to these records." He glanced over at me. "We're leaving."

I scrambled to my feet, not an easy job from such a tall rocking chair. They certainly didn't make furniture like this anymore. If we were leaving, I had nothing to add to Wayne's information. Cautiously, I lowered my mental guard and immediately raised it back up. This place was swimming in sorrow. Not particularly useful in a police investigation.

"Wait!" LA came scurrying toward us, a small object in his hand. "This will get you started. Ms. Korda's address is in there as well as our personnel files. I'll have to get the rest of the requested records scanned and uploaded from our offices in Hollywood. That's all I have access to here. No need to send your guys back out to our offices this afternoon. We hope to resume filming this afternoon. The weather and the tide are perfect for scene twenty-three."

The sheriff scowled and snatched the flash drive. "I need complete access to this house, your records, and your staff. I expect them to be available at my convenience."

I stepped back out of the way, but my foot caught on the area rug by the door. Automatically, I reached for the doorknob to steady myself. The jolt of torrential rage I encountered took my breath away.

At my gasp, Wayne studied me. "You all right?"

"My heel caught the rug. Sorry." I released the knob and thrust my tingling hand into my crystal-filled pocket. The sense of order in my world slowly returned with each heartbeat.

Recognition flared in Wayne's eyes. Under his watchful eye, I trooped down the stairs into the Jeep and buckled up. The kitty jumped in my lap. Not until we were off the property did I speak. "The killer was in River House."

CHAPTER 20

Wayne pulled over on the shoulder of the highway and stared at me through his dark glasses. "Spill it, Powell."

I petted the kitty in my lap and was rewarded with her purr of contentment. "I didn't have a dreamwalk, but I had a flash of insight when I steadied myself with the doorknob. The killer touched it in a terrible rage. He hated so deeply it's a wonder the knob didn't catch on fire, because that's how my hand felt, as if I'd just plunged it into a flame. I didn't see him killing Marv or Bee, but there was a lethal sense about him I recognized from our previous cases."

"A movie person is our killer? Did you see his face? Get a name?"

"Nothing that helpful. All I know is the killer touched the River House doorknob recently."

"That's no help at all, considering how many people are in and out of that house, unless you think Marv was the target all along and Bee was collateral damage."

"I'm not saying that either. This was a crime of passion."

"You profiling now? No way. Stringing those two up and draining their bodies of blood didn't happen in a moment of rage. It was a premeditated act. The killer strengthened the railing ahead of time. This is malice murder from the get-go."

His condescension poked holes in my patience. "Hey. I don't choose the messages I receive. If there's a grand plan in the great beyond, I've yet to figure it out. I'm relaying the information as I get it. I trust my information absolutely."

Wayne stared out the windshield at the empty road ahead. "If what you're saying is true, we have two killers on our hands. One driven by hatred, the other methodical and coldblooded. Two killers would make the logistics of stringing our victims up more feasible."

"Makes sense to me."

"Two killers . . ." Wayne's voice drifted off.

I studied the thin clouds rimming the sky, wondering if LA or Ford were killers. On first glance, neither looked like they'd ever gotten their hands dirty.

Wayne shook his head, drawing my thoughts back to our conversation. "If word of two killers gets out, the GBI will take over my case. We can't tell anyone about this, got it?"

"Got it."

"I'll let you in on a secret, Powell. I've never run across a killing team before, but there's a first time for everything. We need to stop these guys, now."

"Agreed." I cleared my throat softly, chastened by the waves of violence rolling off the sheriff but unwilling to let him intimidate me. He was paying me for my opinion, after all. "I know you think this case has male written all over it, but Marv mentioned his stalker for a reason."

Wayne eased back on the road and accelerated. "We'll conduct due diligence on Cassie Korda, but I need to tighten our focus on our male suspects first. There were eight cars parked outside the actor's local headquarters; no telling how many people were offsite right now. Reed Tyler will be all over me if I shut down the movie people for no good reason. I've been ordered to give them whatever they want. As far as the Tourism Office is concerned, Ford Morrison's bunch is the county's golden ticket to financial security. The movie will draw more film crews and incentivize tourists who want to see the location firsthand."

"Then we'll find a good reason to shut them down."

An edgy silence filled the Jeep, making me squirm in my seat. I could almost feel the gears turning in the sheriff's head as he worked something out. Something to do with me.

"You feeling all right?" he asked.

I shrugged. "Sure. Why do you ask?"

"You just did two woo-woo things in a row and didn't pass out. Seems to me like you're fit enough to go through those evidence bags right now."

Busted. And I didn't like it one bit. Except I did feel better. None of the bone-deep tiredness or sensory overload, and certainly none of the mental fog. Hmm. I didn't understand what this meant, but I wasn't pleased with Wayne's take on the matter.

I gave him a long, considering glance. "You're awful pushy."

"Have to be. I've got twice as many killers to catch."

Crap. He had me there. The sooner we caught these killers, the sooner the threat of the GBI busting in here would vanish. The sooner I'd feel comfortable about bringing Larissa home.

My phone buzzed again. I checked the display screen. Charlotte. I muted and pocketed the phone. "I'll give it a go, but I can't spend all day at the station. I have landscaping to do today, and a personal matter to address."

He gave me a searching look. "What kind of personal matter?"

"My parents. My mom got some bad news."

"Is she sick?"

"No. A friend of hers is."

"Earlene Brown?"

It took me a moment to make the connection. Though Earlene Brown was Gentle Dove's legal name, Mama only called her friend by her Native American name. "Yes."

"Thought she looked different the other day."

"Since when are you scoping out Gentle Dove?"

"Since she's hanging out with you."

"Oh." Funny. I hadn't realized my entire life was under police scrutiny. I stole another under-the-lashes glance at Wayne. At times, he had depth that surprised me. "And while we're not talking about the case, I still need Stinger's contact information. If I don't get Larissa's dog back by Saturday, she'll be brokenhearted."

"I'll have Tamika pull it for you." He switched on the radio to a rock 'n roll station and cranked the volume up loud enough to prohibit conversation.

Fine with me.

I could finally do a silent happy dance. The doorknob jolt signaled good news. My senses had rebounded. That was the best news I could've received. Getting that blast of killer energy had been unpleasant, but the between-the-lines message was clear. The dreamwalker was back in business. The thought of going through the evidence didn't worry me anymore. If I was meant to get a reading, I would receive it.

All too soon, we were back at the cop shop. A knot of cars populated the visitor lot, including Charlotte's vehicle. Had she been waiting here all day?

"Okay if I bring the cat inside?" I asked.

"No. I draw the line at four-legged animals."

"Then forget about the evidence review. I have to head home. There's no shade here and it's too hot now to leave Bee's cat in my truck."

Wayne swore. "Bring it with you then. I need your help more than I don't want a cat inside. But if it takes a dump, you're cleaning it up."

I held the kitty close. "I'll keep her in the room with me. She has the sweetest disposition."

We passed through the back door, and soon I found myself in a room with boxes and boxes of evidence. Wayne glanced at all the evidence bags and then at the cat.

"Gotta do something else with the cat," he said. "Too much in here that it could get into."

"You could put her in your office."

"Not happening. Take her to Tamika."

The office manager and the cat took to one another right away. When I explained the cat was orphaned and I didn't know its name, Tamika offered to call local vets to find out about the animal. I thanked her and headed back to my task of trying to read evidence.

I donned gloves and touched the empty soda cans and chip bags. Nothing. I tried Marv's shoes. Not even a little jolt from my inner eye. Bee's deck shoes jangled my senses, but I got no flashes of insight. The only thing of note was that my rose tattoo itched more with each item I tried to read. Was Rose the demon sending me a message?

After an hour of opening evidence bags, touching stuff, then sealing the bags, I gave up halfway through. I sought the sheriff in his office. "I'm not getting a reading on anything."

"Did you try the items the killer touched?"

"I tried items from the bedroom because I don't know what the killer touched."

"The ropes. The rails. The bodies."

"Can I try that stuff tomorrow? Maybe that spike of bad juju from the doorknob used up all my extrasensory perception right now. I'm willing to come back tomorrow and start fresh."

"In that case, a fresh start sounds good." He pushed a small piece of paper over to me. "According to our records, Connor Simmons, aka Stinger, lives with his mother in the Gibson community."

"Thanks." I tucked the address in a pocket. "Let me grab the cat, and I'll get out of your hair."

He murmured something that sounded like "good luck with that," but I ignored him. At the front, I saw the cat had taken up a perch beside the Plexiglas window to the lobby. Tamika looked sad when I approached.

"What'd you find out?" I asked.

"Bee used Dr. Tara for Ziggy. She's three years old."

"Cute name."

The cat leapt down from her perch and climbed on Tamika's shoulders. "Cute cat." The dispatcher was all smiles.

I could hear the cat purring from across the room. Tamika liked the cat. The cat liked her. I already had a household of pets. "Would you consider fostering Ziggy until Bee's brother turns up?"

Her brown eyes narrowed. "Not a good idea."

"Oh. Sorry. I thought you two were really getting along."

"We are. I wouldn't give Timmy Ray a boa constrictor, much less a sweetie like this kitty."

Hmm. "Chances are he won't want the responsibility. Meanwhile, Ziggy needs a foster home. What do you say? Would you keep this kitty until I can find her a permanent home?"

"We used to have a kitty when I was a girl. I could try it, I suppose. What do I feed it?"

"I took some of Ziggy's food and her litter box from Bee's house. They're in the sheriff's Jeep. That should get you through a few days. If it doesn't work out, please let me know, and I'll come get her."

"Excellent."

Excellent indeed. I headed out, drove down the highway toward town, and noticed a boxy sedan on the shoulder. Not just any sedan. Charlotte's car.

Had her car broken down? Why else would she be parked on the roadside in a heat wave? I stopped, backed up, and hurried to her car door. "Need a lift?"

Charlotte shoved her glasses higher on her nose and stared straight ahead. "I need a new best friend."

CHAPTER 21

Guilt panged my heart. I leaned into her open window, savoring the welcome rush of her air conditioning. "Char, we knew that our jobs would be at odds sometimes. This is one of those times. Honest to God, if I breathe a word of this case to you and it ends up in the paper, I will lose my job."

"If I don't get a story for the paper, I will lose my job. Vandals dug up the Mumford's summer place, the Johnson's cow pasture, and the new playground in town, but Kip doesn't consider that news. He wants crimes with juicy details." Charlotte's shoulders were nearly touching her ears. "My boss is tired of me and Bernard squabbling over who's gonna be top dog. I want the police beat. Thanks to you I've had access to the top cases this year, but Bernard is out for blood. Help me keep the police beat."

Conscious of my butt sticking out in the road, I squatted beside her door so that we were close to eye level. "You are my best friend, and I will do anything in the world for you, except this. For the last few months, I'm finally paying my bills on time with money I've earned instead of borrowing from Larissa's college fund. If I lose this police consultant job, I'll have to sell grandmother's house and move in with my folks. I need my independence. And I wouldn't put it past Wayne to fire my father if I screw up."

"Tab doesn't work for Wayne. His job is safe."

"Not if Wayne makes life miserable for him. You think women are catty and gossipy? They've got nothing on men."

"I need something to work on. Anything."

"Charlotte."

"Okay. Let's do this in reverse. I'll tell you what I've heard and what I figured out from the online photos. Bee and Marv were murdered at June's Folly. Bled out so that blood ran down the stairs, which is so gross I don't want to think about it. So far, so good?"

I smiled. "No comment."

"Word on the street is that a coven of bloodthirsty vampires flew Bee and Marv in the dead of night to the haunted house, where they had their way with them. And then, you know, drank them dry and had a drunken orgy."

I snorted.

"Moving on," Charlotte said. "Rumor number two is that the Ghost of June's Folly literally scared them to death and, channeling energy from beyond, dismembered them to make an example of them. Now the place is a supernatural war zone as Bee and Marv battle the centuries-old ghostly inhabitants of June's Folly."

I covered my mouth to keep from laughing out loud.

"Last but not least, after years of human absence at June's Folly, the movie people invaded the locale, stirring up creatures of yore long presumed to be tales and legends. Swamp monsters and trolls arose from the depths, attacking Bee and Marv as a lesson to all humans to stay the f— away. Anyone who ventures out there will die terribly."

I couldn't help it. A laugh snorted out. "You've got to be kidding."

"Not kidding. People are going nuts speculating about this."

"People believe what they want to believe. Once we catch the killers, people will cling to whatever theory they favor. The truth is irrelevant. That's how legends get started. You don't seriously think we have a sea monster cruising up and down our rivers?"

"The Sinclair Monster is ingrained in local folklore and all our tourism literature. Of course I believe it." Charlotte's face scrunched, her glasses wiggling on her nose. She pinned me with a gotcha look. "You said killers."

Heat rose to my face. "So I did." Dang. How did I let that slip? Wayne would murder me. "You can't print that. This is an active ongoing investigation. We're still trying to figure out whodunit."

"I get what you can't say. I also get why y'all might be looking at more than one person. Logic dictates that it would be difficult for a single suspect to overpower and kill two healthy adults."

"No comment."

Charlotte grinned. "I knew it. Okay . . . No way was this an accident. I don't know anything more than I can find online about Marv, and Bernard has all of that information too. What Bernard doesn't know is that Bee had a very active libido."

"You don't say?"

Confident of my interest, Charlotte stalled by twirling a loop of hair around a finger. "I eat at odd times in restaurants throughout the county because I don't cook. Anyway, I've seen her with different guys on occasion. Nobody notices the fat girl reading newspapers in the corner."

"Charlotte. I notice you. Other people do too."

"Not Bee. I saw her about four months ago, flirting to high heaven with a married man. Because I'm short, I could see their active hands under the table at the seafood place near the shrimp docks. It was quite the show."

That tracked with what Virg had said about being drinking buddies with Bee three years ago. Oddly, I wanted to hear more lurid details. I tamped down that interest and tried to sound like a professional crime fighter. "This is the first I've heard of her having an affair."

"Not the first one she's had. I've seen her at the marina restaurant, drinking at the bar with the guys. She always leaves with a guy. Always."

"I did not know she was so . . . social. I thought she was all about fishing and sightseeing and ecotourism."

"Get real. She was all about getting it on."

"If she was hooking up with Marv, perhaps another companion took offense. Who'd you see her with last? What married man?" A chill snaked through me at a potentially catastrophic conflict of interest. "It wasn't

Wayne, was it?"

"Nope."

The way her eyes slid away from mine was telling. "Charlotte! This is important. If you have information that could help us solve the case, I need to know. Who was she seeing?"

"I want something in return for it. Something Bernard doesn't have."

I gulped in a breath. "Bee had a nice cat."

"That's not newsworthy. Gimme something else. Something I can write a story about."

"That *is* the story. We have no animal shelter for pets of deceased or incarcerated people. Sinclair County needs to have more of a plan than maintaining a list of animal lovers willing to temporarily foster a pet. We got Elvis after his owner went to jail. Sulay's owner is still in rehab recovering from a hip replacement. And I've taken care of the Gilroys' lab, Precious, many times because Louise can't stop thinking of her daughter. And that's just one animal lover's story. You know some of the other folks in town who help out like I do. Tamika offered to take Bee's ginger-colored tabby named Ziggy. Interview her tomorrow or the next day. You could incite a grassroots movement for an animal shelter."

"How is that a police matter? How will that keep me on the front page?"

"Trust me. Animal welfare is a big deal. Your boss will love a heart-tugging story like this. It will sell papers, and you'll get many spin-off stories. Now it's your turn. Who'd you see Bee with?"

"I'm still getting an exclusive from you when the dust settles on the murders?"

"Yes, but I can't promise the sheriff won't talk to Bernard first."

Alarm flared in Charlotte's bright eyes. A muscle twitched in her cheek. "We need to shut that down."

"Nothing we can do about who talks to who. Free country. Now stop stalling. Who was Bee's last conquest?"

"Head of the Tourism Office. Reed Tyler."

CHAPTER 22

As I trimmed, raked, and tidied up a snow-bird couple's yard, my thoughts returned to the news I'd learned. Reed Tyler was the perfect suspect. He knew the locals, some apparently intimately. He knew outsiders. Heck, he even spoke outsider. I remembered the sheriff saying Reed was pushing for extra dispensation for the movie people.

The Tourism Office was very pro-movie industry.

But the sheriff wanted justice, and I was supposed to be on his team. I called him in between yards and told him what I'd learned.

"Thanks for nothing," Wayne said.

"Don't shoot the messenger. Any luck on finding that stalker woman?"

"Not yet. The house she rented isn't occupied. But she used her credit card in Brunswick two days ago. That puts her in the area and not on the west coast. She's definitely a person of interest."

"Will you bring Reed in for questioning?"

"Yes, but keep your eyes and ears open in the community. Right now, my suspect list includes the movie gopher guy, the stalker lady, and now the head of the Tourism Office. We're chasing down other leads, but we're also compiling backgrounds on these three. I've got an image for Cassie Korda, and I'll message it to you. If you see her, phone me immediately."

"Will do." A few minutes later, the message icon lit up on my phone. I clicked over and scanned the driver's license picture. The red hair looked brash, as if it weren't her natural color, but when I enlarged the image, I didn't see roots. Her chin. Poor thing. It was a bit oversized for the rest of her face, which drew my gaze away from her brown eyes. As I stared at the whole face, I was struck by the oddest revelation.

Cassie was a woman who didn't look comfortable in her own skin. I would definitely recognize her if she was dumb enough to still be hanging around Sinclair County.

Onward and upward. I hadn't forgotten about Elvis. Stinger's mom lived in the Gibson neighborhood, which was next on my route. The modest brick structure was nestled between thick woods and a worn-out mobile home. No cars in the chain-link-fenced yard, but the treasure-seeking vandals had been here too. Someone needed to flatten the sand piles out before someone like me twisted an ankle.

I banged on the door. No answer. I tried the mobile home next door. No answer there either. I returned to my truck and dashed off a hasty note telling Stinger to bring Elvis home and I wouldn't press charges.

Not much trimming required in the next client's yard, just lopping off some azalea limbs that had grown into the driveway. Work done for the day, I headed to my parents' house, an open-air concrete block house with ever-changing murals on the exterior and 1960s relics masquerading as furniture inside. As usual, the Weather Channel was blaring. The prediction was for a wet summer all across the states.

Mom sat at her kitchen table, a full mug of tea in front of her. Her pale, lined face made her look twenty years older. "Mom?"

She turned and it took her several blinks before she saw me. "Baxley. What brings you out this afternoon?"

"You do. Mom, what's got you so sad?"

Her hand covered her mouth. She shook her head. "I can't talk about it."

The weather station blared, but the house felt empty. No pot of soup bubbled on the stove. No bustle of my mother caring for others as she always did. I sat beside her and took her hand, opening my senses.

Her fingers closed around mine, and the tension eased from her face. Then she pulled her hand away. "You're reading me."

"I did. Something's terribly wrong for you not to speak of it. I know it's about Gentle Dove. She's sick, right?"

Mom nodded. "She stopped eating yesterday. She's being very Native American and fatalistic about her condition. I can't stand for her to die this way. She doesn't have to die. She could call in a shaman, but she won't do that either. Running Bear is so sad."

I heard a faint cough. "Is someone here?"

"Gentle Dove is staying in Larissa's room. Until the end."

"I need to see her." I pushed away from the table but Mom caught my arm. "Don't disturb her. She doesn't have long. She should've told me sooner, so that I could help her."

I eased down the hall, conscious of my mother trailing me. As I neared the room, the unmistakable odor of illness reached my nose. My Gran had wasted away with something, and her scent changed to this musk a few days before she passed. Gentle Dove's face looked serene on the faded floral sheets. The bright drawings and colors in this room must have seemed garish to the dying woman.

Mom brushed past me and sat beside her friend. She took Gentle Dove's hand. "Someone's here to see you, love."

Gentle Dove's pain-glazed eyes opened. I crossed the room and took her free hand from her belly. Her skin felt dry and hot. Her eyes flared wide at the invasion of her privacy. Too late, I realized I'd forgotten to shield my abilities. My tattoo flared with energy, and my head snapped back as Gentle Dove's thoughts blasted into my head.

She was silently chanting an Indian death song. I knew the tune because I'd heard her teach it to Mom years ago. Somehow, I traveled through her body to the area of illness. Medical acumen from beyond filled my thoughts. Not cancer or heart disease. Swollen appendix.

Appendicitis was potentially lethal without treatment, but it was curable.

"We've got to get her to a hospital immediately," I said. "She doesn't have to die. It's not cancer."

"What?" my mom sputtered. She searched my face, a feverish look in her eyes. "How do you know? You aren't a doctor."

"I don't know how I know, but I'm certain. Absolutely certain."

"The crystals weren't working so I thought . . ."

"You thought she had hours to live? That would be true if you continued to do nothing."

"She doesn't want medical care. She's ready to die."

"Mom. She's got appendicitis. She needs surgery and antibiotics. She should have a full recovery. But if her appendix ruptures, the story changes. We have to go right now."

My mother seemed to weigh the choices for half a second, then she nodded. "How will we move her?"

"Back my truck up to the side door. I'll carry her out."

With a guilty look at her friend, my mother complied. I glanced around the room. "Rose? I know you're here. Show yourself."

A flutter of wings and my guardian angel appeared. She was dressed in bad-ass leather pants and sleeveless vest, ala motorcycle gang. Her dark spiky hair, piercing eyes, and black wings made quite the statement in

184

this colorful room. "Yes?"

"I need your help. My mother's friend is very ill." On cue, Gentle Dove moaned.

"This one is not long for your world," Rose said.

"Our medicine can help her, but I'm worried about her surviving the trip."

"What would you have me do? And remember there's a cost to be paid. I don't work for free."

"Whatever it takes to get her there alive."

"Are you making a habit of trading hours of your life for others?"

"Yes. I would give up anything to help this person. She's like a sister to my mother."

Mom hurried back in the room. "Baxley? Who are you talking to?"

"A friend."

"I don't see anyone."

Rose didn't waver before me. "She's here, and she can help."

Mom glanced around the room. "I don't like this."

I turned to Rose. "How will you do it?"

"Gather her in your arms on the bed, and I will take you to the nearest hospital."

I climbed on the bed. "Mom, I'm taking Gentle Dove. Meet us at the hospital in Brunswick." I nodded to Rose who easily lifted us and enfolded us in her wings. The color faded from the room as reality thinned and bent.

"What? How?" Mom sputtered. "Baxley. Where are you?"

CHAPTER 23

I paced the waiting room, hoping and praying we had arrived in time. Rose bent time and space and delivered us to the Emergency Room's front door in less than a minute. I'd stumbled inside, strangely euphoric and lightheaded after that unusual whole-body transport. Moments later, Gentle Dove was getting the professional medical help she needed.

I wish I'd known of her illness sooner so Gentle Dove didn't have to suffer as she did. My shoulder throbbed. I'd checked the skin there after they'd taken Gentle Dove from my aching arms.

I sported a new rose tattoo on the back of my right shoulder.

Guess that meant I owed Rose two hours of my life now. Mental note. Ask what the payment is before accepting help from otherworld creature. But it wouldn't have mattered. I would have done anything to save Gentle Dove from a senseless death.

At the sound of rapid footsteps, I turned. Mom burst into the room and hugged me. She still looked haggard, but a wisp of hope lit her eyes. "Is there news?"

"Not yet. She's still in surgery." I'd raised my guard on entering the hospital, so I perceived her concern with my normal senses.

"Your father is with Running Bear in Admission completing the paperwork for Gentle Dove's hospitalization." She gave me a sharp look and then sat down with a sob. "I don't know how you did this, but I thank you for helping my friend."

I sat beside her, stroking her head and her silky gray braid of hair. "She didn't have to die, Mom. Appendicitis is curable."

"I'm concerned. About you." My mother's voice trembled, and she gestured with both hands. "How do you know these things? How'd you do this?"

"I don't fully understand it myself. The same entity that helped me bring Dad back when he got lost on the wrong side of the bridge, she brought us here."

"Your father is very worried for you, and so am I. The boundaries must be respected."

"I respect them, but I have been given a chance to help in a different way. When bad things happen to good people. I can right some wrongs."

Accusation filled her eyes. "You can't fix everyone and everybody."

"You're right. I couldn't do these things alone. But I made this choice, and I will deal with the consequences."

Mom's lips pinched thin, then she massaged her temples. For the first time, I noticed how frail her hands were, how bowed her shoulders were. When had my mother become old? She'd always been such a mainstay in my life.

Thank goodness it wasn't Mom on the operating table.

"I shouldn't chastise you for helping my friend because Gentle Dove is the sister I never had. I've been heartsick over her sudden illness, over my inability to help her."

I placed my hand atop hers, needing the comfort of human touch as much as she did. "You helped, Mom. Your crystals bought her some time until I got there."

A white-coated doctor approached, and we rose. Her warm smile quelled the butterflies in my stomach. "I'm Dr. Hanover. Are you Earlene Brown's family?"

"Yes," I hastened to say, crossing my fingers at the necessary white lie. "I'm her niece, and my mom is her sister. Her husband is still in admin finalizing the paperwork."

"She's in recovery, though she's lucky her appendix didn't rupture during transport. Frankly, I don't know how it held together until I got in there to remove it. Her vitals are stable, and if all continues to go well, you'll see her in a few hours."

"She'll be fine?" Mom asked, leaning into me.

I wrapped my arm around her bony shoulders, scarcely daring to believe the good news.

The doctor nodded. "There are no absolutes in this business, but there's nothing to indicate she won't be fine. I conducted the removal laparoscopically, and there were no surgical complications. After she returns home she'll have a few restrictions, but she'll soon be back to doing everything she did before."

My knees trembled, and Mom's arm snaked around me. I had hoped my efforts weren't for naught, and I was so grateful for Gentle Dove's life being spared. "Thank you."

"No need to wait here. Why not relax in the cafeteria for a while? Check back with a nurse on this floor when you return for your sister's status."

The doctor left, and we sank into the sofa. Despite the doctor's suggestion to take a break, neither of us was going anywhere until Running Bear arrived. "She's going to be fine."

"Thanks to you," Mom said. "I'm humbled you pulled this off."

I held her level gaze. "I'm humbled by all you say and do and are. I helped Gentle Dove, but I know what she means to you. We're all connected in this world." And the next, echoed in my head, but I thought it best not to remind my mother that I'd used help from the beyond in getting Gentle Dove to the hospital.

My father and Running Bear joined us in the waiting room. We shared the good news and hugs all around. They were talking about staying overnight with Gentle Dove, and I finally took a moment to think about myself. I needed to feed my animals. "Would anyone mind if I went home? You can call me at any time to come get you."

Mom pulled my keys from her jumper pocket. "Your truck's parked in the lot by the emergency entrance. Don't worry about us. Tab and Running Bear drove separately, so we have another vehicle."

Relief swamped me, made me giddy. "You sure?"

"Absolutely."

Another round of hugs and I left. On the seat of the truck was a mesh bag of fresh crystals, a gift from my mom. I held the crystals, blinking back tears. My mom had known I'd be exhausted after this. Even when she was overwrought with emotion over her friend's illness, she'd thought of me. I kissed the bag and pocketed it.

The twenty-five-minute journey home passed in a blur of headlights and empty road. All I could think about was getting in my bed and going to sleep. And putting salve on my new tattoo.

I held onto the steering wheel with a death grip, focused on the white lines on the highway. It was nearly ten p.m. I should be hungry, but I didn't feel hunger pangs, only exhaustion. I needed to reboot.

Finally, I turned into my driveway, but instead of it being empty, two cars hunkered down in the dark. Dread filled me, ribboning from tendon to marrow. What now, world?

CHAPTER 24

I pulled to the far side of the gravel drive so I wouldn't have to move my truck once my uninvited company left. The cars were empty, and I didn't recognize the white Toyota or the rambling wreck, but at least Charlotte wasn't waiting to sandbag me. To be on the safe side, I pulled the Beretta from the glove box and eased out of the truck.

Feminine laughter carried on the dewy air, followed by a masculine chuckle. Curiosity quickly whited over my fatigue. What was going on here? Who was having a date on my back porch?

"Hello?" Gun in hand, I crept forward. I opened my senses, checking the area. Definitely two people on my back porch. Out of habit, I extended my perimeter check. There. A faint pulse in the woods. My watcher was back, but he didn't seem to be alarmed. His energy was pegged low, to a near sleep state.

I snorted and tamped down my senses. Some burglar alarm I had. A stranger in the woods watching my house wasn't worried by my unexpected, late-night company. Neither was the Shih Poo inside the house.

Suddenly, the events of the day slammed into me, and I couldn't catch my breath. Watcher in the woods. Guardian Angel. Cosmic debts. Murder cases. Sick friends. Daughter away from home. Missing husband. This dreamwalker profession demanded too much from me. I wanted a normal day where I got up and puttered around my house, tending to my family and animals.

Like that was going to happen. But Larissa would come home. Roland would stay in the wind, and all the other stuff would happen whether I wanted it to or not. No point in having a pity party.

I rounded the ligustrum hedge, gun held high, and in the pale twilight identified my visitors. Stinger. And Tamika. How odd.

"Hello," I said again, louder.

"Don't shoot," Stinger said, hands in the air. Starlight gleamed on his dark shaved head. "I did what you asked. Elvis is right here."

I gazed briefly at the Chihuahua curled up in his lap and tucked my gun in my waistband. Despite my relief at having the pet returned, an ugly edge crept into my voice. "You shouldn't have taken a child's dog."

"He was Charlie's dog first, and I needed him, but I know I done wrong. I'm sorry. I made a mistake."

I heard genuine remorse in his voice. He'd admitted his error. Goodness knows, I'd made a few wrong turns myself. "Apology accepted. Are you feeling better?"

"I am, but what's to keep the voices from running me ragged again? What's wrong with me? Am I going nuts?"

"You're not nuts, Connor," Tamika said. "A loon wouldn't have brought the dog back or sat here and kept me company for an hour." The police dispatcher gave me a sheepish grin. "I love little Ziggy, but it turns out my stepson is allergic to cats. I can't keep the kitty, but I couldn't just leave Ziggy on your doorstep."

I took the tabby from her uplifted arms. "I'm sorry to hear about the allergy. You and Ziggy bonded immediately."

"She's a cutie all right, but I can't rock the boat at home. How's Gentle Dove?"

News traveled fast in this county. "She's out of surgery and expected to fully recover."

The smell of fresh vegetables and home-made bread wafted over from the door. One of the perks of being a dreamwalker was the anonymous offerings of food that showed up at my back door. The strain of the day weighed on my shoulders.

"I'm starving. Anyone else up for a tomato sandwich?"

"I shouldn't stay. Kids at home," Tamika said. "But it was nice catching up with you, Connor. Don't be a stranger."

A few minutes later, Tamika was gone and Stinger was sitting at my table, Elvis in his lap. Muffin and Sulay welcomed Elvis home with much tail-wagging and sniffing, then abandoned him to chase Ziggy all over the house. The animals would have to work out their pecking order. Based on introducing other animals into the household in the past, I had no doubt that Sulay the cat would keep her position as top dog.

I placed slices of tomatoes on the fragrant bread, my mouth watering. "I didn't know you were friends with Tamika."

"I worked with her dad some on a shrimp-boat. Then he got into lawn-mowing and I was on his crew for a while." He hesitated a moment as he stroked Elvis. "My wife was kin to some of Tamika's folks."

I remembered the sheriff saying Stinger's

wife recently died of cancer, and that Stinger had been suicidal for the past month. I brought the sandwiches to the table and sat. "I was sorry to hear of her passing."

At that, Stinger broke down into tears. Elvis climbed the man's chest and licked his face. I reached across the table for his shoulder and held on, offering him strength and moral support. I knew what it felt like to grieve. But unlike me, Stinger couldn't hope for a reprieve. His wife's death was final.

An odd thing happened when I touched him. My senses revved, as if he were a charger and I were a dead battery. He didn't seem to notice the transfer. Needing an answer, I opened my senses and stared into the abyss. Stinger was a medium and his extrasensory channels were wide open. That explained a lot.

Not sure of my responsibilities, I shut down my extra senses for the time being. The man had a broken heart. I knew all too well what that felt like. Empathy swelled with me.

"I've been trying to reach her on my own, but she won't answer. I get lots of jibber-jabber from people I don't know, but Necee won't come to me." He put his hand atop

197

mine on his shoulder. "Please, I want to tell her I love her. Ya gotta help me, or I will die trying to reach her."

"I'm sure she knows."

"No. I have to tell her. She thought I had something going on with her sister. But we were only friends. That's all it ever was."

So much for my tomato sandwich. Shoving my plate aside, I abandoned all pretense of eating dinner. I scooted my chair closer to him. "Do you have something of hers?"

He tugged his shirt open to reveal a dainty gold chain. "This necklace. It was hers."

"Hold my hands and concentrate on the necklace. We're going in hot."

In a flash we traversed the void, landing in a sick room. At Stinger's rapid intake of breath, I surmised the woman abed was his Necee. Another woman was tending her, saying hateful things about Stinger. Necee shook her head, tears in her eyes.

"Tell her," Stinger urged. "Tell her it ain't true."

"Tell her yourself," I said as she looked at us.

Stinger glided forward, and I flowed with him as our energies were intertwined. "I love you, Nee Nee. Always have. Always will."

Necee arose from her bed, not quite solid

but not see-through either. "I know, punkin. That sister of mine is nothing but venom."

"Why wouldn't you speak to me before?"

"Couldn't. I heard you trying to reach me, but family is off limits out here unless you have a dreamwalker to make the connection. Please let me go, so that I can move on. You need to move on too. Find someone on the Other Side. I hate to see you so broken and defeated."

"You were my everything. I don't want to live without you."

"Hush up that kind of talk. Be strong. Be the man I knew and loved." The spirit turned to me. "I know who you are."

Her accusatory tone had me backing up. I didn't know what to say, but I needn't have worried. She wasn't finished with me.

"Do you promise to help my man? There's something in it for you."

"Of course, I'll help him. I brought him here, didn't I?"

"You have something he wants."

Elvis? "The dog belongs to my daughter. You can't ask that of me."

"I can and will. Connor needs that dog. It's special. He's special."

"I understand what you're saying, but it doesn't change my mind. Let's compromise. Stinger can stay with me and Elvis until my daughter returns. Then we'll work out an arrangement."

Necee wavered, going ghostly translucent before she burst forward into nearly human solidity. "Your protection won't mean squat if you cross me, but I'll toss you a bone for your concession. The killer you seek? There are two of them. Both men."

"What? Tell me more," I sputtered.

"I've said enough. Take care of my man. I mean that thing."

Wind rushed, the void pulled at us, then we landed in my kitchen. I blinked against the overhead light, catching my breath, getting my bearings. Euphoria crackled in my veins. I had a good feeling about him. Leveling with Stinger was the right thing to do.

That was the quickest, most effortless trip I'd ever made through the veil of life. "Wow."

"That was amazing," Stinger said. "Why'd you make me wait a day for that?"

"I . . ." Should I reveal my weakness to this man? He was someone who could help me. "This is awkward, but I couldn't do it last night. I'd burned too much power on another dreamwalk. But you and I together, we're synergistic."

"What's that?"

"We're good together. Psychically, we fit.

Your medium gift adds to my dreamwalker talent. With you, I can do more and do it faster and better."

"You sound like an advertisement for carving knives on TV."

"Don't mean to." I jumped up, unable to contain myself. Energy seemed to be shooting from my fingertips, fizzing out of my pores. "I've never felt like this before. Giddy. Drunk on power. I don't understand the how of it, but we're meant to be a team."

"Did you mean what you said in there? That I could stay with you and Elvis?"

"Stay as long as you like. We'll make this work."

"What about the voices? Will I still hear them?"

"You're a medium. Did you know that?"

"A medium what? I take a large in shirts."

I flashed him a grin as I drew us both glasses of water from the tap. "A medium. Someone who senses messages from dead people. Not a fake one, but the real deal."

He shook his head. "Isn't that what you do?"

"Sort of. But this is different. On the way back, I closed down your open channels, but you should learn how to do that yourself. I can teach you. Seriously, you never did anything like this before?"

"Nope. Just started hearing the voices after Necee died. Thought she needed me so I kept listening."

I circled the kitchen, stepping aside as the dogs and new kitty thundered through. Sulay watched the chase from the doorway. "Grief must have triggered your latent talent. This is amazing. Last time I took someone on a dreamwalk, I couldn't make it back home by myself. I have to figure out what this means."

"Figure all you like. I'm eating this sammich."

My stomach rumbled, and I slid my plate over. "Good idea."

CHAPTER 25

I awoke to the sound of a male voice talking. Downstairs. Fear drove me to my feet,
had me groping in the bedside table for my
Beretta. The events of the previous night
came to mind, and I realized Stinger was
downstairs. I had a houseguest, not a serial
killer, under my roof. Not an emergency. I
put the gun away and dragged in a few deep
breaths to steady my nerves.

Sunshine streamed through the window
sheers, painting the room with cheery
brightness. The alarm clock showed the time
as half past seven. I'd fallen asleep in my
clothes. Never a good sign.

My door was cracked open, and there
wasn't a pet in sight. I needed to feed them
and to let the dogs out. I shuffled down the
stairs, sniffing the breakfast-scented air with
delight. I could get used to a houseguest
who cooked.

"Morning," I said, my voice rusted with sleep.

"Morning," Stinger replied, handing me a steaming mug of coffee. "Your phone rang twice this morning. First time was the sheriff. Second time was your daughter."

"You took both calls?"

"I did. Thought they might be important."

"Were they?"

He shrugged. "Your people asked for a callback."

I walked over to my counter, checked the call log to verify what he said, and pocketed the phone when his story checked out. "I could've picked up those messages later. We need to talk about boundaries if you're staying here."

"Sure, but something weird happened to me in my sleep." He shoved his hand toward me. "I woke up with this flower on my hand. It looks like your tat."

I stared at the familiar rose on his dark skin, appalled. "Oh, no."

"What's it mean?"

"It means Rose had something to do with our journey last night."

"Rose? Who's she?"

"Hard to explain, but basically someone on the spirit realm with lots of power. I didn't ask for her help last night, and I didn't see her or sense her. My tat happened the same way. Woke up with it on my hand. I have some salve that helps with the discomfort. Let me get it."

I retrieved the first-aid kit from the downstairs bathroom and hurried back, noticing the cats eating side by side and the dogs curled up on their beds. "Thanks for taking care of the animals."

"You're welcome. Elvis stuck with me all night, the others came and went. Figured taking care of the critters is the least I could do. Fixed something for you too."

"Thanks." I handed him the tube of salve, sipped my coffee, and looked longingly at the breakfast on the stove. I'd eat, but first I needed to call my daughter. "I'm headed to the station this morning. What are your plans for the day?"

"Thought I'd tag along with you. Seems like I need you or Elvis around until I learn how to manage the voices."

Possibilities tumbled in my head. With Stinger, I'd have twice as much power to read the evidence. That could speed the investigation along. "I'll check with the sheriff. If he says no, you can keep Elvis with you today."

Stinger nodded and smoothed the salve over his raw skin.

"Excuse me. I need to return my calls." I stepped outside and called my mother-in-law's cell number.

Larissa answered. "Mom! What's going on? Who's that man who answered your phone? What's he doing in our house?"

"He's a friend, and he and Elvis are buds, from before we got Elvis."

"Oh. He must be okay if the dog likes him."

"Yeah. You ready to come home on Saturday?"

"I'm ready to come right now. The kids down here. They're different."

Maternal concern clouded my thoughts. My hand closed over the truck keys in my pocket. "Are you all right? Was someone mean to you?"

"I'm fine, but I don't like it down here anymore. These kids pretended to be polite. And that guy I liked? He used me to make another girl jealous. I'm the oddity of the month around here. They make fun of me when they think I'm not listening."

"Have you spoken to the Colonel and Elizabeth about this?"

"No. They'd only order the kids to be nice and that would make these kids hate me. Will you come get me?"

Dilemma. If I rescued her, I would earn

points with my daughter and alienate her grandparents. Worse, the Powells wanted full custody of Larissa after Roland, and I wasn't going to let them have her. Larissa belonged with me. Her mother.

Even so, Larissa deserved better than she was getting from her father's side of the family. "Your grandparents went to a lot of trouble to arrange your visit. Could you spend the rest of your visit with them instead of the kids?"

Larissa groaned. "I guess. I miss my Elvis. Does he miss me?"

"He does, though he's happy to reconnect with his friend from his life before. Tell you what. Give it a few hours and call me again. If you still want to come home, I will drive down there this afternoon."

"You've got a case, don't you?"

I didn't rise to the bait in her accusatory tone. "I'm helping the sheriff with an investigation."

"What happened?"

"We can talk about it when I pick you up." And I hoped that would be on Saturday, which would give me two more days to locate the killers and make our county safe once more. "May I speak with your grandmother?"

"Sure. Hold on while I find her. Love you."

"Love you too."

Elizabeth's voice came on the line, strong and self-assured. "Yes?"

"Keep smiling at Larissa, Elizabeth. She called me because the kids you stuck her with at tennis camp are rude and insensitive. She asked me to come get her right this minute, but I know you don't want her to cut her visit short. If you want her to stay, try a different activity today."

"Of course. Hold on just a minute while I check my schedule." Footsteps sounded. A door closed. "What is this about? Who slighted my granddaughter?"

"Larissa doesn't want you to interfere with the other children. But know this. If she's still unhappy and homesick this afternoon, I'm coming to get her, regardless of our agreement. Her happiness comes first."

"On that, we're agreed. What do you suggest?"

"She loves animals. How about the zoo?"

"The heat."

I heard the dismissal in her voice. "Try the animal shelter then. They often need volunteers to walk the animals or socialize them."

"I have a friend who's on the shelter

board. I'll try her first."

"Larissa wants to get to know you, to know more about her dad growing up. Share those memories with her, and you'll both have what you want from the visit."

"I will." Elizabeth sighed deeply. "This isn't easy for me, but thank you for the suggestions. I want Larissa to be content here. I didn't know she was unhappy with the activities at the country club. She didn't say a word."

"She's not a complainer, but she's my world. I trust you to make this day be about her, not about the grand life you think she should have."

"Message received. I will bend over backward to make her happy here."

I ended the call and dialed the sheriff. "Having a sleepover?" Wayne asked.

"I got my dog back, but I also landed a temporary houseguest. I learned Stinger's a medium, and his channels were stuck on wide open. I'm helping him hone his ability, but it turns out, he can help me too. His ability attenuates mine."

"What?"

"Attenuates. Makes it better."

"I understand the two-dollar word. What I don't understand is you taking a marginal character like Connor Simmons into your home."

"Long story, but can he assist me today in the evidence room?"

"This isn't part of our agreement."

"But there's a strong possibility I will be more receptive with him there. He might be the catalyst we need to speed things along."

The sheriff took his time answering. "We'll try it today, no promises. If I change my mind, he's out. Got that?"

"Got it."

"Good. And another thing." He paused. "You did right by Gentle Dove. Word is she's coming home tomorrow."

Tears welled in my eyes. "My mom must be so relieved."

Wayne cleared his throat. "I don't say this often enough, but this is a small community, and we're glad you came home. Taking care of each other is important. Word of how you helped Gentle Dove is spreading through the community like wildfire."

"I didn't do anything you wouldn't have done." My tattoo warmed uncomfortably on my hand. "She was sick, and I carried her to the hospital."

"Right."

I didn't care much for his wry tone. He knew there was more to it. Did we still share

210

a subconscious bond after traveling to the afterlife together?

I shrugged off that uncomfortable notion. "Stinger and I will be there in half an hour. We're bringing the dog."

"No dogs. Bad enough you brought a cat here yesterday."

"Elvis is a therapy dog. He helps Stinger. Stinger helps me. I help you. It's a chain. Break a link, and it doesn't work."

He sighed heavily into the phone. "Do you know how many rules I break for you?"

"Appreciate that, and Sheriff?"

"Yeah?"

"I received another lead on the case. This time from Stinger's wife when we contacted her last night. We've got two killers all right. Necee says they're both men."

CHAPTER 26

Despite the fact that the month was June and the heat felt like August, Elvis curled up inside Stinger's shirt, his alert little Chihuahua head peeking out above the placket. I didn't see how that could be comfortable for Elvis or Stinger, but nobody asked me.

Stinger drifted closer, as if my body offered him protection from the institutional-looking corridor and the banks of fluorescent lighting at the cop shop. I'd been here enough that the surroundings felt familiar, but this place throbbed with negative energy. I was thankful for my new sack of crystals, which I'd tossed in my pocket before leaving home.

Should I hit Wayne's office first or the conference room where the evidence must surely still be stacked? Wayne's office was on the way. Always good to check in with the boss.

I summoned a professional smile and

poked my head in his doorway. "Here I am, reporting for duty."

He glanced up from his writing and scowled. "Inside, Powell." He pointed to Stinger. "Wait in the hall. Shut the door behind you."

I gulped. So much for giving the sheriff time to think while we drove into town. Had I crossed a line with my glib remark? "Yes?"

Tension rolled off him like breakers freight-training off the ocean. "Explain yourself. Two killers?"

He hadn't invited me to sit down and, truthfully, I'd rather stand. That way I could run if needed. "When Stinger and I were working on his problem last night, his late wife told me there were two killers."

"A ghost? I can't put her on the witness stand. We need solid evidence."

"We can use that angle to focus the investigation. Two killers imply an association. We have to figure out how your top suspects know each other. If they don't know each other, we can move on to other choices."

"Ah. An exclusion tool." He leaned back in his chair, steepling his fingers, studying the grid of the dropped ceiling. I glanced up and saw a corner tile was discolored. Must be a leak somewhere in the roof. Probably not a good time to voice that observation.

Wayne lowered his gaze to me, inscrutable. It irked me that I couldn't read him at times. Cycling through my mind was the strong possibility the sheriff had more than just a cop's keen intuition. He could block my mental probes, whether consciously or not. People used to say he made opportunities on the field as a football quarterback. I had the strong feeling Sheriff Wayne Thompson still made opportunities for himself.

Which begged the question, how did I fit into his picture?

"As it happens," he drawled, "I had a development last night as well. Barry Campazzi got himself arrested."

Barry was our resident protestor. If a live oak was chopped down without due process, Barry wrote letters to the newspaper editor and picketed city hall for a day or two. Once, an antagonistic attitude displayed by a Board of Education member got Barry so riled up, he'd been banned from all future BOE meetings. Lately, he'd been on a mission to make lights-out at nine p.m. mandatory along the Georgia coast. Claimed the sea turtles were being harmed by human activities, and the lights tricked them into nesting at the wrong places.

"And?" I asked. Two could play at the inscrutable game.

"The movie people. They got a restraining order against him last week, and yet he was onsite at sunrise today. That gopher guy, LA, called me to come get the trespasser. Barry kept yelling the movie people were unnatural. I couldn't calm him down. He's had a few hours to chill out in jail. I want you to talk to him with me."

"First, I'm not surprised Barry's in jail. Second, I don't understand the unnatural part. Does he think they're zombies or something? Third, LA and Barry know each other. That's a connection."

Wayne snorted. "They hate each other. I can't see those two collaborating on anything."

"Their posturing could be a pretense."

A sly smile crossed his face. "Lucky for me I've got a human lie detector on my staff." He got to his feet. "Ready?"

"What about Stinger?"

"Tamika can babysit him while you're busy."

"Ooookay." Did he know Stinger and Tamika were loosely related? That they'd spent a few hours last night on my back porch? Hmm. Odds were he did.

I followed Wayne to Interview Room Two

and heard Stinger and Tamika's voices from the next corridor. Yeah, Wayne knew they were friends. He'd planned this all along.

Barry startled awake when the door opened. Dressed in a plain tee, basic jeans, and yellowed shrimp boots, he resembled every waterman in the county. A few years back he'd sold his shrimpboat and hung up his fishing nets. He spent his days protesting abuses in Sinclair County.

He blinked rapidly as I followed the sheriff in and closed the door behind us. Even though there were two chairs on our side of the table, I elected to stand while Wayne sat with Barry.

"What's she doing here?" Barry asked, his work-thickened fingers brushing his flat-top haircut. The grizzled shadow of a beard on his face attested to a night spent in jail.

I couldn't miss the quiver in his gravelly voice. We weren't best friends, but we weren't enemies either. What was his beef with me?

"I asked her to sit in on this interview," Wayne said. "You were arrested for violating a restraining order. Ford Morrison doesn't appreciate your protest, and the county won't tolerate your out-of-control behavior."

"They had it coming," Barry muttered.

Cautiously, I opened my senses. The negativity of the station house washed through me like a red tide. My teeth pressed together as I adjusted to the baseline negative vibes of the place. The urge to touch my moldavite necklace was strong, but I didn't want to call attention to myself at this point by moving.

"How's that?" the sheriff asked.

"Hellfire and damnation will rain down upon them," Barry said.

It chilled me to my core that Barry believed his words a hundred percent. Loon or truthsayer, he wasn't lying to us.

"The movie people are good for the county," Wayne continued in a gentler voice than I expected. "You can't antagonize them and not expect to pay the consequences."

"The sacrifices are confirmation. Evil has a foothold in our county. We must root it out at all costs."

Another truth. I shivered and accidentally clunked into the wall, drawing a sharp look from Wayne.

"I'll catch whoever killed Bee and Marv," the sheriff said.

"Will you catch them before they kill again?" Barry asked.

My heart leapt at the use of a plural pronoun. How did Barry know?

Wayne leaned forward. "Did you see something?"

"If I tell you, I'm a dead man. But I'm already dead, so what does it matter? On the night of the murders, I saw two hooded figures coming at me, one with the biggest fish knife I've ever seen."

I couldn't help myself. I stepped forward. "Did you have a vision?"

Barry shrank from me as if I was infected with the plague. "I'm not crazy, despite what people think. I was in the woods, watching the place they rented. People come and go from River House at all hours. They don't sleep like normal people. They're unnatural, I tell you."

Wayne sat back in his chair, which I took as a go-ahead. I edged toward Barry, knowing I needed to touch him to get the whole picture. "Go on."

Barry gulped, and his eyes widened as he shot a quick glance my way. "I'll tell you, but please, don't come near me."

My feet remained immobile, but I leaned forward. Expectation hummed in the tiny room, and a walking-across-a-grave sensation skittered across my skin. Had Barry seen the murderers?

"They worship the devil," Barry said in a whisper-light voice.

It took everything I had not to scoff. I schooled my features as if I heard that sort of news every day. "And?"

"And, they run around in robes and chant and drink from a chalice with odd symbols on it. They speak in strange tongues."

"Freedom of religion is guaranteed in our constitution," I said. "I'm not keen on all styles of worship, but I don't condemn people for their faith. You're not telling the whole truth. Stop lying."

He cowered in his chair, the color draining from his ruddy complexion. "I can't. They'll kill me. That's why I came out of the woods when I did. That's why I got arrested. I'm safer in jail."

"Who threatened you?" Wayne asked.

Barry shook his head.

"You need to tell us," I said, hoping Wayne would let me continue the questioning. "The sheriff will protect you."

Barry gazed at his hands. "I can't."

"Don't you want justice for Bee?"

"Bee was my friend." His voice sounded strained. "But I wasn't good enough for her."

"Go on," I urged.

"She said the movie people were her salvation. That her future was tied to them. She said I couldn't come around her place anymore. But I saw her with that Marv guy. What they did was unnatural."

He'd spied on them? "They conducted private religious ceremonies?"

"Nah. But the way he treated her in the sack, it wasn't right. Worse, she enjoyed it."

I couldn't remember if Bee's skin had any sort of abuse marks. All I remembered was the alabaster sheen of her entire body. "Did he hurt her?"

"Yeah. But she liked it. And she hurt him too. The way that man screamed and hollered, you'd a-thought the world was ending. We don't want that kind of people around here. I don't care how much they help the economy."

I was pretty sure what he was talking about, but to be on the safe side, I patted his shoulder. The image of Marv choking a naked Bee flashed into my head, as did their cries of ecstasy. Not my cup of chowder either. I probed deeper and saw the hooded figures Barry mentioned. In the midnight vision, I couldn't estimate their relative sizes, much less make out any features.

He shrugged off my touch. "You can't do that."

I stepped back to the wall. Wayne's gaze burned into me. I nodded to show I'd gotten something.

"To recap," Wayne said, pushing his chair back from the table and making a loud noise, "you and Bee had an intimate relationship, and she dumped you."

Barry hung his head. "That's right."

"She played rough in the sack with Marv, but it was consensual."

Barry didn't say anything.

"Answer me," the sheriff said.

"Yeah. She liked him better'n me."

"The movie people have private religious ceremonies," Wayne continued.

"They're a perversion," Barry growled. "They have to be eradicated."

I stepped forward again, gentled my voice. "Easy, there. We'll get this straightened out. Tell us about the hooded men. Were they also watching Bee's house?"

"Yes. And they know I saw them."

Wayne edged into Barry's personal space. "Did you see their faces?"

"It was too dark. But I followed them through the woods and heard their vehicle crank up. A diesel."

"You're sure?"

"Damn straight. I've been around engines all my life. I know a diesel when I hear one."

His bitter words rang with truth. The sheriff didn't need my lie detection skills on that statement.

"What else can you tell me about the vehicle?" Wayne asked.

"It was a pickup. Must have been a dark color because I couldn't see a thing as it drove off."

My thoughts whirled. From the sound of it, Barry had seen the killers. "Why didn't you come forward right away?"

"I didn't want anyone to know I was spying on Bee. Thought I'd be a suspect 'cuz we'd had a falling-out."

"You are a suspect," the sheriff growled. "Give me one good reason why you didn't kill her."

"I loved her."

"Even more reason to kill her," Wayne taunted. "If you couldn't have her, no one could."

Barry let out a sob. "No. It wasn't like that. I couldn't hurt her. I would never hurt her. She . . ."

"She what?"

"She's the mother of my child."

CHAPTER 27

"What?" Wayne and I asked at the same time in a creepy gender-neutral blend of our voices. The walls of the interview room seemed to close in around me.

"We was kids," Barry said. "Neither one of our families had two nickels to rub together, and Bee got pregnant in high school after we, you know. She spent the summer at her uncle's place up at the lake, had the baby at home, then gave it to an adoption place. Weren't nobody outside of her family and mine who even knew. She couldn't look me in the eye for ten years afterward. A few years ago, she took me home one night and said we weren't going to talk about it. So we never did. But I always wondered what happened to my kid."

My head spun with the possibilities of a secret baby. Could this child have a vendetta against his parents for not wanting him? Could the child have murdered its own mother? If so, how did Marv fit into the picture? He didn't fit. Hmm. This scenario didn't work.

Wayne shifted in his chair. "Did you contact the adoption agency?"

"Didn't think of it until about ten years ago when I got dried out. Turns out, the place burned down five years after she gave the baby up, and their records were destroyed," Barry said, hanging his head. "I ain't never finding out what happened to my boy."

"It was a male child?" Wayne asked.

"Naw. I don't know jack about the baby, but I dream I've got a son. Never had any other kids. This 'un is the only one I got." He looked away and blinked a few times before pinning me with a watery stare. "He's the only Campazzi in the next generation, and I don't know his name, where he lives, what he likes, nothing."

At the look of abject sorrow on the man's face, my heart softened. "There might be a record of the adoption somewhere. Have you contacted the Department of Human and Health Services for help?" I asked.

"Didn't think of it, but what kid would want me to come looking for them? I still got next to nothing. At least Bee made something of herself with her charter business, and now she's gone. My boy's all I have left, and I don't even have him."

"I can see it's important to you to find him. If you're innocent, after we catch Bee's killer, I'll help you get started with your search." I'd become something of an expert on red tape and government bureaucracy after Roland's alleged death.

"That'd be mighty fine." He gazed up at me. "You look in my head?"

I held my breath, not knowing if he'd explode or cry. I wasn't accustomed to men who wore their emotions on their sleeves. "I did."

He squinted at me. "You ain't scared of what you saw?"

Seemed like he didn't take issue with my snooping. I risked a small breath. "No."

"I guess my thoughts aren't as scary as the ones you get from dead people. You're one tough cookie, ain'tcha?"

"We do what we have to do," I answered with a shrug.

"Where were you the night Bee died?" the sheriff asked.

"Shooting pool."

"Anybody verify that?"

"The regulars at the pool hall. That afternoon, I was out working in my clamming fields off the point when Bee and Marv cruised by in her Boston Whaler. I knew she'd be spending the night with him, so when I got done and got cleaned up, I headed to the pool hall to keep from thinking about it. About her. With him."

Wayne nodded, his poker face rock solid. "We'll check your story. Meanwhile, you'll be our guest in the back."

Barry shrugged. "The longer I ken stay here, the better. I don't wanna wake up dead."

Wayne summoned a jailer to take Barry back to a cell. He motioned me to join him in his office. "Well?"

I closed the door behind us. "He was telling the truth."

Wayne leaned against a corner of his desk. "He said a lot of things."

"He meant them all. His love for Bee. His revulsion for the movie people. His longing for his child. Those are all truths to him."

"Did he kill her?"

"He said he didn't."

"Not good enough for me. We'll check his alibi."

"I was stunned about the kid."

"Same here, but I doubt it's relevant to the case. Happened too long ago."

"I disagree. It's a loose end worth pursuing."

"Let's focus on finding the killer before we go haring off on any tangents. Right now, I need you to examine the evidence we've collected. Grab up Stinger and do your woo-woo thing in the conference room. Get me something useful."

"Will do, but Barry gave us confirmation of our two-killer theory. That's progress."

"Barry's a whack-job. A good prosecutor will tie him up in knots on the stand. We need corroborating evidence, which is your job. Get busy with my evidence."

He leveled a finger at me. "If you don't get a hit, I want you to read the bodies. We need a solid lead, today."

I shuddered, thinking of the last time I'd seen Bee and Marv. That gruesome image of them strung up on the stairway would be forever embossed in my brain. "Let's hope we find something in the evidence."

We used an assembly-line process to go through the collected items, starting with the stuff I'd vetted yesterday. Tamika handed me items from the evidence boxes. Stinger sat beside me, his hand on my shoulder. We sorted through empty soda cans, chip bags, and other junk food wrappers. Nothing unusual there.

Which left the clothes.

It felt good to know I hadn't missed anything yesterday. Wayne finished up whatever he was doing and came in to watch. I nodded at Tamika. "Ready."

She handed me Marv's shorts, polo, and sandals. I felt static. Nothing good, nothing bad. Same with Bee's outerwear.

Bee's bra was next. Somehow, I'd missed it before. The lacy garment was clean, no blood on the white fabric, but I didn't want to touch it. I drew my hand back.

"What?" Wayne asked.

I gulped, curling my hands protectively into my belly. "Can't explain it. This one's different."

"You do different."

I screwed up my nerve. "You're right. I do." With that, I touched the lingerie and fell down a rabbit hole. The steady beam of a flashlight shined on the sagging wooden ceiling. Below, Bee and Marv were grappling with each other, rolling on that stained mattress in the June's Folly house. She was clad only in her bra. He wore nothing.

Bee moaned and writhed. Marv shouted. I closed my eyes, not wanting to see, yet finding myself peeking through my eyelashes. Bee's breathing evened first. She opened her eyes and made cooing sounds, then she stiffened.

228

"Who are you?" she demanded.

Marv roused. "What?"

"Someone's here," Bee said. "He saw us."

"You're dreaming, babe. I need a minute."

She punched him in the shoulder. "Get off me. This isn't a dream. A man in a black sweatshirt was standing in the doorway a second ago."

Marv grunted and complied.

The sequence of events in the vision slowed to a molasses drip. Marv's shift on the mattress seemed to take forever. Bee pushed up on her elbows. "I hear footsteps," she whispered.

Marv rolled to his feet, finally taking her seriously. "Who's there?" he called.

Each event flashed by in a freeze-frame sequence, each word uttered lengthened in slow motion. My heart beat faster and I wanted to tell them to jump out the window, to run, to do something, but my voice was silenced during this vision.

The man appeared in the doorway. Rushed to Marv. A wicked blade pressed on Marv's throat. "Move."

Marv lashed out at the man. A trickle of blood ran down Marv's neck.

"Stop it, Marv. Do what he says," Bee shrieked. "We'll do what you want."

Marv inched out the doorway, more blood

on his neck.

Bee scrambled for her clothes, but her hands were shaking too badly to do any good.

"Don't."

Bee looked up. The hooded man returned, his features indistinct in the shadows at the edge of the flashlight beam. With his blade, he pointed to her bra. "Take it off."

"Please," she pleaded. "We'll do whatever you want."

He gestured at her torso again with the gleaming knife. "Off."

Bee unhooked the lacy bra, tossed it to the side. Tears ran down her face, and she covered herself with her hands. "Where's Marv? What have you done to him?"

"Move."

She stumbled off the mattress, hit her knees on the floor. An unmistakable gurgle sounded from the other room. Bee cried out. "No!"

The knife-wielding assailant yanked her up by her hair. Bee screamed as he marched her out the door.

I followed, but it was so dark. I couldn't see anything.

I heard a soft sound. A gurgle. Then an anguished yip of pain. Then nothing.

Darkness.

The killer or killers moved easily in the night. They'd killed with precision and needed no illumination. How odd. Not once had I seen their faces. I wasn't even certain there were two men. One man could've killed Marv in the hall and then come back for Bee. But the blade he'd brandished at Bee had been clean. Not a smear of blood on it.

"I don't understand," I said, hoping the spirit would hear. "Bee, please show me more."

I heard a noise behind me, in the mattress room. The scene played out again. Exactly the same way. Except this time, I noted the height of Marv's assailant. His head was as high as the top hinges on the door. Bee's assailant was shorter. Definitely two men.

Then I heard it. A low rumble of a voice in the darkness. "I'm coming for you next."

CHAPTER 28

"That was intense." Stinger clutched Elvis to his heart. They stared at me with wide eyes.

I nodded, tears misting my vision. Intense? How about awful, gruesome, macabre, brutal, and downright horrible? White noise trumpeted in my head as I shoved the bra back into the evidence bag. I skittered away from my chair and stopped by the hospitality station near the door. I didn't want a cup of coffee. I needed to mainline sugar and caffeine, and even that might not be enough to keep me going.

"Omigod." It was all I could get out. Knees trembled. Hands quavered. Someone in the spirit world knew I'd watched that death scene. That someone was coming for me. I needed to run. To hide. Where?

"Tell me." Wayne blocked the exit, not venturing closer, when I would have welcomed a hug, even from him.

"Two of them," I managed, shaking sensation back into my fingers. My heart galloped out of control, and I felt my breaths coming too fast. I had to pull it together, had to get past the personal threat and give my professional report. I took control of my shallow breathing, deepening each inhalation until the panic ebbed.

"Two what?" the sheriff asked.

"Definitely two killers. A tall man came in the dark. Took Marv first. Did him. A shorter man entered, made Bee strip off her bra, then marched her into the hall and killed her."

"Details."

I relayed the vision, noting with disgust Wayne's eyes heated when he heard about Bee and Marv having sex. "Marv's assailant was about six feet. I used the hinges on the door as a yardstick. Bee's assailant was shorter. Maybe five-five or five-seven."

"The murder weapon?"

"Each man carried a knife. Some kind of Bowie knife, I think. The blades were wide and long. Maybe two inches by ten? Bee's assailant's knife had an S-shaped hilt."

"Not something you'd pick up at the local hardware store."

"The victims weren't drugged. The first guy got the drop on Marv and dragged him out of the room, knife to throat. Bee grabbed her clothes, but the other guy came in right away. She saw the blade and froze."

"Makes sense that they'd separate them to kill them. But are you sure about the height? No one on our suspect list is six feet tall. Our suspects could pass for the shorter assailant, but we're back to square one for Marv's killer. Could you see anything distinctive, recognize something in their voices?"

"It was dark. They wore black hoodies. I didn't see anything helpful. There's nothing else to tell."

Stinger did a fake cough. I silenced him with a glare. Wayne didn't need to know I'd been threatened in a dreamwalk. Successful police consultants didn't whine about the dangers of their jobs.

"You got something you want to add?" Wayne asked Stinger.

"No, sir. This is the dreamwalker's show."

"It isn't a show," I said, feeling my heart kick into fight-or-flight mode. "I saw their last moment together, heard them take their last breath."

Wayne smacked the tabletop with his palm. "I want to know who killed them. Why the hell don't the victims come right out and tell you what happened?"

"They do tell me, in their own time. But they have their own way of spinning the story."

It was their story to tell, not mine. Bee and Marv had run afoul of a killing team. Bad things happened to them. Not me. I was seeing a replay of the event. I had to separate myself from what I saw, or the visions would eat me up.

This didn't happen to me, I repeated for my own benefit. Words mattered, so I repeated them silently until my heart rate slowed and my skin felt like it fit again.

Wayne swore up one wall and down the other. "This sucks. And now for the other bad news. The coroner is releasing the bodies to family today. Bee's funeral is at two tomorrow afternoon, and Marv's wake is in the evening. I expect you to attend both functions."

A cold wind shivered through my blood. Dread built inside me. I did not want to follow my boss's orders, and I had no good excuse to get out of the duty. I tried to bow out anyway. "That is bad news for the investigation. I knew Bee to see her and didn't know Marv at all."

His confounded expression put me on notice that I'd overstepped. "We're attending their funerals as investigators, not friends of the deceased. Observe people's behaviors, look for pairs who are the same height as you noted in the dreamwalk. You'll be on the clock."

I gulped. Easy for him to say. I got paid by the job, not by the hour. I didn't finish the job, I didn't get paid from the sheriff's slush fund.

The sheriff's gaze rested heavily on me. "What? You scared? I thought dead people were your wheelhouse."

His cop-vision made me squirm, despite all the dirt I had on him. "It's not the dead I'm afraid of. The living are much worse."

"Take your sidekick here, or the little rat dog, if you need moral support."

Stinger shook his bald head, the overhead lights gleaming on his mahogany skin. "I'm not going to no funeral. That man brought this trouble to Bee. She was good people. Bee would understand if I don't see her into Zion."

"And Marv?" the sheriff asked.

Stinger's lips thinned before he spoke. "The hell with that movie scum."

Wayne reached for the doorknob. "Baxley? Can I count on you?"

I was half-tempted to say no, but the realities of bills shaped my answer. Until this case closed, I was at the sheriff's beck and call. "I'll be there."

"Good." He waved me to the door. "Come on, you're not done yet."

I planted my feet solidly on the floor. "I got you new information from the dreamwalk. I need some downtime to recharge."

"You can have downtime tonight. Right now, you and your motley crew are headed to the morgue. This is our only chance for you to examine the bodies."

"But-but-but," I sputtered. Two dreamwalks in a row? Was that safe? Wait. I did two dreamwalks in a row to rescue my father when he went too far in the spirit world. Rose had bailed me out, or I would've been condemned to wander the afterlife too.

I touched the rose tattoo on my hand, realizing it was warm. Rose wanted me to do this? I didn't trust her motivations. I'd better ask someone I did trust. "I'll do it, but I need to make two phone calls first."

"Make it snappy."

"I will. I'll just step outside —"

"Think again. Too many reporters out there. You want privacy, you hit the head."

I gave Stinger a nod. "Give me a sec, okay? We'll knock this out and then grab some lunch, on me."

"Sure 'nuff. Me and Elvis will hang with

Tamika while you catch your breath."

His easy tone confused me. "You're not zonked?"

"Me and Elvis are good."

So was I, come to think of it. I didn't feel tired or punchy or flooded with adrenaline. I felt morning fresh. How was that possible? Other dreamwalks temporarily sapped me of energy, but a dreamwalk with Stinger had a different outcome. Huh. Good to know.

My steps quickened. Before I opened the bathroom door, my phone rang. I stepped inside and answered, leaning into the phone. "Mom?"

"You have a question for me?" she asked.

The Weather Channel droned in the background. Mom's favorite program was on. "I do. How did you know?"

"Your father told me. He's sitting right here, finishing his lunch. You want to talk to him?"

I didn't realize I'd broadcast my thoughts. I'd better be more careful in the future. "No. At least, I don't think so. I wanted to ask about the crystals you sent. They're getting a workout. How will I know they're still helping?"

"Easy. Put your hand on them."

I reached into my pocket and pulled out the mesh sack of unpolished stones. "Okay."

"What do they feel like?"

"They feel hard."

"The other kind of feeling," Mom prompted.

"Let me check." I tuned out the buzz of fluorescent lighting, the faint murmur of Tamika and Stinger's nearby conversation, and the warmth of my cell phone. My eyelids drifted shut as I focused on the crystals. A sense of joy came over me, a humming joy.

I dampened my extra senses and opened my eyes. "They feel good."

"Then you can use them again."

"How will I know when to get them re-charged?"

"They'll feel different."

Relief spread through me like a warm hug. "Thanks. I did one dreamwalk for the sheriff just now, and he's asked me to do another right away. I wasn't sure if that was a good idea, for me or the crystals."

"You know what it's like to feel spiritually exhausted. Heed the signals from your body, and you'll be fine."

"Thanks, Mom. I feel much better about this."

"We're so proud of you. You're making a real name for yourself with your good deeds."

"I don't know about the last part, but thanks for believing in me, even when I didn't believe in myself. You and dad saved me by helping me accept who I am, what I can be."

"You would have come around on your own. Destiny isn't something we can hide from forever. It follows us no matter what path we take."

Cryptic words from a wise woman. Standard fare in my neck of the woods. "Gotta go. Love ya."

Next, I dialed my mother-in-law's cell phone. Larissa answered on the first ring. "Hey, Mom," she said. "What's up?"

"Checking on you. Making sure you're feeling better about Jacksonville."

"I am. We're at the zoo, and the animals are awesome. I want to be a veterinarian when I grow up. I want to work at the zoo."

"Glad you're enjoying the day. I won't keep you, but I needed to make sure you were feeling better about Jacksonville. You sounded so sad this morning."

"I was sad, but now I'm happy. Very happy. Wait. Elizabeth wants to speak with you."

My teeth gritted together. Elizabeth refused to be called any variation of grandmother. "Put her on."

"Baxley?" Elizabeth's shrill voice commanded the airwaves.

"Everything all right?"

"It's fine. Thank you for your advice this morning. I am sweating like a pig in this heat, but I've never seen Larissa so happy. I feel like our week with her is just beginning. Which brings me to my point. I insist she stay here another week."

Disbelief dropped my jaw. My spine straightened. "I insist she come home on Saturday. We can talk about another visit later in the summer."

"I don't agree to those terms."

"We're not negotiating a legal contract. We're talking about my daughter."

"My granddaughter," Elizabeth corrected. "We need more time with her, and there's so much to show her in Jacksonville. She's out of school for the entire summer. What would it matter if she's here or there?"

Panic squeezed my throat. "Larissa needs to come home on Saturday. I know what's best for her."

"We'll see about that."

The connection ended, and I sagged against the wall. A wily adversary in any skirmish, Elizabeth had been a successful trial attorney when she met the Colonel. So far, I'd escaped her full attention, unlike the various charities that she ran with a heavy hand, but I had something she desperately wanted. Larissa.

CHAPTER 29

The morgue was a fancy name for the refrigerated room with human-sized cold lockers. It smelled of bleach and death, a repelling combination under any circumstance. Elvis whined pitifully and curled his head into Stinger's chest. I felt the same way. I was capable of doing another dreamwalk, but I needed the scents of nature to lift my uneasy mood.

Something about this situation wasn't right, only I couldn't get a handle on the source of my discomfort. I jammed my hands in my pockets, careful not to touch the walls, doors, or tables in this room.

"Tox screen came back clean. These two weren't drugged," the sheriff said.

"Which corroborates my dreamwalk," I added, wishing my feet hadn't gone cold inside my work boots. Elvis whimpered in Stinger's arm. My uneasiness grew to a new level. *Something is very wrong.*

"What's the matter?" the sheriff asked.

Did I say that out loud? I was losing it. "I don't know, but every spidey sense I have is telling me to run out of this room. The dog feels it too."

"Get a grip, Dreamwalker. Do your job. These bodies are outta here in a few hours, and we won't get another chance to examine them."

"I'll do my job," I snapped, angry that I'd been pushed into a corner. "Give me a minute to see what's wrong."

"I can wait outside," Stinger offered hopefully.

"Stay put," I gritted through clenched teeth. "This won't take long. If I zone out, grab my shoulder like you did in the evidence room."

Cautiously, I lowered my guard, one hand on the sack of crystals in my pocket, the other on my moldavite necklace. Whatever was after me, I didn't want to be surprised. The room fogged to an acid yellow. I fanned the mist from my eyes, squinting into the murk. My tattoos heated to the point of pain.

"Who's there?" I called, walking this way and that in the nothingness.

It's a trap kept running through my brain and the urge to run from the unknown hammered me. But I hung in there. This was my job, dammit.

"Dreamwalka . . ." an insidious voice rumbled in my head. My sense of humor flared wildly. Must be a Southern ghost with that accent. "You try my patience."

The last syllable of patience drew out like the hiss of a snake. "Who are you?" I asked, gasping at the instantaneous chill in my body. The very marrow of my bones seemed to have crystallized. Talking became a monumental effort.

"I am many. Your kind isn't welcome here. The dead must be silenced."

"Well, Many." I croaked as boldly as I could, despite the ice crystallizing in my veins. "You have a problem because I'm staying, like my father and his mother before him. This is what we do."

My energy flared. A bolt of warmth followed. Stinger. Bless him.

"You have been warned," Many said.

The ground trembled and roiled, an earthquake and a mighty tsunami rolled into one. A howling wind followed. I held my stance, determined not to let this bully win. I would have shouted a reply, but it took all my concentration to remain standing. Fury built within me at the remembrance of playground bullies who'd tormented me because I was a Nesbitt, of service wives who'd shunned me because I didn't shop at the right stores, of the army and their solid roadblock of red tape regarding my missing husband.

"No." I stated, fighting the roaring wind to be heard. "I have a right to be here."

The wind subsided by degrees. Heartened, I continued. "I am a natural being, and this is my place in the order of things."

The ground quit trembling. "I seek justice for the dead and solace for the living." My voice sounded stronger, firmer, authoritative. Righteousness drove the arctic chill from my bones, hastened my thready pulse.

I felt a disturbance behind me. Rose? I whirled, half-hoping it was Rose and not another entity with a beef. Half-hoping it wasn't Rose because it cost me every time we interacted.

"Well done, Dreamwalker," Rose said in a sulfury blast of air.

"I didn't summon you," I stated matter-of-factly. "I've got this."

"You are strong."

"You sound surprised."

"I am often disappointed."

I pondered that a moment. Uneasiness swirled within me. "Wait. You did this? You set me up with that, that *thing*? You expected me to fail?"

"My expectations aren't the issue. You performed well under pressure."

"I'm here to learn who killed Marv Kildeer and Belinda Donlin."

Marv and Belinda appeared behind Rose, their mouths obscured, their eyes dull. "The answers you seek aren't with the dead. I've silenced these mischief-makers."

"You won't let me talk to them?"

"You're needed elsewhere, Dreamwalker. And ease your fears. I will collect on my debt soon."

Like that would relax me. I feared what she'd do with two hours of my life. "Any chance we can change the terms of our deal?"

Lancing pain radiated from my tattoos, dropping me to my knees. I regretted saying anything, but damned if I would apologize.

"Don't annoy me, earthling. I own you."

With that, Rose faded, and the darkness thinned. Cold seeped into my body from the concrete slab floor, and light gradually returned to my field of vision.

My face felt wet. Something sandpapery lathed my chin. Elvis. I tried to reach for him and couldn't.

Stinger hovered above me. His round face gleamed like polished wood, his dark eyes

247

radiated concern. "Miss Baxley? You okay in there?"

He had a tight grip on my hand. The ceiling looked miles away. The floor pressed against my back. I struggled to get my bearings, but I was too spent to do more than breathe. I'd drained my crystals. I'd drained my energy, too. There would be no more dreamwalks today.

"I'm here," I managed, my tongue thick in my cotton-dry mouth. "But I'm spent. I need my mom."

The sheriff leaned over my face. His eyebrows drew together in a stern line. Deep grooves of skin etched his cheeks into his cheekbones. "The bodies. Today."

I tried to moisten my lips, but my tongue was too dry. "Water."

A faucet ran. A cup appeared. Stinger lifted my head, and I drank. Funny how good morgue water tasted. Like nectar. Did that make me a god? I would've laughed at the notion if I wasn't six miles past exhausted and my crystals weren't drained.

"Do your job," the sheriff said.

He could bluster all he wanted, but I had nothing left. "I saw Bee and Marv on that dreamwalk," I replied, carefully choosing my words. "The answers we seek are on this side of the veil."

The sheriff's face flushed Christmas stocking red. "Don't go all cryptic on me."

My eyelids weighed as much as my truck. I couldn't keep them open. It was too hard. They fluttered shut. "My mom. I need my mom."

CHAPTER 30

I floated on the softest clouds, drifting through dreamy skies of baby blue. Sunlight burnished my pale skin, and I slid into the drowsiness of complete warmth and love. I heard my name now and again and roused enough to shift positions, then faint melodic chanting lulled me back to a peaceful sleep.

Wood smoke. I breathed deeply, thinking fondly of campfires and marshmallows and my family. I hummed with energy and stretched drowsily. My eyes gradually grew accustomed to the dim light. The angled walls seemed quite near.

How strange.

I moved, feeling the luxurious slide of animal fur against my bare skin. Elvis and Muffin were curled against me. Sulay and the new kitty were tucked into my right side. I had no idea of where I was or why, but oddly, I wasn't panicked. If my pets were here, someone had gone to the trouble of fetching them to comfort me.

After what I'd been through, it would take a lot to scare me. There. A sound. I turned my head to the faint thread of soft voices. Outside of this cozy space. I sat up, the covers sliding down to reveal I still wore my underwear. The pets stretched and demanded my attention. I gave it to them, hugging them each in turn. Even the cats, who purred in my arms.

My skin felt different. Oiled. And the bone-deep satisfaction reminded me of the massage Roland had bought me one Mother's Day. Instinctively, I reached for my necklace, another gift from my allegedly dead husband. It was gone.

I dampened my automatic alarm response. Everything else was good. There must be a reason my necklace was missing. I'd drained the crystals in my pocket. Must've drained the necklace too.

Objects in the relative darkness became distinct as my vision adjusted. My clothes. My boots. And the space. It was conical. Like a teepee.

I dislodged my pets and dressed in my tee and jeans, crawling on hands and knees out the narrow opening. Three people sat by a campfire under a canopy of twinkling stars.

My mom. Dad. Running Bear. Ah, I was at Running Bear's lodge. No wonder I felt energized. This place had great vibes.

"There you are," Mom said, arising gracefully from her cross-legged position.

She'd saved me. I knew it as well as I knew my name. My heart swelled with love. I ran the last few steps and threw myself into her arms. She drew me close, and I savored her warmth and strength. Mom was my mighty fortress, my metaphysical rock.

"You're okay," she said, patting my shoulder. "I have something for you."

She'd pulled me back from the brink of total exhaustion. That was gift enough. As the fire crackled, I struggled to speak. "Thanks. I'm . . . I owe you so much . . . I'm overwhelmed by your selfless giving. I'm at such a loss for words. Thank you doesn't seem like enough."

Mom gestured to her companions. "I had help. Lots of help. Many hands made light work." Then she clasped a new moldavite necklace around my neck. My center of calm restored, and it felt as if a flame deep inside me burned steadily once more.

This gem was my touchstone. It anchored me through hard times in this world and the next. With all the wear and tear my other necklace had been receiving, this was the best gift she could've given me.

"Thanks." I hugged her again, filled with love and wonder.

My father and Running Bear stood beside us. I hugged and thanked each of them for their help. They invited me to sit down by the fire, and Mom handed me a mug of something warm to drink. The taste was bitter, but I knew better than to complain. It was what I needed.

The cats squatted beside me, mesmerized by the dancing flames. Muffin and Elvis vied for a spot in my lap. I tucked them side by side in the cradle of my folded legs. Questions bubbled from my subconscious, one from every "w" category, but I let the who, what, when, and wheres alone.

"Are you ready to speak of the trial?" Running Bear asked when I'd finished the broth.

That got my attention. I set the mug aside and hugged my knees. "How did you know?"

"It is their way. To test the dreamwalker."

Annoyance flitted through me. "Why didn't y'all warn me?"

"Worrying about it wouldn't help. You did fine," my father said.

"They did this to you?"

His gaze met mine. "They did. I'd been helping people for a few years, sure that I knew everything, and something big in the spirit world ambushed me." He looked away. "I nearly died, and would've crossed over permanently without your mom and Running Bear. They knew what to do."

I didn't remember him being near death during my lifetime. He'd only been sick one time in my childhood. Recognition flared. "When you had pneumonia?"

He cleared his throat. "It wasn't pneumonia. I was literally at death's door for most of a week, drained of energy. The spiritual warfare I endured during my ordeal took a terrible toll."

"I remember lots of people coming to sit with you."

"They helped me. Same as people helped you."

I tried to construct a timeline. Couldn't. I had no idea of how long I'd been recovering from the ordeal. My mouth went dry. "How long was I out? What about Larissa? Did someone pick her up from the Powells?"

"It's still Thursday, and Larissa is fine," my mom said. "You'll get her on Saturday as planned."

"She doesn't know of the incident, does she?"

Mom gave my hand a reassuring squeeze.

"She would've called if she felt the disturbance."

"You're a dreamwalking powerhouse," my dad crowed. "Eight hours of rest was all you needed. Eight hours. My mom took two days after her trial, and I needed a week. You're amazing."

"Not so amazing. I had Stinger and Elvis with me at the trial. Elvis seems fine. What about Stinger?"

"He seemed none the worse for wear," my mother added. "We sent him home with Tamika. She said she'd look after him tonight."

"You're already building your own support team," my father said. "You're intuitively doing what it took me years to do. And animals. I never would've thought to use them as helpmates, but they're your natural companions. It all works."

"You make my new vocation sound so organized and purposeful. It didn't happen that way. More like serendipity."

"Good word," Running Bear grunted.

"How is Gentle Dove?" I asked, finally remembering my manners.

"My wife is fine, thanks to you. Bubba Paxton is sitting with her this evening, though she wanted to come here more than anything. I owe you, Dreamwalker."

"I'd say we're more than even. This place.

255

This healing. Whatever y'all did to me. It accelerated my recovery."

"We've learned a few things over the years," Mom said, her wry smile both proud and sad. "We're glad to pass our knowledge to you. With Gentle Dove's recent illness, we've realized how fragile life is for our generation. I hope to be here for most of your dreamwalker journey, love, but you must absorb what we know to help Larissa when her turn comes."

My protective instincts surged. "I don't want her to go through a trial. Not ever."

"She will, whether you want it or not. It's best to be prepared."

I sighed. "I get what you're saying, but I'll find a way to protect her. She's a kid. She doesn't need to stand at death's door and wrestle with angry spirits."

"Isn't that what you do every time you dreamwalk, dear?" Mom asked.

"Not on that level. The trial was creepy-scary. I never want to do that again." I turned to my father, the fire crackling before me. "Tell me this is a one-time thing. Tell me it had to do with Bee and Marv's case."

"I can't. The framework dreamwalkers operate in is fluid. There are few rules, and I imagine, based on your tattoos, that you've already broken most of them."

The disappointment in his voice tore at my heart. My decisions were my own, the best I could do at the time. "Have you met Rose?"

"Not to my knowledge," my father said. "I never dallied over there. I did what I could for our people and came home. Crossing the veil always exhausted of me."

"But you did the job. You helped others despite how hard it was for you personally."

"It's in our blood." He shifted on his blanket. "I was worried for both of us when you denied your heritage and moved so far away. I knew at some point you would come into your power, and if I didn't do my job to shepherd you, you could be lost."

I shivered at his dire tone. "Lost, as in over-the-bridge lost?"

"Yeah."

A snicker built in my throat. I squelched it. "And yet, you got lost on the Other Side."

"I did it for you. Same as you rescued me. We're bound in this life and the next. Never forget that, daughter."

I stared into the flames to absorb the weightiness of an eternal connection. "Will I see Granny Nesbitt in my dreamwalks?"

"Only if she wants to see you."

"There's so much about this I don't understand. I wish there was a manual."

He shook his head. I noticed how deep the lines were etched in his face. "Too dangerous to write this down. It must be relayed in oral tradition."

"Why?"

"It's our way. For our protection. The less normals know about us the better."

"Because we're weird?"

"Because ignorant people are scared of things they don't understand."

Chapter 31

Heavy dark clouds clogging the sky slowly gave way to dawn on Friday morning. I awoke at home fully rested, but the sense of well-being fled as the day's schedule came to mind. Bee's funeral and Marv's wake were today. Tomorrow I'd drive to Jacksonville to bring my daughter home.

I wanted to solve this case before she returned, but the possibility of that seemed as slim as summer snow. I had a little over twenty-four hours to work this out. As I tidied up the house and vacuumed the tumbleweeds of dog hair, Bee and Marv's murder filled my thoughts. They deserved justice.

Whether the sheriff's suspect list included the killer was anyone's guess. Among the local folks, the sheriff fingered Bee's brother, the protesting waterman, and the county's top tourism director. His suspects from Marv's world included Marv's stalker and his gofer of an assistant. I ran a mental recap of the players.

Timmy Ray Donlin benefitted from Bee's death because, as her brother, he inherited Bee's waterfront property. He'd grown up hunting and fishing, so he was no stranger to big knives. Which meant Timmy Ray had the means, motive, and mental fortitude to kill his sister.

Barry Campazzi's impassioned quest to protect the waters and the county from unnatural influences bordered on scary for me. A former waterman, he knew his way around the county and the law. He'd had an intimate relationship with Bee in the past, and they had a secret kid together. Barry had means, motive, and opportunity to kill Marv and Bee.

Reed Tyler moved here a few years back to become the top tourism executive. Charlotte said he'd dated Bee, so his reason to kill Marv might be jealousy, but we'd yet to verify their romantic connection. Various natives tried to oust Reed because of his pro-tourism mindset, but Reed dug in and landed his biggest triumph ever — the movie deal. If the movie crew picked up stakes and moved elsewhere, his job was toast. How far would he go to keep his job?

I had little information about the other

suspects. Cassie Korda, Marv's stalker, was the only female in the bunch. According to two different spirits, our killers were male, which disqualified Cassie. But my gut wouldn't let me take her off the list.

Why would Cassie fixate on Marv? Was it jealousy? If so, we had good cause to investigate her. In a recent case I'd worked, a woman had killed because of jealousy.

And Marv's assistant, Lou "LA" Alfredo. He'd already stepped into Marv's starring role as superstar Ford Morrison's number one gopher. Was Marv's job worth killing for?

Even so, this individual consideration wouldn't solve the case. We had two killers and two pools of suspects. When did the movie people scout us? Six months ago? A year? Either way, the locals and the movie people had time to become acquainted. Two suspects banded together to snuff Marv and Bee. But which two?

Today I'd focus on figuring out how well these people knew each other. Easy enough at Bee's funeral. I should know everybody there, but Marv's wake might be full of strangers. Worse, they knew I was connected to the police investigation and would be on their guard. A savvy killer could easily hide in plain sight.

It was up to me to use every talent I had to solve this case.

I put the vacuum away and realized I had company. A plus-sized woman in electric blue stood at my back door knocking. The coral-colored starfish pendant she wore was a favorite of mine. Charlotte.

I opened the door and ushered her inside. "Since when do you knock on my door?"

Both doggies danced around her heels, expecting coos and attention, which they promptly received. Charlotte straightened, her merry eyes alight with mischief. "Since you became a dreamwalker and God only knows what's going on in this grand old house of yours."

I barked out a laugh. "Didn't you hear the vacuum?"

"I did."

I waved my friend to the kitchen. After fixing us both glasses of iced tea, I joined her at the table. "What's up?"

"I know you can't tell me about the case, but I miss you. Staying away when you're on an investigation is killing me."

The emotional distance between us didn't sit well with me either. We stayed in touch when I got married and bounced from army base to army base with Roland. We reconnected when I moved home. Charlotte and

I always took on the world together, no matter the geography separating us. Now my police consulting job and Charlotte's newspaper ambition put us at odds.

"Killing your career?" I winced immediately, wishing I didn't blurt that out.

"No. Don't ever think that. I push to get ahead because Bernard has an in with the boss. They are so good-ole-boy connected it isn't fair. With me covering the top crime stories this year, he's out for my blood."

I shuddered, thinking of all the spilled blood I'd seen recently. "Don't mention blood."

Her shoulders drooped. "Oh. Sorry. Was it awful?"

"Beyond awful."

"I'm sorry. Your job sucks."

"It does. But getting justice for victims makes it worthwhile."

"Being a crusader for the underdogs and victims suits you."

I snorted. "Who'd a-thought you'd grow up to be a crack reporter, and I'd end up hanging out with cops?"

"Don't sell yourself short. You're more than a cop groupie. I've always known it. The people here were slow to see your value, but they're catching on fast."

"Mutual appreciation society, Char. You

bring an element to the news Bernard doesn't. You care about this place and its people. He's only in it as a stepping-stone to a bigger venue. You're a weebie."

"What's that?"

"A term I picked up on my travels. The grammar isn't perfect, but the sentiment is right. Weebie is short for 'we be here when he be gone.' "

She digested that a moment then nodded. "Definitely a weebie, because he surely will be leaving soon, even if all I have to report on is the number of lawns dug up by the vandals. We had two more yards hit last night."

An awkward silence swirled over the hum of the refrigerator, the sound of a dog scratching. I gazed out the window, caught between wanting to help Charlotte and needing to keep my mouth shut. Would our career choices do what time and distance couldn't? We'd faced this precipice before, but the stakes had never been as high. I froze, unable to get past the thought that she might choose ambition over friendship.

Charlotte shifted in her chair, drawing my attention her way. The insecurities that lay beneath her bright facade showed in her tremulous expression, the tightness of her clasped hands. I may be the only person in the world to know she still had a teddy bear collection in her bedroom. The thought of Charlotte walking out that door and never coming back made me sick to my stomach.

Please, don't let it come to that, I silently pleaded.

"Friends again?" Charlotte asked.

An olive branch. I seized it. "I never stopped being your friend, but we have to respect the new boundaries."

"About that . . . I was hoping to be your wingman at Bee's funeral today."

Hmm. A new quagmire. I stepped cautiously on the uncertain footing. "Don't you have copy-editing tasks due at the paper?"

"I said I'd do my Friday work over the weekend. Bernard liked to split a gut. He's got concert tickets in Macon tonight."

"Leaving the door open for you. Smooth move. Only, how does one cover a funeral? Isn't that a bit morbid?"

"One chats up everyone in sight and hopes for a human-interest story, that's how. Even if I don't get a story idea, I might be able to help you, which would in turn help me to write a Page One story once you arrest the bad guy."

It was on the tip of my tongue to correct her with the plural of guy, but I knew better than to remind Charlotte we had two bad guys to catch. "Wayne won't like it, but I don't care. It's a date. You, me, and Elvis."

Charlotte's eyebrows shot above her glasses to hide behind her wispy bangs. "Since when do you take dogs to funerals?"

"Since I found out Elvis is a therapy dog. And there might be one more in our group. Stinger."

"Odd choice. Is he connected to the killings?"

"Nope. He's connected to me. To my dreamwalks. Found out the hard way."

Questions danced in Charlotte's eyes, but she merely nodded, pushing her chin-length hair behind her ears. "Cool. Entourage, here we come."

CHAPTER 32

Charlotte and I arrived an hour early at Bee's funeral to make sure we had a good seat. Good thing, because the other early birds were already warming the pews. While waiting for the service to begin, we proofread a stack of newspaper copy Charlotte carried in. For a dog carrier, I'd borrowed a large tote bag from Charlotte that we'd stuffed with towels. Elvis looked like he'd died and gone to heaven sitting in such fine comfort.

The church filled to capacity twenty minutes before the service. People stared with unabashed fascination at the sealed coffin, which was positioned front and center in the country church. I might be one of the few who'd physically seen her corpse, but chances were someone else here watched her bleed out.

Stinger said he didn't do funerals, so he agreed to meet us at the reception afterward.

Attendees ranged from deeply tanned boat captains, to familiar-looking locals, to out-of-towners that I presumed had been Bee's friends and clients. Of the movie people, only Ford Morrison and LA attended. Ford caused a stir when he entered, but the buzz dulled to a heated whisper-fest after he sat across the aisle from us.

To his credit, Ford neither looked right nor left. He faced the altar as if his life depended on it. Was he praying for salvation or repentance? LA glanced around the church several times, once locking gazes with me. His eyes narrowed with suspicion, but he turned away so quickly I wondered if I imagined his expression.

Before the service began, I surveyed the entire crowd in the packed church. The sheriff stood in the back, scanning the room as well. Our eyes met, and he nodded before continuing his perp search. Was there a killer in this place of worship? Or worse, two killers?

I looked for the rest of our suspects. Our watchdog waterman, Barry Campazzi, wasn't here, which seemed odd since he'd been released from jail this morning. Over-flow mourners stood on the lawn near the open windows to pay their respects. Barry could easily be out there, and I'd never know.

Tourism president Reed Tyler sat in an aisle seat across the way from us. He was dressed in a brown suit the color of his eyebrows. Though his color seemed off and worry lines framed the stern set of his mouth and his eyes, Reed had oiled his way into the sanctuary like a politician, greeting people and shaking their hands. Was his friendly behavior compulsive or the act of a desperate man who wanted to keep his job? Either way, I wanted to talk to him after the service.

I gazed at the lazy ceiling fans whirling overhead, wishing they could spin faster. I didn't like being packed in so tightly like this. I didn't like breathing used air.

"See anyone who looks guilty?" Charlotte whispered in my ear.

"Too many people," I muttered, reaching down to pat Elvis's head. We'd packed five adults into this narrow pew, which meant I had to hold the dog purse in my lap. Elvis took it all in stride, as if he rode in a padded purse to funerals every day. I held a very tight rein on my extra senses in here. Besides the crush of people in this place, decades of emotions seeped through my defenses. Despair. Joy. Grief. Guilt. Loads of guilt.

The combination made my skin feel too tight. I couldn't wait to get out of there.

Bee's brother, Timmy Ray, entered with the minister and sat beside Bee's next-door neighbors. He wore a dark suit, while the neighbor ladies were adorned in Easter egg colors. One of the ladies dragged an oxygen tank, making these fragile seniors unlikely suspects.

I'd only seen Cassie Korda's picture, but as far as I could tell, she wasn't here. I expected she'd show up for Marv's wake later today. I'd never met a stalker before, but obsession about another person was rarely a good thing. Jealous women weren't rational. That was a fact, Jack.

Not ten minutes into the service, Reed Tyler fidgeted, withdrew a phone from his pocket, glanced at it, and scurried from the church. What was up with that?

Timmy Ray's behavior puzzled me also. Throughout the music and prayers, his shaved head stayed down, and his shoulders were bent as if he could hardly function under the burden of grief. But there was an unmistakable lightness to his step as he strode down the center aisle during the recessional. What emotions were riding him?

I didn't have time to dwell on Timmy Ray because Elvis started singing along to the final hymn, "Amazing Grace," doggie style. Not quite a howl, but not a human sound either. More like a tremulous croon, and not the melancholy notes the organist was hitting either.

Heat flushed my face as I tried to shush the dog. He was having none of that. He raised his head and ramped up the volume. Oh, my God. I ducked down in my pew, thrusting my sunglasses over my eyes.

I leaned over to Charlotte, who looked like she was one microsecond away from bursting out laughing. "Do something!"

She grinned. "What? It's funny."

"This is a funeral."

People were looking around the church, murmuring to themselves. In such a small space, they'd surely figure out where the noise was coming from in short order. The familiar standard played out, and I hoped like anything the organist would transition to a new tune, but no. He bridged to another verse.

My only choice to avoid complete disgrace was to brazen it out. I elbowed Charlotte. "Verse one. Sing with me. Now."

Charlotte could bring people to their knees with her powerful singing. But she

271

held back as I erupted in song, alone. She calmly motioned me to continue, and once I'd started, pride wouldn't let me stop. After I sang the first line, she joined in, melding her voice with mine into a louder version of the hymn. Relief came out in my voice as I warbled the high note at the end of the second line.

I could still hear Elvis singing along, so I motioned with my hands for Charlotte to sing louder, but she shook her head. To my amazement, the man next to her joined in, then the woman in a scooter across the aisle. By the end of the first verse, the entire church had joined in. The minister, sensing the groundswell of emotion, strolled up the aisle and began directing us like a conductor. People sang as I've never heard them sing before. I guess everyone was pondering their own mortality as they sang Bee into heaven.

By the third verse, my eyes were watering. I couldn't say whether it was from the perfume in the packed church, the natural harmonies coming at me from front, back, and side, or just the zaniness of a dog inspiring people to cut loose and give Bee a rousing sendoff.

The organist ended with a flourish worthy of Carnegie Hall, and the minister raised his arms and shouted. "Let the church say, Amen."

Everyone in the church shouted back, and the noisy exodus began. Elvis hunkered down in the purse as if his job was done. I leaned into Charlotte, grateful her instincts had been spot-on about the song. "Thanks."

Her eyes glistened with emotion. She wrapped me in a mama bear hug, not an easy thing to do in these tight quarters. "Thank you. That was beautiful. People will be talking about this funeral service for generations."

My eyebrows raised in question.

Charlotte smiled. "No matter where Bee is, I'm sure she heard the beautiful music, and it eased her transition through the pearly gates. I want you and Elvis to sing at my funeral. Promise me you'll do it."

My throat spasmed. First off, Elvis was a tiny dog with a minimal lifespan. The likelihood he'd outlive Charlotte was very small. Second, I couldn't think about Charlotte dying. Third, from what I'd seen of the spirit world, I wasn't as convinced of heaven as I was of hell. Life after death seemed to be shades of gray.

But Charlotte was my friend. A true friend. "If that's what you want, I'll do it."

She hugged me again, holding me a little

longer than necessary. "I absolutely want it. And I'll do the same for you. It was so beautiful."

"I'm hoping people don't remember how the singing started."

She pulled herself together, adjusting her blouse, and snickered. "Good luck with that."

CHAPTER 33

"I never knew you had such a pretty singing voice," Deb Holt gushed over a paper cup of pink lemonade at the reception. "You should sing the national anthem at our athletic events."

Doused in sparkling jewelry and industrial-strength perfume, Deb offended two of my normal senses at first glance. But her words struck fear in my heart.

"Uh. No, thanks. I don't sing in public," I managed.

"Nonsense. A talent like yours should be brought out from under that frumpy bushel basket you've been hiding under. Have you thought about joining the community chorale group?"

I worked to loosen my back teeth. The goal here was to be friendly and chat people up, not put them in their place for rudeness. "I just . . . can't, but thank you for thinking of me."

"Baxley's shy, but she was so moved by the service that she began singing," Charlotte explained from beside me. "She's been getting in touch with her spiritual side lately."

"Even better." Deb's face took on a fervent glow. "Let me call the organist over here. They're always looking for soloists in church. Why, we could plan an entire revival featuring you."

My parents stood in the threshold with Stinger, who was looking decidedly uncomfortable in such a crowded space. Stinger needed Elvis to silence the human voices in this room, that much was clear, and I seemed to be holding my own with the people here. Time for a changing of the dog.

"Excuse me," I said to the town's matriarch. "I need to speak to my mother."

Charlotte trotted after me. Elvis lifted his head out of the purse, sniffing the room, then he yapped excitedly. In the hubbub, no one noticed. Except Stinger. His worry lines smoothed out into a big smile.

"There's my boy," he said as Elvis leapt into his arms, licking his face.

As hugs went around the group, Charlotte finked on me to my mom, and then vanished into the crowd. "Won't you come on in?" I asked my parents.

"Not our scene," Dad said, with a step backward. "But we're proud of you. Leading the singing at a religious ceremony. Imagine that, Lacey. Our Baxley, stepping up like that."

"I'm not surprised," Mom said. "You have many talents yet to discover."

Someone tapped my shoulder. The sheriff. With a smirk on his handsome face. "Ready to get to work?" he asked, "or will you break into song again?"

All kinds of retorts jammed into my brain, but fortunately the only response that came out was the one Charlotte uttered earlier. "I was moved by the service."

With a nod to my parents, he cupped my elbow and steered me along the wall, away from the refreshments. His face suddenly wreathed in smiles, and he laughed aloud. "I heard the dog howl."

"All right. I had to bring Elvis with me to tolerate being in such a densely populated setting. Laugh all you like, the dog is better than a prescription anxiety reliever. Elvis makes things better."

He glanced over his shoulder at Stinger who was following closely. "That runt is no therapy dog."

"You, of all people, should have an open mind."

"Me? I'm the most skeptical person in this room."

"You hired a psychic consultant, didn't you?"

"Well. There is that. And if the doggie helps you amp up the woo-woo factor, go for it, but, dang, girl, that was funny. Good save, Powell."

"Sometimes I amaze myself. What do you want me to do here?"

"Get me a lead. Three of our suspects are in this room. I thought Reed Tyler would still be here, but he left already. We'll corner him tonight at the wake."

"So, we've got Bee's brother, the movie gopher, and who else?"

"Barry's here. I saw him smoking outside during the service."

"Gotcha. Who first?"

"Barry. He's talking to the art association woman over there."

I glanced back at Stinger. "You coming?"

"I don't like being around so many people, but all things are possible with Elvis."

"Let's get this over with." I trudged away from Wayne, dodging compliments about my impromptu stroll down Songbird Lane. I dove for the vacant spot beside Barry, who seemed to be trying to divine the future from the pulp in his lemonade. For the funeral, the waterman had changed out of his normal faded jeans and stained tee into a pair of black trousers and a button-down collared shirt. His black shoes had that just-bought sheen.

"You doing all right?" I asked as I sidled up to him.

"What? Oh, hi. Not all right. Bee's dead, and the punch is pink."

"It is."

"Pink is, I mean, it was, Bee's favorite color. She didn't wear a lot of it, but she had a secret fondness for girly things."

Did he know about Bee's pink bathrobe? "I never saw her in pink. She wore a white polo and khaki shorts every time I saw her."

"Not to speak ill of the dead, but Bee had this hot pink number that she wore on dates that would make a man's heart nearly jump out of his chest. She was something else."

I parsed the information quickly. He definitely knew about the robe. "Sounds like y'all spent a lot of quality time together."

"I shoulda paid more attention to her instead of chasing the polluters out of the county. Then she wouldn'ta lost her way or gotten herself dead. Bee was a fine woman. She deserved better'n she got."

I nodded sympathetically, lightly touching his shoulder with my senses at half mast.

An image flashed into my head of music, old-timey jazz. Ella Fitzgerald. With Bee dressed in the pink robe and singing along. Then Bee moved toward the open arms, Barry's open arms. I released the connection, and the image vanished.

I did a quick check of my facts. "That she was. And her taste in music was the best. She sure loved her Ella."

Barry nodded sadly, then tossed the lemonade down his throat like a shot of hard liquor. "Yep. Excuse me."

The waterman wandered off, and I joined Stinger, who was stroking Elvis.

"I've got two more murder suspects to chat up," I said. "There's still a crowd around Timmy Ray, so let's mosey over to LA Alfredo."

"That skinny movie dude?"

"Yeah. You know something about him?"

"He's into the club scene. Partied at the Oasis the other night."

Oasis was one of those mostly black-attended clubs in the county, though whites were welcomed inside. I'd never had a surplus of friends in the county, being a weirdo Nesbitt and all. And being a military wife had me picking up traces enough times to avoid making friends on our last two stops. Someone who acted like LA baffled me. Why bother making friends here if you're leaving soon and never coming back?

"What was he doing way out there?" I asked.

"He wanted to party, but the singles weren't interested in what he had to offer."

"Singles." Stinger's word choice baffled me. Was there a hidden context? "We talking women or something else?"

"Women. Sorry. I was cleaning up my language for you and nearly steered you down the wrong path. Pasta Boy chatted up every woman in the club, but he left alone."

"Pasta Boy?"

He shrugged. "Alfredo, pasta. It fit."

Great. A stranger had earned a nickname from the locals, but I didn't rate one. A quick glance verified that Timmy Ray was still talking to a tall tow-headed man who looked vaguely familiar. I gestured toward the movie star flunky who was by himself. "Let's go see what Pasta Boy has to say."

We joined LA over by an ancient, upright piano. Even in the heat of the crowd, LA managed to look cool and at ease in his pressed white slacks and starched lavender button-down shirt. The diamond shapes on his silk tie ranged from lavender to deep purple. He might not have Ford's charisma, but his style of dress set him apart from the locals.

He looked up with a guilty start, smiled, and hefted a shiny hip flask our way. "Hey there, my brother. Want some hooch?"

Stinger offered his cup and a similar greeting. I didn't have a lemonade to doctor, not that I would've drunk on the job. "Big day," I said to get the conversation going once the libations were dispensed, and LA had cooed over the dog.

LA nodded, one eye on his boss, who was engaged in conversation with the mayor a few people away. "It's a day all right."

The noise from the crowded room paled as I zeroed in on the movie flunky. "You expecting a large turnout for the wake this evening?"

"Probably not this big, but everyone is welcome. We plan to do Marv proud. Even hired a musician to liven things up."

Not scintillating conversation, not much help at all in solving a murder. "Are his family or friends flying out?"

"His mom's in a nursing home and his brother's doing time. Marv has lots of acquaintances. Hardly any close friends. So, no. We're Marv's family."

"Sounds like the friendliest man in the movie company was lonely," I observed. So far, LA's words were all truthful. Nothing had a false ring to it.

LA snorted. "Marv never lacked for company. This broad, no offense, ma'am, was one of a long string of his playmates. He had a golden touch when it came to seduction, but women and booze flowed around him like the tides."

"He had a drinking problem?"

LA raised his cup. "Who doesn't? This is a volatile industry. You can be on top of the world one day and unemployed the next based on a chance remark or your hair color. Like Marv, I'm a survivor. This is the third production company I've worked for in two years. You want to talk survival of the fittest? Work in the movie industry."

"But you're doing well. The filming is going well."

"Maybe. You never know in this business."

His words clunked in my ears. He was lying. I leaned in, cautiously placed a hand on his shoulder. "Are you worried about your job?"

Lights flashed and streaked out into a narrow rainbow, sounds collided in my ears. Caught in the void, I couldn't breathe. Couldn't move. LA shrugged off my hand, and the world returned to normal.

"Damn straight. Ford's being nice to me

right now, but he has an investment group coming out before the wake. My replacement could be part of the new deal. I might wake up tomorrow morning and find myself out on the street."

"Surely not," I said, hoping I sounded like myself. Stinger seemed to know something bizarre had happened to me, and he held the dog up for me to take. Elvis curled into my arms like he belonged there. My anxiety level calmed as systems returned to normal. "That would be cold."

"Welcome to Hollywood, baby. The stakes are higher than Vegas."

Another truth from Pasta Boy. I shrugged off a shiver. Had Marv died for his job? Why couldn't I tell from LA's voice if he was innocent or guilty? What was that crazy mishmash of lights and sounds I picked up from LA?

LA sat his cup on the piano and nodded at Ford's right hand brushing back his hair. "That's my signal. The boss is ready to bolt. Come on out to the wake. Bring your friends. We've roasted an entire pig."

He sauntered off, extricated Ford, and managed to get out of the building.

"That boy's got no home training," Stinger said, removing the discarded cup from the piano and tossing it in the trash.

"Ya don't put drinks on a musical instrument."

I stroked Elvis's soft fur, and he made little humming noises in his throat. "Something's off with that man. When I touched him, the world got all weird."

Stinger nodded. "I could tell."

"From how I acted? Did he notice?"

"Nah. He didn't notice anything except his paycheck standing over there." He gestured toward Ford Morrison, then nodded toward the Chihuahua cradled against my chest. "You feeling better now? 'Cause I could help lighten your load by holding Elvis."

I handed the dog to him. "One more person to read, then we're done."

"Good."

As we crossed the room to Timmy Ray, I saw Charlotte chatting up a former county commissioner. The sheriff had joined a group with Barry in it. Barry took one look at Wayne and bolted for the door. Uh-oh. Nothing said guilt like running. Wayne pivoted and followed Barry outside. So intent was he on his prey that the crowd parted like the Red Sea before him.

I would've loved to hear that conversation, but I had another suspect to read.

"How're you holding up?" I asked Timmy

Ray once the Carters, who'd been consoling him, moved on to another conversational grouping.

He surveyed the room. "Bee would've loved this party the church ladies threw. So many people are here. I never knew she had so many friends. Everyone says you're the one who started singing her home with 'Amazing Grace.' That was moving, even to a broken-down nonbeliever like me."

"Thanks." Timmy Ray spoke the truth. And if he didn't believe in God, that accounted for his discomfiture inside the church walls.

"They say funerals are for the living, but you made this one about Bee. Made it special. She would be pleased." Timmy Ray glanced down at his shiny shoes. "She wasn't proud of much when it came to me. I was never good enough. Never lived up to my potential. Never stood on my own two feet."

More truth. "She'll be missed."

He nodded and nearly met my gaze. "I loved her."

A lie. A big, fat, bright red lie. It was all I could do not to jump up and down and point and yell, "Liar!" Timmy Ray did not love his sister. I was certain he hated her guts, but Timmy Ray's lie wasn't evidence of a crime or murder. I needed more.

"What will you do now? Are you moving back home?" I asked.

He glanced around the room. "I dunno. Got no job. Been bumming places to stay from my friends, but some friends they are." His voice roughened. "Not one of them came to my sister's funeral."

"I'm sorry." And I was. People needed friends. They kept us grounded. Kept us from doing stupid stuff. *Like murdering your sister.*

Is that what happened? Timmy Ray ran out of options, and hit his sister up for money? Knowing what a hard worker Bee had been, she would've eventually gotten tired of doling out her earnings to her brother. The Donlins had grown up in the sand hills on the west side of the county. A solid blue-collar family, but no family money and no social connections. Bee's success had been her own doing. Had it also been her undoing?

I went to pat his shoulder, but Timmy Ray skirted me to face Stinger. "Look at that cute little doggie. What's his name?"

Interesting. Bee's brother didn't want me to touch him.

Like a pro, Stinger stepped up, close to Timmy Ray. "This here's Elvis. He's a therapy dog. For my nerves. I done stared too hard into the bottle. Know what I mean?"

"I hear ya." Timmy Ray focused on the Chihuahua cradled on Stinger's chest.

Someone passed by, jostled me a little, so I gave Stinger a little nudge into Timmy Ray. We all staggered a bit. I held onto Stinger's belt loop, he held onto the suspect, and Timmy Ray held onto Stinger. The psst-zap of sheer energy through the link felt like a contact burn and I let go. The painful sensation eased.

Elvis started his nervous sounds. In two seconds, he'd amped up to a full howl. Timmy Ray cocked his ear to the sound, shook his head, and burst out laughing. "That dog is a trip." He backed away, his hands in the air.

People stared at his odd funeral behavior. Stinger turned so Elvis couldn't see Timmy Ray, keeping a tight hold on the struggling pooch. "It's okay, little dude. We won't let that creep near you again."

I touched Stinger again. No bug zap of energy. That pulse had come from Timmy Ray. "Did you feel it?" I asked.

"Sho' did. Right down to my ingrown toenails. That man is turned wrong."

CHAPTER 34

Charlotte appeared at my elbow. "What? No bursting into song to cover for the dog?"

"Not this time." I ignored her silly grin, focusing on Timmy Ray circling the reception crowd. "Something's off with that man. The dog doesn't like him."

"The dog's got good taste," my friend said, light glinting on the sparkles of her oversized watch.

People often underestimated Charlotte because with her big and beautiful figure, she didn't resemble a mastermind. But they were wrong. She'd thought rings around me and everyone else in town for years.

I steered the three of us to a quiet corner. "You can't tell anyone I said that."

"Timmy Ray has always been weird. Took me a while to string this factoid together, but Kyle Branch confirmed my suspicion. Timmy Ray showed a marked interest in Percy Madison's daughter about six years ago, then suddenly he was gone, gone, gone. The Branches paid him to leave town."

Roland and I were living on the west coast then in our whirlwind tour of military postings. Larissa had been learning to count and going to preschool. Events happening in coastal Georgia had seemed more than a world away.

"Do tell," I said.

"Skye Madison lasted one semester in college before she came home, hooked on white powder. She hung out with a different crowd when she returned, one unbefitting a bank president's daughter."

In the time I'd been home, Skye had cycled through town twice. She looked emaciated, and rumor was her parents had frozen her trust fund. She graduated from rehab clean as a whistle, drifted into her old ways, got in trouble again, then was shipped to rehab for more treatment.

I inclined my head to Stinger, who'd been listening intently to our conversation. "You know anything about this?"

He flashed a bit of teeth. "Miss Skye was lucky her daddy ran Timmy Ray off."

"Huh. Is this common knowledge?"

Stinger shrugged, Elvis sighed, and Charlotte sparkled. Great. So what if Timmy Ray had been Skye's youthful indiscretion? Being a leech and a crappy boyfriend weren't stepping-stones to murder. "What other off-the-books trouble did Timmy Ray get into?"

Charlotte's sparkle faded. "Isn't that enough?"

"If everybody knows about his history with Skye, then Wayne knows. Timmy Ray Donlin isn't a model citizen, but was this an isolated incident or did he get caught doing other bad things?"

"He mooched off his sister," Charlotte said, chin rising.

"A good lawyer would make that accusation go away. Family helps out in tough times, and we've certainly seen tough times lately." I tried to think of somewhere to go with this information, hoping it wasn't another dead end. "Where's Skye row?"

"On a cruise with her mom," Charlotte added. "Her dad died of a heart attack three years ago, and her mom made it her life mission to keep Skye too busy to screw up again."

My pocket buzzed. I checked the new message on my phone. It was from the sheriff. *Outside. Now.*

"We've gotta go," I told Charlotte. "Will you be at the wake this evening?"

"The boss assigned Bernard to cover it. If I go, I'll be stepping on his toes."

I snorted. "When has that ever stopped you?"

"Can I come as part of Team Baxley?"

Wayne would kill me if Charlotte rained on his investigative parade. "Too dangerous. Char, someone brutally murdered two people."

"And yet, you, a single mother, will be at this party risking life and limb."

I groaned. "Let me think about it."

"Recap," Wayne demanded.

We were sitting in his Jeep, me in the front, Stinger and Elvis in the back. Elvis jumped up on the back of the rear seat and patrolled its length. I angled the air-conditioning vent to blow on my hot face.

"Charlotte told me about Timmy Ray and Skye," I began, since that was fresh in my mind.

"Old news. She's been with at least five other ne'er-do-wells since Timmy Ray. You got anything on him?"

"He lied about loving his sister."

"I'm paying you for this?"

"He was onto us from the start. Evaded my questions. Wouldn't let me touch him, but he was interested in Elvis. Stinger and I dosey-doed, and long story short, when Timmy Ray touched Stinger, we both got

292

blasted with bad energy."

Wayne gave me a slack-jawed look. I hastened to add, "The dog didn't like him either."

The sheriff's eyes flicked quickly to the pacing dog in his rearview mirror. "I'm beginning to think the dog has the most sense of anyone else in this vehicle."

I wrinkled my nose at the insult. "What about Barry? I saw you chase him outside."

"He was a mite concerned I'd take him back to jail."

"Oh. What'd you do?"

"Called Virg and Ronnie to follow him. What was your take on Barry?"

"I got a read on him. He knew about the pink bathrobe. He and Bee had been intimate."

Wayne nodded. "And the movie guy?"

"LA Alfredo is a bundle of nerves. He's insecure about his job, envied Marv, and tried to get laid at the Oasis."

Wayne glanced in the mirror at Stinger, who nodded and added, "Poor home training too. Pasta Boy put a drink on the piano."

I cleared my throat. "I touched LA, and something weird happened."

"Define weird," the sheriff said.

"The room bent around me. The light streaked out. Sounds blared. I didn't have a

293

chance to sort it out because he shrugged my hand off before I got my bearings."

"Doesn't sound like evidence to me."

"It might be. What if he was involved in something before? Something off the books like Timmy Ray and Skye. He outright lied to me about the movie filming. It isn't going well. I didn't like him one bit. Oh. And he said Marv had a drinking problem."

"The autopsy showed Marv had liver damage." The sheriff rolled his neck as if it had a crick in it. "Too many years of boozing it up."

I reflected on that for a moment. My information didn't yield new leads, but I wasn't the only one working the room. "You get anything else?"

"Nothing I can use in a court of law."

Surely we'd learned something for our efforts. "I didn't see Barry or LA approach Timmy Ray."

"Doesn't mean they aren't acquainted." He paused for a beat. "Charlotte?"

"She isn't stupid. She saw who I spoke to at the reception. She wants to come to the wake with me."

"You told her no."

It wasn't a question, but I treated it as such. "I told her it was a bad idea."

"Did you recognize the tow-headed man

talking to Timmy Ray?"

"Yes, but I couldn't place him. You?"

"Never met him. Thought he might be Timmy Ray's friend."

"Don't think so. Timmy Ray was bummed because his friends didn't attend the funeral."

"I snapped a photo of the stranger with my phone and sent it to Tamika to plug into our facial recognition software. He doesn't live around here and that makes me suspicious. Let me know if you remember where you've seen him."

"You've got good cop instincts." I stared at my feet for a moment. "I, uh, may have forgotten to mention Bee's cat to her brother. Figured that would be okay as long as he was still a suspect."

"No rush on that notification." Fluffy white clouds raced across the edge of the sky. "Storm's coming," Wayne said, in the knowing way of watermen.

Despite my lack of weather acuity, I too felt as if there was a disturbance in the atmosphere. "Larissa is coming home tomorrow. I want us to solve this case tonight."

"Get some rest this afternoon. You may get your wish after all." He turned to Stinger. "Stick with her. We've rattled cages with our questioning here today. Three of our five suspects have secrets and another acted suspiciously."

CHAPTER 35

After the funeral, I went home, changed into old clothes, and drifted out in the yard. I grabbed my good snippers and began trimming the ligustrum along the driveway. Stinger and the pets stayed inside in the air conditioning watching reruns of old sitcoms on TV. Either way, I figured we were both relaxing.

As I cut away six inches from the sides and tops of my hedge, I wondered if the sheriff was right. Could we solve this case tonight? So far this murderer hadn't killed anyone else, but I didn't want my daughter returning to an unsafe situation. The truth lodged in my stomach like a heavy stone. If we didn't close this case before early afternoon tomorrow, I should allow my daughter to spend a few more days in Florida with her Powell grandparents.

Everything in me rebelled against that notion. I grabbed hold of a thick branch and hacked my frustration out. My protective instincts battled with my need to see, hold, and delight in my child. A smile from Larissa could brighten every minute of my day.

When the sheriff and I had come close to solving previous cases, the guilty parties had lashed out without fail. The sun darted beneath a cloud, and I realized how isolated I was out here. A chill swept over me. I hadn't thought to bring one of my guns outside. Woods surrounded three sides of my property, and a county road marked the other boundary.

Was someone hiding behind a tree right now? Still snipping away at the greenery, I expanded my senses in all directions. I picked up Stinger in the house right away. I pushed farther. My watcher didn't register, and that worried me. Had the killer immobilized the silent stranger who often watched my house from the woods?

I'd discovered the watcher months ago, but in all the time he'd been out there, he'd never lifted a finger against me. And in fact, he'd hogtied someone who meant to do me harm and left him as a present for me.

An odd thought occurred to me. The nearest house was that of my neighbor, Mr. Luther. If a lurker wanted an outpost near here, his house would be the logical spot. Was my neighbor in danger? His only relative, his son Morley, was off serving the country. I pulled out my cell phone and called Mr. Luther. He answered on the fourth ring. After a few pleasantries, I asked if his doors were locked.

"Why?" he asked.

"We're getting close on this June's Folly killer. You live close to me, and I was concerned that you might be in danger."

"How's that?"

My suspicions sounded dumb now that I was sharing them. Heat flamed my ears. "This killer is different. Organized. Strategic, even. If he comes after me, I'm worried your place may also be a target by proximity."

A chair scraped across a wooden floor in the tomb-like silence over the line. "Don't you worry about me, Baxley. I've been taking care of myself for a long time."

Was that a murmur of voices I also overheard? My shoulders rose to my ear as I contemplated hightailing it through the woods to his place. "Is someone there with you now? Do you need me to call the cops? If so, say something about the weather so I'll know."

"I'm fine."

His words rang true. I relaxed, allowing my senses to quest outward. Since I was facing Mr. Luther's place, the strongest sending was in that direction. I picked up one signal. Then another. Alarm crept back into my throat, causing me to finger my moldavite necklace. I leaned into the phone and whispered. "Be careful. You're not alone."

He chuckled. "You're right. Someone is visiting, at my invitation. Please, don't worry about me. You catch this killer and make Sinclair County safe again. I've about had enough of these bad actors."

Actors? Did he know something I didn't? "We're working on it. Just stay safe. And lock your doors. These are uncertain times."

"I have every confidence in you, Madam Dreamwalker."

I hung up the phone, still staring in the direction of Mr. Luther's house, senses on wide open. And just like that, the second life-form I had detected powered down.

Dang if that didn't get my curious up, but Charlotte chose that moment to barrel into my driveway. Gravel crunched as she hit the brakes. I retreated into the safety of my shrub line and thanked the sweet heavens my dogs were inside.

Charlotte waved as she grabbed up her

stuff and exited her sedan. She'd changed from her conservative charcoal gray power suit to soft blue slacks and a jeweled top. "I'm here for my pre-op briefing!" she said.

My back teeth gnashed together. This was so not a good idea. "You're just in time. I'm mulling things over as I trim my hedge. You're welcome to help me finish the line."

Moisture beaded on Charlotte's upper lip. Rivulets of sweat ran down the side of her face. June in coastal Georgia could be brutal, especially to those who carried extra weight.

Charlotte gave my yard an assessing gaze. There was no immediate shade to be had, no chairs to sit in. "I don't want to spoil my complexion."

I grinned at that absurdity. Freckles peppered Charlotte's pale skin, giving her a perpetually youthful appearance. Unlike most women who sought to constantly look younger, Char sought respect that came with maturity and intellect. Only recently had she dropped the neon colored clothes in favor of pastels to reflect her role as ace reporter.

Despite her efforts to blend in, deep in my heart I knew she'd always stand out. She was a force, and her sense of right and wrong stemmed from childhood bullying incidents. Victims deserved justice. Bad guys deserved punishment. But in between her strict code, she found time for me and I loved her for that.

"No-o-o, I don't think so," Charlotte said with a flip of her chin-length hair. "I'll get myself a glass of ice water and wait for you at your kitchen table. Connor's inside, right?"

Stinger was inside, and he'd be defenseless against Charlotte's nose for the truth. I pocketed my snippers and gestured toward the back steps. "Water would be a good idea. I'll take a quick break with you."

"Thought you'd see it my way."

I bustled past her to open the door. The rush of air conditioning felt great on my heated face. "We've got company," I hollered inside to Stinger. Elvis and Muffin trotted out to see what the fuss was about, both of them going into high excitement mode when Charlotte said, "It's just me."

After the dogs settled, the three of us sat around my kitchen table nursing glasses of water. "You'll never guess what I found out from my source in California just now." Charlotte's voice crackled with emotion. "Funding for the movie has dried up."

"Because of the murder?" I asked.

"Nope. The backers are dissolving their

company. Irreconcilable differences."

I snorted back an inappropriate snicker. "Sounds like a divorce."

"You're right. Her money. His project. And he got caught with his pants down."

My laughter fled. "Another woman?"

"Another man."

"What?" I asked, working hard to close my gaping jaw. Not that someone's sexuality mattered to me, but it was rare here to have partners of both genders.

"Yeah. Boggles the mind that someone's mid-life crisis in California could wreak havoc with people on the Georgia coast."

Working with the sheriff had me focusing on means, motive, and opportunity. When love soured and money was involved, criminal behavior flourished. Charlotte's findings could very well prove relevant to the case. The trick was to find a direct link between events.

My pulse jumped. Could it be so simple as connecting the dots? I very much wanted to put this case behind us.

My hand strayed to the moldavite necklace I wore. This pendant was my touchstone in all the ways that mattered. A sense of profound clarity came over me. Certainty followed. We could solve this case tonight.

Feeling everyone's eyes upon me, I nodded. "I need more information."

Charlotte whipped out her notebook. Her expression sobered. "So do I."

CHAPTER 36

Alarm flared in my gut. "No dice. Last time you made notes about a case I was working on, Bernard stole them and used them in the paper, so no notes. All is not fair in love and publishing."

Charlotte put her pen down, but the notepad stayed on the kitchen table in silent challenge. "You're no fun at all."

"Put it away. Seriously. I'm trying to keep my job without getting us killed. Someone out there is murdering people. They know the cops are trying to catch them. Trust me, you do not want to end up naked, tied upside down on a stairway landing, and bloodless."

The corners of Charlotte's lips lifted ever so slightly.

I cussed myself to the road and back once I realized what I'd done. "You can't tell anyone I told you. No one. Honest to God, Char. This is life and death stuff."

"I won't."

"No finger crossing under the table. No rough outlines on your home computer. No heading out to remote places alone."

A calculating gleam came into her eye. "I want exclusives with you, your dad, and the sheriff."

"I can't promise access to anyone but me. I'll tell you what I know when it's over."

Stinger had been quiet throughout the exchange, but Elvis made a squirming noise and repositioned himself on Stinger's chest. I watched Stinger stroke the small dog absently. His gaze was fixed on Charlotte. What did he make of her?

"Great!" Charlotte said. "I'm part of Team Baxley." She reached over and high-fived Stinger.

Once Stinger recovered from his surprise, he flashed a genuine smile. Charlotte was officially part of our collective. It boggled the mind to think that a scrawny landscaper, a plus-size reporter, and a jittery senior toting a therapy dog might outwit two stone-cold killers, but I reminded myself that in situations like this, the sum was often greater than what the math indicated.

Synergy. We had it. Plus, my contacts in the underworld gave us an edge on solving the case. My spirits lifted.

Charlotte leaned forward, crossing her arms on the table. "I know you're looking at Timmy Ray, Barry, and that movie assistant, what's his name."

"His name's Lou Alfredo, but he goes by LA," I said.

"What about the movie star?"

"Ford Morrison doesn't have anything to gain from the deaths, and everything to lose. The sheriff ruled him out as a suspect."

"But he could be acting a role," Charlotte said firmly. "We have no idea what he's really like. I'm sticking close to him at the wake."

I groaned. "Don't tell me you're going to have him autograph your chest."

"I might." Her eyes turned dreamy for a second before her focus sharpened. "Who else we got?"

Wayne would absolutely kill me if he knew I was spilling his suspect list to a reporter. But Charlotte needed to know who to watch out for tonight. For her own safety. As a member of Team Baxley, she needed as much information as I could afford to share.

"There are two other people we're investigating. Marv had a stalker. She has a history of showing up at his worksites, stirring the pot, and creating messes for him to clean up. Her name is Cassie Korda. I haven't met her, but according to her ID photo, she's tall, slender, and has red hair. I think she'll be there tonight."

"What do you know about her?"

"Not a whole lot, but her unruly behavior in the past makes her a suspect. She tried to get parts for Ford's movies several times but never made the cut. She was possessive of Marv and didn't want him to date anyone else. And then he moved here and started dating someone steadily."

"Very interesting, but I can't help wondering, how'd she find out about his dates?"

My fingers skimmed the condensate on my glass as I thought aloud. "Marv and Bee kept their relationship on the down-low. They spent couple-time at her place and on her boat."

Charlotte squirmed in her seat. "Remind me not to sit down on those boat cushions."

It was on the tip of my tongue to say the sun would've detoxed any body fluids, but it wasn't the chance of contamination that bothered Charlotte. Merely the idea of it. Ideas had power. I waited for the thought to purge from my friend's head. Sure enough, she came back at me with another question.

"That's four suspects. Who else is on your list?"

I threw caution to the wind. "Reed Tyler."

Charlotte gasped. "Reed? No way. He's such a cutie. I've spoken with him a kazillion times at tourism functions for the last three years. He's way too busy to be a killer. The man juggles three phones all the time."

"According to the sheriff, Reed's job is at stake. The powers-that-be told him to boost the economy or get out of town. He brought the movie people here, but from what you've said, the movie people are slap out of money and will close up shop. Which begs the question, does Reed know about the money drying up?"

"I could mention it to him in conversation tonight," Charlotte said.

"Over my dead body." My cheeks heated at my poor word choice. I cleared my throat. "What I meant to say is that's a bad idea. We don't want to be confrontational or incendiary. We want to observe the suspects interacting with party-goers."

"We're outnumbered," Charlotte waggled the fingers of one hand. "There are five of them and only three of us."

"The sheriff will be there. What we're most interested in is groupings of any two of our suspects, so that evens the odds right there."

"Because you have two killers," Charlotte

added smoothly.

I smiled briefly. "You should be a cop. You're good at piecing together information."

We took my truck to the wake, parking along the dirt lane leading to the house. Cars were lined up along the access road. Few trucks, though, and no diesels that I saw. I took the time to turn around so that we'd be facing in the homeward-bound direction when we returned. The muted din of conversation and music drifted through the sighing pines.

No sign of security at the gates. Ford Morrison must've concluded the local press wouldn't crash his private party. I hadn't seen any TV crews, so he'd guessed correctly, except for Charlotte. Could I keep her safe? I sure hoped so.

The air under the moss-shrouded oaks felt heavy and damp. Oppressive, even, and the hair on the back of my neck tingled. My nerves were wound tight as a grapevine on a wire fence.

Charlotte, on the other hand, looked like she was about to explode with anticipation. Her leg kept jumping on the ride over, her hands had twitched her trousers twenty times at least, and she kept glancing around and smiling like a camera crew was in the vicinity.

"You don't have to look so happy about being here," I grumbled as I shifted into park. Making sure she understood the gravity of the situation wouldn't be easy. Once we left the safety of my truck, we were potential targets. "We're here to catch a killer, not audition for the evening news."

"I can't help it. My presence here will upset Bernard, it will help you, and I'm hoping it will land me a wrap-up feature I need to write. If it doesn't do any of those things, I won't lose any ground. But if this works, I'll be sailing straight to the top."

Her determination took my breath away. She yearned for excitement, which concerned me, but I wanted her to have a rewarding career. The trick was to encourage her without coming off like a downer. Was I up to the task?

"I've seen the top," I began slowly, switching off the engine. "Those big-name television reporters look all glossy and professional, but they're not nice people. I believe in you, and you're a good person, a decent person. Angling for a big-gun slot at a daily or even the tube would change your life in ways you can't begin to imagine. Be careful what you wish for. Everyone in this town appreciates you. We love you for you who are, not who someone else thinks you should be."

"Not everyone thinks that way," Charlotte said, an unexpected edge to her voice. "This chance to prove myself is what I need. You had a chance to see the world. I respect that you chose to come back. I'm asking you to respect my need to spread my wings."

I let out a long breath. "Of course I do. But I'm a worrier. The Mom gene corrupted my sense of adventure."

Charlotte laughed, a rich, hearty sound. "Good one." She opened her door and popped out of the truck. "Let's do this."

I glanced over my shoulder at Stinger sitting in the back seat with Elvis. "You ready?"

He met my gaze with glassy eyes. "This place has a strange vibe."

That got my attention. I'd felt something when we pulled up, but I'd ignored the icy sensation to sensitize Charlotte to the potential danger. "Go on."

"Hurry up," Charlotte called from outside, lightly rapping on the driver's-side window.

"Just a minute. This is important." I turned to Stinger in the backseat again. The illumination from the dome light showed his eyes were closed. Was he channeling someone's energy? Would a spirit's voice come out of his lips? Charlotte would freak out. Heck. I would freak out.

"Stinger?" I asked whisper-soft.

His dark brown eyes opened. His pupils contracted slowly and his breaths came in shallow bursts. "The spirits here are unhappy. Someone has been performing rituals that anger them. This is their place. They do not want to leave. Or join with another."

My skin crawled for real. "What are you talking about?"

"A very bad man is in that house."

I glanced in the direction of River House. It looked the same as before to me, but I trusted Stinger. He was telling the truth. "Right now?"

"Yes."

"Who?"

"They call him Janus."

Charlotte opened my door and leaned in. "What? Did I miss something?"

"Stinger got a spirit message just now." I filled her in.

To her credit, Charlotte didn't scoff. She took the news in stride as if people around her received spirit messages every day. The overhead light glinted off her glasses as she nodded, her gaze darting from Stinger to me. "Janus. He was a Roman god. He looks to the past and the future. He's known for having two faces."

I vaguely remembered mythology, but I remembered Charlotte yammering about it endlessly when we were kids. "Two faces? A public face and a private face? Or something else?"

"I don't know," Charlotte said. "That's all I remember from mythology class. I can look it up on my phone, if you like."

"You still want to do this?" I asked Stinger.

He said nothing as his fingers mechanically stroked the dog.

His silence spoke volumes to me. "Get in the truck, Charlotte. I'm taking Stinger home, and you can't stay here without me."

"I want to help you," Stinger said. "We don't have to leave, but I don't like this place."

Were his medium channels stuck on wide open again? I exited the truck and slid in the back beside him. Touched his arm. He was indeed hearing a lot of chatter from the spirit world. I dampened that din instinctively. Waited.

His smile was slow and sure. "How did you quiet the noise?"

"I don't know exactly, but I think of it and I do it." I released his arm. "You don't have to stay here. I understand why this place creeps you out. The offer to leave stands. Your call."

He nodded out the door. "Your friend is a distraction."

"Always has been, but Charlotte is razor sharp and determined to nose around. I need to watch out for her."

"Understood." He took a long breath. "Elvis and I are ready to snoop, but you gotta stay close to me. The voices . . . they're so angry."

"We catch these killers, and we'll fix a lot of things. Justice will be served. Our community will be safe again, and the dead can rest in peace."

"Amen to that, sistah."

Chapter 37

The party was in full swing as we walked onto the front lawn. Elliot Peters crooned into the microphone on the flatbed truck stage. Sparsely populated chairs dotted the lawn. Tiki torches lined the stone path and ringed the seating area. Knots of the county's business elite huddled together under the trees, on the porch, and inside the illuminated house.

On the porch, I recognized the college interns from my prior visit here. The lanky man who worked with them listened intently, broke away, and disappeared in the house. Ford Morrison stood nearby on the porch, deep in conversation with Reed Tyler from the Tourism Office. Ford looked like a fashion plate in pressed khakis, black shirt, and tie. Reed looked rumpled in his black suit and open-collared white shirt.

LA stood in a clump on our way to the house. Instead of his usual picture-perfect appearance, LA's head glistened with sweat. Perspiration soaked his long-sleeved shirt. He waved and moved to intercept us.

His smile of welcome made it seem like we were old friends, though I'd only met him once before. Warily, I introduced my companions, adding, "Looks like you have a nice turnout for the wake. I'm sure Marv would be pleased."

LA beamed. "It came together in the best way. The interns created a montage of film clips and stills from Marv's life, which are running in the media room inside. Help yourself to the seafood buffet in the dining room and the wine bar in the great room."

"The music is great," Charlotte said. "Elliot Peters is practically a local legend. How'd you get him?"

"Marv and Elliot were jam buddies," LA explained. "Marv knew a lot of the old standards and liked to play a few licks in his spare time. Mostly they played in Elliot's studio, but once, not too long back, they sat on the porch and sang the sun down. It was magical."

"I didn't know they were acquainted," I said, scanning the clusters of people with interest. "Did any of Marv's California friends make it?"

"Only Cassie, though her relationship with

Marv was rocky to say the least."

I inched closer, wondering if I could accidentally brush against him to get a better reading on him. "Could you point Cassie out to me? I'd like to meet her."

"The wine bar most likely. She's bummed about Marv's death."

"What's she wearing?"

"Black cocktail dress. Killer heels. If she wasn't a complete whack job, I'd hit on her."

My eyebrows rose. So much for the sheriff's speculation that LA was gay.

"But that would be wrong. At Marv's wake and all," LA quickly amended as a group moved past us to stand in front of Elliot Peters who was playing the devil out of a saxophone.

Charlotte edged forward, moving into LA's personal space. He responded by crabbing sideways. Sensing my opportunity, I intercepted him and we collided, arms tangling.

As before, colors and lights flashed like a kaleidoscope. Sounds drew out like an audio track on slow speed. Emotions slammed me next. Anger. Lots of bright red anger. A gauzy scene started to fill in, of people in robes and oaks, and then just as quickly, vanished.

"Pardon me," LA said, disentangling

himself from me. "I need to speak to Ford about his remarks."

He ran from us, causing Charlotte to snicker. "What'd you do, Bax? Goose his privates?"

"Nothing like that." I glanced over at Stinger, found his gaze on me, found his hand on my belt loop. "You see it too?"

Stinger nodded.

"What?" Charlotte asked. "Y'all share a spirit-world video feed or something?"

"Don't know what it was, but two sets of eyes are always better than one," I said, catching Stinger's eye and barely shaking my head. If Stinger and I discussed the spirit message now, it would end up in the newspaper. Neither one of us wanted that.

"And three makes it a lock," Charlotte said. "That man is hiding something."

"Anger," I blurted out. So much for discretion. I shrugged and continued. "He's very angry."

"At what?" Charlotte asked.

"Don't know." I turned to Stinger. "The woods?"

"Yeah. I saw that. The rituals my spirits were complaining about. LA's seen them."

"He might be involved. Or, he could've been excluded, which would account for his anger."

"Y'all are talking in code again," Charlotte said.

"LA knows more than he's letting on," I clarified for her, "but I didn't get the sense of him being two-faced. If he's part of the killer duo, he's able to conceal it from me. But he doesn't have a killer vibe. Does that make sense?"

Charlotte nodded. "Check him off the list as the mastermind. I say we follow LA to Ford. I can't wait for you to check him out."

"Ford can wait. We should identify Cassie first," I said. "I want to make sure she doesn't blindside one of us. She's an unknown so far. We can get refreshments as props."

"Speak for yourself," Charlotte said. "I could use a tall glass of wine."

Stinger and I followed Charlotte up the steps and into River House. Every room glowed with light. Massive flower arrangements were everywhere, so many that I sneezed from sensory overload. My friends looked at me in alarm. I didn't normally sneeze around plants, which would be awful since I was a landscaper as well as a police consultant.

"I'm fine," I said. "The strong floral scent caught me by surprise."

Charlotte gave me another searching look,

then we got drinks to hold. Stinger refused a drink and a snack. His eyes darted around the room uneasily. I took hold of his arm, found out his channels were wide open again. Spirits were screaming at him. I dampened the noise, but the din ramped back up immediately. The loud roar of internal conversation made my temples throb.

"We have to get you out of here," I said, noting Reed Tyler texting away in a corner of the montage room. Charlotte's nemesis from the paper, Bernard, lurked at Reed's elbow. No redheaded women were in sight, though black cocktail dresses abounded in this crowd.

Charlotte ran over to Reed before I could tell her of the change in plan. Scowl locked in place, Bernard joined her conversation with the Tourism VIP. With Bernard nipping at her heels, Charlotte wouldn't exactly be alone.

Stinger shuddered. We had to get outside. My fix wasn't holding. The voices wouldn't stay silenced in this house. The chaos gave me a pounding headache. We couldn't stay in this toxic environment.

Charlotte caught my eye and waved from across the room. I gestured with a jerk of my thumb that we were going outside. She nodded her understanding. I cupped Stinger's arm and aimed for the exit. From being here before, I knew the doorknob was jacked with emotion, but Ford Morrison did a two-step around us as we tried to leave. Elvis snarled and made a low rumble in his throat. Stinger stumbled into the movie star. "Sorry," Stinger mumbled. "This is too much for me."

Ford clapped him gently on the shoulder. "We're all sad at Marv's passing."

I nodded because I couldn't speak. The loud voices in Stinger's head spilled into my head, giving way to robed people chanting in the darkness. One perfect face was clearly illuminated: Ford Morrison. He was involved in the rituals. He was the two-faced person the spirits hated. And hate him they did. The voices returned with a vengeance. They were so loud and scathing that I wanted to hold my head and moan in agony.

Somehow we made it off the porch and into chairs near the empty music platform before we collapsed. Slowly, the evening air cooled our bodies as the voices of the dead dialed back to a normal level. Nearby tiki torches provided soft light and kept the shadows at bay.

"That was horrible," I managed, thankful the band was on break.

"No shit," Stinger said. "I don't like this place. That man is evil."

"Who knew? He's a big-time movie star."

"He drew the spirits here to trap them."

"Why do they call him Janus? Is it because of his inner persona being so different from how he looks?"

"I couldn't . . . I didn't . . . It was too intense. The voices. They were awful. So angry. So upset. If they could, they'd kill him."

"I got that." One-handed, I massaged my throbbing temples. I didn't dare turn loose of Stinger. One or both of us would go crazy if the voices bushwhacked us again.

But Charlotte. I needed to get her out of the house. I turned to Stinger. His face was drawn and his eyes were wide as he stared away from the house.

Coming here had been a colossal mistake. We needed to leave right away.

"Stinger, touch me with your leg, so that I can use my hand and arm. I need to call Charlotte."

His thigh snugged next to mine. Quickly, I whipped out my phone. The call went to Charlotte's voice mail. I left a message for her. "Come outside ASAP. We have to leave."

I shot her a text with the same message.

We waited. No return call, no Charlotte striding outside. Then a text message appeared on my screen. "Five minutes," it read. I showed the communication to Stinger.

Someone approached, walking on tiptoe across the lawn. From the long stride, I knew it wasn't Charlotte. I dreaded having to converse with anyone. Holding these clamoring voices at bay was taking all I could manage right now. Even so, I slowly dragged my glance up from the ground. Stilettos. Tanned legs. Black dress. Lanky figure. Red hair.

"I heard you were looking for me," Cassie Korda said in a whiskey-roughened voice.

CHAPTER 38

Why now? I didn't feel like I could stand to talk with her, much less interrogate her. Not a drop of spare energy in my tank. I introduced us and gestured to a nearby seat. "Please, join us."

Cassie glanced around as if to see if anyone was watching her. She perched on the edge of a chair. "What's this about?"

I tried for a look of sympathy. "I wanted to express my condolences. I heard you were close to Marv, and his passing must be hard for you."

Cassie lost her erect posture, hunching forward to bury her face on her hands. Even in the dim light, I could see the gleaming white tips of her French nail manicure. To my horror, the woman started sobbing.

If ever there was an opportunity to touch someone for consolation, this was it. But I couldn't move without releasing Stinger. What a fine pickle this was.

After a long moment, Cassie drew back up to a stiff sitting posture, swiping at the moisture on her high cheekbones. "I'm sorry. I'm just . . . This is just . . ." She took a slow breath. "I miss him. Marv was everything to me."

She spoke the truth. Of that I was certain, but she hadn't said much, had she? "It's hard to lose a close friend. Y'all were friends for, what, five years now?"

"Three," she said quickly. "We dated at first, then we just hung out. I wanted more, but Marv didn't." She fanned her face with those white fingernail tips. "He was the love of my life."

A lie.

A big, fat lie.

What did it mean? "I understand," I murmured softly. The longer I sat there in her presence, the more I felt a sense of wrongness. I couldn't put my finger on the disconnect, but something was very off about this woman. "I know what it's like to lose someone. You feel like you can't breathe."

Cassie nodded. "Exactly. Part of me wants to stop living right now. To go to him and be with him wherever he is."

Not quite the truth, but not a full-on lie either. Hmm.

"How long have y'all been together?" Cassie gestured to Stinger and me. "It couldn't have been easy with the May–December gap in your ages and your different races. I imagine people around here have a lot to say about your relationship."

I couldn't explain our true relationship, and I couldn't let go of Stinger either. I glanced over at Stinger, who regarded me closely. I gave him a nod.

"We haven't been together long," Stinger said, "but as soon as we met, I knew Baxley was special. She . . . completes me."

Cassie gave us a long, considering look. "There is a certain energy about the two of you."

Another truth. It occurred to me that Cassie was very good at this. She managed to give me enough information to think I was reading her, and then she turned the tables on me. Time for me to do my job as a sheriff's consultant.

"Where will you go from here?" I asked. "Are you returning to California?"

"I'm considering a job with the film company," Cassie said, her voice breaking. "That was my dream all along. I can't believe it took Marv's death for it to come true."

Liar.

"Will you be working behind the scenes with LA or with Ford in front of the camera?" I asked.

"I'd like to be in front of the camera, natch, but I have to earn my spot. The other interns have the same goal."

Another truth. Stinger elbowed me. I followed his nod to see Ford Morrison on the porch, his attention directed our way. His interest sparked questions in my head. Why did he care if we talked to Cassie?

Were Ford and Cassie the killer duo we were seeking? If so, they knew exactly what I was doing at this party. I'd better watch my step or I'd be their next victim. I hoped Charlotte would stroll outside so we could leave. That's what I wanted more than anything. To get away from these movie people. Wayne would have to observe these people by himself.

"I wish you luck with your career," I murmured to fill the gap in conversation.

Cassie beamed, but instead of the expression lighting up her face, the effect was sinister. "I'm certain I'll be successful. You can deposit that in the bank."

Truth, but it glittered like an ugly toad. I had no doubt Cassie was involved with Marv's death, only how would I prove it? Wayne couldn't use my intuition or special skills as evidence in a court case. Worse, he didn't believe a woman was strong enough to string victims up over the stairs. My only move with Cassie was to pretend I had authority and question her closely.

I cleared my throat for good measure. "You may have heard that I consult with the sheriff's office. Where were you the night Marv died?"

Alarm flared in Cassie's eyes, then her gaze narrowed. "I don't have to answer that."

"No, you don't, but a solid alibi will eliminate you as a suspect."

Her voice sliced into me. "I was en route to this place. My flight was delayed in Atlanta. You can check."

"We will."

"We're done here." Cassie sneered and stalked off as best she could, tiptoeing in her stilettos so the sand didn't grab her heels.

"That was intense," I said.

"She's a piece of work," Stinger said. "I didn't believe a word she said. My gut says she's mixed up in this."

"Can you prove it?"

"No more than you can. I thought you'd touch her for a reading."

"Couldn't reach her. Didn't dare risk letting go of you."

"I'm better. The voices are quieter outside. I don't feel like I'm going to throw up anymore."

I did a systems check on both of us and agreed with his assessment. "Thanks for covering for me. Her observation caught me off guard. I didn't expect for us to be mistaken as a couple."

"I thought of it. Made me smile 'cuz I ain't never loved nobody but my Necee. I first laid eyes on her when she was five years old, and I knew she was the one for me."

"How nice. So many people struggle with loneliness for years, and y'all spent every day of a lifetime together."

"I miss her, same as you pine for your man. I feel your sadness."

Roland. I hadn't consciously thought about my missing husband in days. I sent up a quick prayer for his safety. Whatever he was involved with must be dangerous indeed for him to abandon his family.

Charlotte's five minutes were up. I texted her again. "Must leave now." No response. Was she ignoring me? I didn't like her being out of touch. I scanned the lawn and the porch but I couldn't see her, which made me anxious. Was this how Wayne felt about me playing amateur detective?

The tiki torches flickered, and, as if I'd conjured him up, Sheriff Wayne Thompson appeared before us. "What're my ace detectives doing outside the party?"

"Recovering," I said.

"Do tell." Wayne started to sit in the chair Cassie vacated.

"Not there!" I shouted, my voice shrilling through the mossy oaks.

CHAPTER 39

Adrenaline surged, and I clambered to my feet. "Don't sit in that chair."

Wayne paused in mid-squat. "What's going on?"

"I need to . . . um . . . check the chair." Surprised at my ability to stand without psychic backup, I glanced over at Singer. He waved me on. I took a few cautionary steps away from my lifeline.

The sheriff stepped aside and scanned the area for armed threats. "What?"

"Cassie sat there," Stinger said. "We think she's involved. Might even be our killer. One of the killers anyway."

"A woman?" Wayne scoffed. "She'd have to be strong as an ox. And your ghosts say we've got two male killers. She doesn't fit the profile."

"Have you met Cassie?" I asked. "She's very direct and intense. And she's not a small woman. I'll bet she's strong as any man. And I bet she drives a diesel pickup truck."

The sheriff shook his head, his face law-man tough. "No betting at this point. We have to be certain. What proof can you offer me?"

"Let me read her chair, then we'll tell you about our other discovery."

"You're killing me, Powell."

"This is important, even more so since Cassie vacated that seat moments ago." I drew in a long breath, then grabbed the back of the chair. The roar of Cassie's life invaded my head at warp speed. Lights pinpointed and blurred, sound shrilled and dragged out to clumps of nothingness, and red, red was everywhere.

I smelled the taint of copper and knew blood had been spilled. Through Cassie's eyes, I scanned the scene. It was the murder house. June's Folly. Marv and Bee's bodies dangled over her head.

"Stand under it," Cassie commanded.

Her accomplice sobbed openly. "No."

"Do it, or I'll gut you like the others." Cassie's voice conveyed the threat and left no doubt as to her intention.

"I've done what you asked. Please, let me go."

"You're mine now, Janus. Mine to control,

mine to use as I see fit. You even think of sharing what we've done with another, and your acting career will be over. Your life will be over."

"My life isn't worth anything. I don't know who I am anymore. You're out of control, and I'm bound to you by blood. By our crime."

Cassie reached under the blood drip line, caught a handful and rubbed it on Janus's face. Then she did the same to herself. "I anoint thee, Janus, to be my apostle, from now until evermore."

Janus dry-heaved, but nothing came up. "Kill me now and be done with it."

Cassie pressed the large knife against his Adam's apple. "I gave you exactly what you asked for. You wanted to live again, to feel the pain and suffering, and to savor the glory of a job well done."

Janus hung his head. "I am ashamed."

Cassie removed the knife and drew him close. Kissed him. Fondled him. "Be ashamed no more. You are a glorious vassal, and I shall reward you handsomely."

A sly, calculating look crossed the actor's face. "Now?"

"Outside, under the moonlight."

The image faded, to my relief. I came to my senses, saw Wayne and Stinger watching me. Crickets chirped, the ordinary sound so reassuring after the horror I'd witnessed. "We were right. Two killers. Cassie and Ford. I saw them at June's Folly with the bodies."

My knees trembled. I stumbled back to my seat. Stinger handed me Elvis and wrapped his arm around my shoulder. Warmth flowed into my limbs. Better. Much better.

Wayne pulled up another chair, casting a wide berth around Cassie's vacated chair. "Explain."

"Both of us got independent confirmation Ford Morrison is involved," I said. "He's not the squeaky-clean guy he appears to be. He leads rituals in the woods and angers the spirits."

"Not a crime to do stupid stuff in the woods. Freedom of religion and all that."

"The spirits call him Janus, because he's two-faced," Stinger continued. "That veneer of civility you see is a shell. He's an evil man. The spirits he summoned here hate him."

Wayne shook his head, a baffled expression in his dark eyes. "I did a cursory check of Morrison at the beginning of the investigation and he came up clean. I'll dig deeper into his background, call a few contacts out in California. He may have gotten a pass on some of his misdeeds, but the local cops will know if he's dirty."

I cleared my dry throat. "For what it's worth, Ford's involvement with the murders seemed involuntary in the scene I witnessed. Cassie holds some big career-wrecking secret over his head. And that Cassie, let me tell you, she's a piece of work. She's an accomplished liar. Only when she told a whopper could I get a sense of truth or lie."

"What'd she lie about?"

"Something about acting being her dream and a job opening up with the film company and how sad she was that it came about through Marv's death."

"Sounds reasonable. You sure it's a lie?"

"Absolutely. She also lied about Marv being the love of her life. She said the night of the murder, she was stuck in Atlanta on a flight delay. Can you check that?"

"I'll check it. I'd like to question her myself. Where is she?"

I waved toward the house. "Inside. Tall, lanky redhead in a black cocktail dress. Stilettos."

"Sounds like my dream date," Wayne quipped.

"You can't be serious."

"It was a joke, Powell. Stay put. I'll be

right back." Wayne melted into the house.

I still wanted to leave, but Stinger was right. We were no longer under spiritual attack. We could wait a few more minutes for Charlotte. If the voices came back, Charlotte was resourceful enough to catch a ride home with Wayne.

Elliot Peters came back onstage and treated us to another blue-ribbon musical performance. Lovely. I let my thoughts drift along on the sultry music as my strength returned. Elvis climbed over and snuggled with Stinger.

Odd that Charlotte hadn't come out to check on us. I texted her again. "Call me." As Stinger and I clapped at the end of a song, the sheriff charged out of the house. "Cassie's gone. A black dress and shoes were in the upstairs bathroom. Ford's gone too. I've got an APB out on both of them. I'm taking LA and Reed with me to the station house. You guys meet us there."

It wasn't a suggestion. Stinger and I rose. "All right," I said. "Why take the other suspects when we know Cassie and Ford are to blame?"

"We can't prove anything, and until I can, I want to know where the key players are." He fixed us each with a harsh glare. "That includes the pair of you. Something about this stinks, and I don't like it."

Wayne was in his glory, his cop instincts firing on all cylinders. I suppressed an inappropriate smile. "You might solve this thing tonight, but I can't go without Charlotte. She's somewhere in the house."

"I'll send her out to your truck. Y'all don't look any too steady on your feet, so get started."

I nodded. "We're leaving now."

CHAPTER 40

Arm in arm we shuffled down the lane of parked vehicles. I expected Charlotte to join us any minute, so my ears were keenly attuned to the noises of the night. At the sound of a low moan, I halted. "Did you hear that?" I asked Stinger.

"What?"

I held up a hand, my white flesh ghostly pale in the twilight of sunset. "That sound. Hold still a minute. Someone's in trouble."

"Wayne said to go to the truck."

"He thinks he's boss of everyone. I'm not leaving someone out here if they're hurt. We could call for help or give them a lift back into town."

"I don't like this."

The moan sounded again. Louder. We followed it. Elvis made a keening noise, which set my arm hairs on edge.

There, in front of the parked cars. A body on the ground. In the faint light, I recognized the light blue shirt. I swore under my breath. "Hold up. That's Ford Morrison."

Ford moaned and stirred.

Stinger tugged me back around the cars and whispered, "You trying to get us killed? Call the sheriff."

I pulled out my cell phone. Turned it on. No signal. "I can't."

"Why not?"

"It won't connect to a tower."

"Sounds fishy to me."

"It's the God's truth. What should we do? Should one of us go for help?"

"Nope. We're not splitting up."

The moans intensified. It sounded like he was saying Charlotte. Alarmed, I peeked over the hood of the car we'd put between us and him. Ford was sitting up. He clearly said, "She has Charlotte."

"Who has Charlotte?" I asked.

"Cassie. She's crazy. She had Charlotte at gunpoint and hit me over the head with something. I'm bleeding."

Prudence and caution fought against self-preservation and lost. Oh, no. My friend was in danger. "Where's Cassie taking her?"

Ford tried to get up. Fell. Pushed up to a seated position with another deep groan. "We were going to June's Folly. Where Marv and Bee . . . died. Cassie says Charlotte is next."

I couldn't breathe. Couldn't think. Charlotte was in trouble. She would die if we didn't get there in time. I had to save her. I tried my phone again. Nothing. "Stay right there. We'll get a medical team for you as soon as my phone starts working, but we have to go."

"Take me with you," Ford said, sobbing. "I have to stop Cassie. I should have stopped her before."

I was getting a very bad vibe. I backed up. "We're not taking you anywhere, but we will send you some medical help." And hopefully a pair of handcuffs.

I nodded to Stinger. "Come on. We've got to hurry."

My truck wasn't too much farther. Four more vehicles. We unlocked it and got in. Cranked the engine. And there was Ford Morrison, standing in front of the truck with a Beretta in his hand. My mouth went dry as I stared straight down the barrel.

"Duck," Stinger yelled.

I dove for the seat as the gun roared. The bullet tore through the windshield and out the back glass, right where my head would've been.

"Don't do anything stupid," Ford yelled.

"Open the door nice and slow, or I'll shoot you both right here, right now."

No way. Ford was a killer. I wasn't letting that man in my truck. If I hit him with my vehicle, so be it. I punched the accelerator and the truck lunged forward. He must have leaped out of the way because we moved ahead without incident.

Ford Morrison was a dangerous man. A liar. A Janus. I eased my head up to see the road and to glance in the rearview mirror. Would he follow us?

"You all right?" I asked Stinger.

"Scared."

"You gotta right to be scared after being shot at. I didn't expect that. Hang on, this will be a bouncy ride."

Neither one of us said a word as we bumped down the lane to the highway. Once on the pavement, my phone worked again. I tried the sheriff's direct line. Nothing. I called 9-1-1 and identified myself.

"Ford Morrison tried to kill me," I said, mashing the accelerator to the floor and peering around the bullet hole. "He shot a hole in my windshield. Then he tried to force me out of my truck, but we got away from him."

"Where are you, ma'am?" Dusty Jorgenson said.

I'd never felt less like a ma'am, but I let it slide. "Heading from River House to June's Folly. Morrison told me his partner in crime, a woman named Cassie, took Charlotte hostage. She plans to kill Charlotte the same way she killed Marv and Bee. I tried calling the sheriff from the driveway, but the call wouldn't go through. My phone wouldn't work at River House a few minutes ago, but it worked fine earlier and it's working right now."

"Something must be jamming the signal out there. I'll route a deputy to June's Folly immediately. Do not go out there. Report to the station. The sheriff is on his way here with two suspects."

"Charlotte is my friend. I have to save her."

"Virg and Ronnie are working that zone of the county. I'll send them to the house. Baxley, the sheriff wouldn't want you to go out there without police escort. Come into town and wait for him here."

"Sorry, you're breaking up." I hung up the phone and studied my companion. In the relative darkness of the truck cab, his dark skin appeared ashy. "I'll drop you off at the crossroads convenience store. You'll be safe there."

My phone buzzed again. Dusty. I muted

343

the call.

"We're in this together," Stinger said. "I'm coming with you. You need me."

Was he channeling Clint Eastwood? Or was this male bravado? "I've got one gun in the glovebox, but that's it for my weapons stash. Charlotte likes to talk a big game, but she's a marshmallow. I can't let them hurt her. I have to find her."

"Even if it comes to shooting a person?"

I swallowed around the lump in my throat. I was no killer. "Charlotte is family to me. I believe Cassie will drain her like Bee and Marv. Time is of the essence. Virg and Ronnie mean well, but they're not a SWAT team. I won't pin Charlotte's life on them getting there in time."

Stinger took his time answering. A dip in the road sent us both off the seat. "We need to arrive in one piece. Slow down a little."

I eased up a bit on the gas. "I'm worried. And scared."

"Me too."

CHAPTER 41

Though it was only a little after nine, the hour felt like midnight. I had that out-of-phase feeling where houses and yards beside the highway passed in freeze frames, each one searing into my thoughts. Not wanting to alarm my father, who could receive telepathic messages from me, I dampened my worries.

This wasn't my father's battle.

There'd been no traffic on the cross-county road to speak of, which seemed odd for a Friday night. Was it too early for folks to go juking? I wasn't part of the carousing scene, so I didn't know when the club crowd went out. Not that I cared right now. I had to rescue Charlotte. And capture two killers.

Not too big of a deal.

Unless I thought about details.

Nope.

Not thinking about guns or killers or consequences.

What good was being a psychic police consultant if I couldn't protect my best friend? Charlotte deserved my best effort. She'd get it.

Stinger'd been quiet once I'd quit bouncing us all over the truck. As I turned down the road to June's Folly, I searched the swamp beside the road for a place to pull off. If I drove up to the house, the killer would know I'd arrived. I needed the element of surprise on my side for this to work.

I passed by a place that looked big enough. Braked. Reversed. And slotted the truck in the spot. "You should be safe here."

His hand went to the door handle. "Nah. We're a team. Though, I get to pick our next outing because this one blows. Big time."

I grabbed the gun and hopped down. The soft ground dulled the thud of my nice shoes. The thick, swamp air was harder to breathe, and it reeked of rot and decay. The darkness here seemed absolute, so we waited impatiently for our eyes to adjust. It wouldn't do any good for one of us to twist an ankle. Faint stars appeared overhead, and a wash of moonlight silvered the sandy road.

We hurried toward the house. Soon we were huffing for breath. "I should've parked closer."

"Ya done fine, Dreamwalker." He cradled Elvis in his arms. "What's our plan?"

My stride shortened. "I'm playing this by ear, unless you've got any suggestions."

"One of us could go in the front door while the other circles around back," he pointed out.

Icy cold assaulted my legs. I stopped altogether. "Oliver?"

The ghost dog materialized, his pinkish tongue lolling to one side.

I heard Stinger's sharp intake of breath and his nearly inaudible "God almighty."

I gave the dog's triangular head a quick pat. "I don't have anything for you. Can you help us find Charlotte?"

The dog cocked his head as if listening, but that was it. He fell into stride with us as we walked toward the house.

"Is the ghost dog still there?" Stinger asked, whisper soft.

"Oh, yeah." Though Oliver's shape had returned to a thin wisp, the cold he emitted was tangible.

"I didn't know you could command ghosts."

"I don't. The dog is choosing to accompany us. Big difference."

"I can't hear him. In my head, I mean."

"He's not barking or anything. Just seems

lonely. Like he's waiting for someone."

"I haven't been out here in years. Not since the last owners had a big party and needed folks to help out. Necee got both of us a job for the bash."

The chatter should have calmed my nerves, but it put me on edge. I needed to focus on what we were doing. Focus. I stopped again and sent out a mental scan for life signs. One strong life sign registered. In the direction of the house.

Was I too late for Charlotte?

"What?" Stinger asked.

"Someone's in the house. No one's in the yard or waiting outside to ambush us. Just the single person in the house. No one else is around for miles. We should use your plan. You take the gun and go around back." I could call in another chip from Rose my guardian angel/demon if I got into a jam.

He shied away from me. "I don't hold no truck with no guns. Don't want it. Don't need it. I'll circle around back and find a brick or something."

I fished my cell from my slacks pocket. "Take the phone and call for help if I get into trouble before Virg and Ronnie arrive."

"Good idea."

I searched his face. "What about you? You getting anything? Any voices talking to you?"

348

"You want me to do this now?"

We were standing in the middle of the dirt road. I latched onto his arm and pulled him to the nearest tree. Oliver lay down at my feet. "Yes. We need all the intel we can get. Let's look together."

"All right already." He closed his eyes. I did the same and felt the rush of air on my skin. We dropped into the void, Oliver barking and dancing around us. I knelt for the dog, then glanced up at Stinger. "Anybody talking?"

He pointed to my left. "Over there."

We hurried over, opened the door. Marv and Cassie. On the lawn at River House. "You don't love me?" Cassie asked, her lower lip trembling.

"I don't. I'm sorry. I know you have strong feelings for me, but I don't return them. There's always been a distance between us, one that time and familiarity haven't bridged. I don't know you. If I can say anything for certain, you enjoy acting the part of my girlfriend."

Cassie laughed, a harsh, grating sound. "You're smarter than you look, Marv Kildeer. And for that transgression, I'm going to kill you and ruin this production company."

"Because I won't sleep with you? Isn't that harsh?"

"It's the way I roll. You've been warned." Cassie stalked off.

Marv stared after her, muttering, "Crazy bitch. I'm getting another restraining order to keep you away from me and my friends."

The image faded from view. Night sounds stirred again. My leg was numb with cold. Oliver. I nudged him aside and stomped my leg to get sensation back in it.

"She threatened him," I said once I could talk. "She warned him, but he didn't take her threat seriously."

"Now she's inside. Waiting for us."

"She's waiting for me. I have to draw her out, get her to tell me where she stashed Charlotte. If I die, hightail it out of here. The keys are in my pickup. Take it and the phone and get as far away from here as possible. Tell Larissa and my parents I love them."

Stinger shook his bald head, the faint sheen catching reflected starlight. "We not gonna die tonight. There's been enough death in these here parts already."

"Are you revising the plan?"

"I am. We got another weapon. Oliver."

My uneasiness grew as seconds ticked off Charlotte's life clock. Was my friend already dead? Where was she? "How's that?"

"Elvis and I'll still sneak around the back, but you send that ghost dog in the house first. Sic it on the bad person in there. Cassie won't be expecting a ghost."

"If she's not a sensitive, it won't matter. Oliver could walk through her multiple times and she'd never know."

"They's something off about this woman. Something I can't quite get at yet. What will it hurt to use the dog? He wants to help."

Why was I quibbling? Adding the dog to our sneak attack might help. I nodded my agreement and pushed away from the tree. I stopped to rack my handgun. "Off we go."

CHAPTER 42

Mindful of the potholes still marring the lawn, I eased toward the front porch. Stinger and Elvis edged off to the right. I pulsed energy into the air again. Got two ping-backs. The killer and Stinger. Where the heck was Charlotte?

The porch steps creaked as I mounted them. So much for stealth mode. The fingers of my right hand tightened around the grip of my gun. I held it by my hip, not concealed, but not so someone could knock the weapon out of my hand either.

Could I take aim at a person? Other than shooting at rattlesnakes in my truck and a lot of paper targets at the range, I preferred not to think about the guns I owned. I didn't have to shoot anyone, I reminded myself. The gun was a deterrent.

The front door of June's Folly gaped wide, crime-scene tape dangling beside the door frame like last year's Christmas lights.

Inside the house, everything was dark and still. Oliver leaned against my leg.

"I know you're in here, Cassie," I said. "What did you do with Charlotte?"

In a back room, a match flared, then another. Light flicked. The sulfur smell drifted out to me as shadows shifted. My courage faltered, and I gritted my teeth. "Hello? Come on out, Cassie. Ford told me you'd be here."

Edgy silence filled my ears. My pulse hammered in my head, making it hard to think. I brought the gun up in a two-handed grip shoulder high and inched toward the light. I wasn't a marksman, but this outsider didn't know that. For all she knew, Georgia rednecks were born with silver-plated trigger fingers.

"Cops are on their way," I said. "After I found Ford, I called 9-1-1. The sheriff knows what you did. You won't get away with murder, battery, and kidnapping."

Every instinct screamed at me to get out of this house of death. I forced in a breath. I'd stare down the hounds of hell for Charlotte. The woman had stashed Charlotte somewhere, and I needed to find her before it was too late.

I studiously avoided looking at the blood-stained staircase where Marv and Bee had taken their last breaths. With each step I took into the house, the soft glow ahead beckoned. Lungs stilled, I glanced inside the lighted space. Six votive candles glowed on the floor inside a chalked pentagram.

"About time," Cassie said from a shadowed corner of the room. "Did you stop off for a latte on the way here?"

She'd changed into black trousers and a snug black tee. Her hair was different, shorter, but the voice was the same. The white skin of Cassie's bare feet gleamed in the darkness. Near her thighs something shiny glinted momentarily. The knife. Oh, God. It was the curved knife that killed Marv and Bee.

Cassie brought the knife forward, slashed it in the air. She was trying to scare the shit out of me. It was working, except I'd brought a gun to her knife fight. I kept the gun held high.

"You're done, Cassie," I said. "We know you and Ford teamed up to kill Marv and Bee."

"Knowing's one thing, proving it is another." She circled to the right toward me. I edged left until she stopped. With dismay, I realized she'd maneuvered me into the corner and the doorway was behind her.

I was trapped.

I may have a superior weapon, but Cassie was a wily and practiced adversary. She'd killed before and wouldn't hesitate to do so again. "Where's Charlotte?"

"Don't know. Don't care. But you. You're going to squeal like a pig when I slice you open. You're going to beg for mercy on your knees, but there's no mercy in this house. Only death."

"Ford said you took Charlotte hostage."

"Ford lied. He'd do anything for me. Why would I take the reporter hostage when I could lure you out here just by saying I did?"

She'd tricked me. I hadn't questioned the actor. I'd acted impulsively. Worse, Cassie had counted on my rash behavior. She had cunning on her side, but I couldn't let her win. She needed to pay for her crimes.

"You're the one who's trapped, not me." I managed a shaky breath. "Even if you hurt me, they'll catch you. Your only chance to escape is to leave right now."

Cassie snorted. "The powers of life hold no claim on me. I've channeled dark energy from the Other Side. It seethes inside me. Two overweight cops with a Taser gun are no match for me. I can defeat them easily. Should I give them flat tires right now so they don't make it? I can do that."

The flower tattoo on my hand heated. So

did the one on my back. Rose. Was she here? Would her presence balance the evil forces?

Cassie lunged across the room at me, knife blade slashing in the vicinity of my belly. I should've pulled the trigger, but I couldn't. I ducked to the side. "Get her, Oliver."

A micro-second later, Cassie screamed, dropped the knife, and grabbed at her throat. Her vocal protests went deeper instead of shriller as I expected. She cursed a blue streak and bolted out the door. I kicked the knife into the corner of the room and followed her, hope warming my ice cold insides.

In the hallway, the darkness seemed absolute. After the candlelight, I couldn't see worth a darn, but I had to keep moving. I had to see this through. Night blind, I heard someone cry out in pain. Stinger.

My heart thumped like a kettle drum. I hurried in the direction of the cry, keeping an elbow along the wall to my left. In the kitchen, I came upon them. Starlight illuminated the windows. Cassie held a butcher knife on Stinger's throat.

"Come one step closer, witch, and I'll cut him. I'll cut him good," Cassie threatened in a low rumble.

Where was Elvis? Stinger didn't usually make a move without the little Chihuahua.

For that matter, what happened to Oliver?

I sent out a probe for the dogs, but I kept my gaze locked on Cassie. "Don't hurt him. He's an innocent."

"No one's innocent, girlie. Everyone has blood on their hands. Even Christians talk about the purifying effect of the blood of Jesus. This man's blood will sanctify me, just as Marv's blood did."

"You killed two people."

"The woman wasn't absolutely necessary, but it was a pleasure to watch Marv realize I wouldn't spare her. Now I get to experience that rapture again as I take the life of your witchy familiar. I'll anoint you with his blood before I kill you. I'll take every one of your secret powers while I'm at it."

I must have started.

"You didn't think I knew about your psychic talents?" Cassie laughed, a harsh sound that grated on my nerves. "I know exactly who and what you are. I move freely across the veil, and the disturbance you've caused in the spirit world won't be tolerated."

"Says who?" I gripped the gun, sure that I had to shoot this woman, not sure if a bullet or three would stop her. If her alliance in the spirit realm was with someone as strong as Rose, Stinger and I wouldn't survive this

357

encounter. I needed help.

Oliver and Elvis were hiding in the hall. I sent Oliver a mental command to attack and hoped like anything that I spoke dog.

"Says me. And Many." Cassie laughed again, the action causing the knife to dig into Stinger's throat. A crimson trickle ran down his neck.

I heard the thunder of dog claws on the planked floors. Heard Cassie scream. Saw her reach for her throat to dislodge Oliver and at the same time try to shake little Elvis off her ankle. Stinger broke free and ran toward me. I motioned him out into the hall with a jerk of my head and waited for my chance.

As Cassie careened toward the window, I cried "Heel," hoping both dogs would obey. Upon gaining relief from the dogs, Cassie laughed, an evil, diabolical sound that echoed through the empty house.

"You fool. You shouldn't have called off the dogs. You'll pay for your mistake with your life."

"Stop or I'll shoot."

"You won't shoot me or I'd already be dead."

I retreated a step. "Stop."

Cassie rushed forward, the tip of the sharp knife slashing through the darkness, inches from me. The choice was clear. Shoot or die.

I squeezed the trigger three times in rapid succession. Cassie fell at my feet. I sagged into the doorway. Moisture dripped from my face, and I felt horror, remorse, and shame at what I'd had to do. The room wavered and faded into the nothingness of the other realm. There, before me, was Many, a dark glob of pure evil. I recoiled inside, but I held my ground. I'd beaten Many before. A flutter of wings sounded beside me. Rose.

My odds of surviving this encounter were getting better by the minute.

"You!" Many snarled.

"I kicked your butt once, and I can do it again," I blustered. With Rose for backup, I had a winning team. "You're not welcome here. Crawl back into the dark hole you came from."

"I will crush you," Many said.

"You will not touch a hair on my apprentice's head," Rose said, the ground trembling as she roared her threat.

Many puffed to twice the size, a living cloud of utter darkness. "This will not be tolerated."

Rose breathed fire over my shoulder. "Welcome to the new order of the world.

Get used to heeding my words."

Many howled his displeasure and dissolved before my eyes.

"Thanks." I turned to Rose, expecting to see her in her angel or demon guise, but she towered beside me, a terrible nightmare from ancient mythology texts. Multiple eyes, oversized body, snakes writhing in her hair. I cringed and slammed into the wall behind me. Stinger fell beside me.

I couldn't breathe. Couldn't think. Couldn't run.

I was going to die.

"Fear not," Rose said, toning down the appearance to her equally terrifying demon shape. Her eyes glowed red in the murk of the spirit world. "The only way to get that bully to back down is to out-bully him."

I sipped some air, relieved it wasn't pure brimstone. Every time I thought I had a handle on who Rose was, I'd guessed wrong. Angel, demon, or something else, she hadn't killed me, so I was in her good graces for now.

I dug deep for more courage. "In that guise you would scare the worst monsters ever imagined. My heart is still about to burst out of my chest."

She smiled, showing a lot of sharp teeth. "That was the idea."

"Is it over? Did I kill Cassie? Am I going straight to hell for killing someone?"

"The being you call Cassie isn't dead, though his life force is draining away."

Her words slowly penetrated my brain fog. Cassie wasn't dead. Relief washed through me. I wasn't a killer. I studied Rose as I processed the rest of what she'd said. "Cassie's a man?"

"An evil man. He tortured and killed more than a dozen people. I can take his life if you so desire."

The thought alarmed me. "No. Cassie needs to be brought to justice. Her confession, I mean his confession, won't be enough to close the case. The sheriff requires evidence."

"You'll have it."

"What will it cost me?"

"Consider this one a freebie. I haven't had this much fun in centuries."

"Fun?" I pointed down at Stinger passed out on the floor. "My friend and I nearly died tonight."

"But you didn't. Good triumphed over evil. Like it's supposed to."

"Evil plays a dirty game."

"It's the way of the world, sweetling."

Rose started to fade. I had something I needed to ask. "Wait. You called me your

361

apprentice. Am I like you?"

Rose brightened momentarily. "You are a fledgling in the scheme of things. What you become is up to you."

I stood alone in the world of death, reeling from recent events. I'd shot someone. Nearly killed them. I'd confronted a monster and won. I'd had my own monster at my side. Hell. I might even be a monster myself. Only one thing was certain. I stood on a threshold.

I liked winning.

I liked being powerful. It was no fun to always lose. If I followed in Rose's footsteps, I might someday be like her. Strong. Powerful. Mysterious. Multidimensional.

But was that what I wanted? To spend the rest of my life fighting bullies and chasing down supernatural baddies?

I snorted. It wasn't even on my top one hundred list of things to do. Nope. I wanted to be Baxley Nesbitt Powell. A woman getting up every day and putting one foot in front of the other.

Life called to me.

My daughter, my parents, my friends. Rose's suggestion weighed me down. Like taking a bite from the tree of good and evil, I now realized the responsibility I bore as dreamwalker. Sure, I helped people talk to the dead, but the ease with which I traversed the veil had become second nature to me. I felt comfortable over there, though it was still scary as all get out.

Whatever I was, I was on my way to becoming something else. Would my friends and family fear me? Would I like myself?

A voice called to me from the distance. I knew that voice. I listened intently until I could make out the words my mom was saying.

Time to come home, Baxley.

CHAPTER 43

I opened my eyes to a familiar setting. My ceiling. My dresser. My windows and bed. I was home. Tears welled in my eyes. I shifted in the bed and had the sense of objects falling off of my bare skin.

"She's back," my father said.

My fingers closed around a small object beside my hip. A gemstone? I felt along the mattress. More similar objects. Faces crowded over me. My dad. My mom. Running Bear and Gentle Dove. Charlotte and Stinger. Elvis in Stinger's arms.

I blinked in astonishment. "Charlotte! You're alive!"

Charlotte beamed. "I am."

"I was so worried about you." I glanced at the smiling faces, needing to ground myself in reality. "What day is it?"

"Saturday morning, hon," my mom said. "We've got everything under control. You take your time waking up."

I did a bed stretch, careful to keep the covers in place. Didn't want to flash anyone. "I'm awake, but first, what's the news? Did Cassie survive? Did the sheriff arrest Ford Morrison?"

"Cassie's alive," Stinger said, "though that woman is a total waste of human flesh. You should've put her down for good. That critter was turned wrong."

"Him," I corrected. "Cassie was a him. And how's the neck?"

"Barely a scratch. I'm fine."

"I want to go with you to Florida today," Charlotte said, her face aglow with reporter's fervor. "You can give me the whole story on the way down."

Out of the corner of my eye, I saw my parents exchange a sharp look. What was that about? I'd find out soon enough. Clutching the covers around my neck, I wiggled to a sitting position in the bed. More gemstones slid to the mattress. "You're really okay?" I asked Charlotte.

"Never better," she said. "Stinger told me y'all went out to June's Folly to save me. I didn't know anything about your heroic act until the dust settled. I apologize for losing track of time. I was still talking to the movie people at the wake when everything went down. You could've knocked me over with a palm frond."

"I'm glad you're safe and sound."

"You're the best friend ever. I can't wait to tell you all the movie gossip I learned."

I held up my hand to slow the torrent of words. So many people I wanted to talk to . . . so many questions I needed answered. I glanced around at my friends and family, each of their faces glowing with love and empathy. "How about if I get dressed and meet everyone downstairs in a few minutes?"

"I'll have you a bowl of stew cooling on the table," Mom said. "You missed dinner, so you should eat something substantial for breakfast."

I didn't quite follow her logic, but I was starved. "Gimme some privacy, and I'll be right there."

After I had the room to myself, I stumbled out of bed, stiffer than normal. Shooting bad guys and wrestling with supernatural monsters sure took it out of you. If not for today's drive to Jacksonville to pick up my daughter, I'd eat the stew and go back to bed. Later. I could always sleep tonight.

I took a quick spin through the shower and jumped into jeans, a tee, and my work boots. My nice shoes had been neatly placed where they belonged on the closet's top shelf, my good slacks and blouse were in the hamper. I shuddered at what I'd been through last night in those duds. Hopefully, I wouldn't have to dress up again anytime soon or wrestle with any supernatural monsters.

The stew was delicious, as were the two cups of mom's special tea blend. Once my belly was full, I felt like myself again. I'd prearranged to pick up Larissa in mid-afternoon, so it was too early to leave for Jacksonville. First, I needed to do something about my full house.

Charlotte seemed to be biting her tongue, and from the frequent glances she shot my mom, I guess she'd been put on notice to let me eat in peace. Or at least that's the inference I drew once my mom collected my empty bowl and my best friend whipped out her notepad.

"We could get started on your interview right now," Charlotte said. "What did it feel like to solve the case?"

The barely audible murmur of Gentle Dove and Running Bear's conversation in the next room quieted. My parents stopped puttering around the kitchen, and Stinger stared at me intently. I met his gaze. We were older and wiser for last night's encounter with a crazy man, but I didn't want that in the paper. And now that the case was solved, I didn't want to think about it at all.

"Don't be mad, but I can't give you an in-depth interview. Don't write this down either. I shot someone. Shot that person with intent to harm. I can't talk about my reaction to what went down. I can tell you what happened, but my thoughts on the matter are now and will ever be, private."

A predatory glint appeared in Charlotte's narrowed eyes. "You said you'd tell me everything."

"I have to get clearance from Wayne on what's okay to tell. I could cause a lot of trouble if I release the wrong information."

Charlotte shook her head, sending her chin-length locks into a mini frenzy. "I'm not scared of Wayne."

"You should be. Wayne takes the safety of our community seriously, and so should we. The case against Cassie Korda and Ford Morrison depends on our discretion right now. If we make a misstep, they'll walk."

"That's not fair. And besides, Wayne already gave Bernard a canned press release on the case. Without your take on the psychic consultant angle, I'm screwed."

"Sorry. I have to take that position, and I'd prefer not to spin up a media frenzy about Sinclair County's psychic consultant.

I don't need loons from all over creation camped out on my lawn. That's exactly the ammunition Elizabeth and the colonel need to file a custody suit for their granddaughter. I can't take that risk."

Charlotte started to say something. Stopped. Then she stared right through me. "You've changed. Being in this job has made you harder, colder."

"I'm not the same person I was a few months ago, that's true, but I can't unsee the things I've seen. This isn't easy for me to admit, but I'm not very good at being the dreamwalker. Dad didn't have nearly this much commotion during his term."

"Different times, different dreamwalker," my father added. "For what it's worth, you're the best dreamwalker you can be. This is a darker time. I couldn't do what you've done."

Charlotte painstakingly lowered her pen to the table. Her head and shoulders drooped. "I promised Kip I'd have a story. He's holding a page one slot for my feature. I have to give him something."

How could I help my friend without losing my kid or my job? I wanted to help her. An idea slowly formed in my thoughts. "Would a related story do?"

Her head came up. "Like what?"

"Like the odd goings-on in the woods. Ford Morrison was conducting rituals that got spirits here and in the next world all stirred up."

Light glinted off Charlotte's glasses. "Before last night's mention of them, I hadn't heard a hint of a rumor about these Satanic rituals. A story like that would be breaking news. You've got more information?"

"Not me." I pointed at Stinger. "He does. His spirit guide showed him the ritual. He might be able to identify local people who participated. They might talk to you about it, off the record. Maybe Wayne would let you ask Ford about his nonlethal activities."

"I'd need someone to go on the record about the rituals, and I'd have to pull everything together by Sunday evening. That's only eighteen hours to find sources, interview them, and write the piece."

"You could get that activist waterman to comment about it. Barry Campazzi would give you a good quote about the sanctity of nature and how these outsiders disturbed the natural order of the environment. According to Barry, he observed the ritual one evening."

Charlotte nodded, her pen moving swiftly across her notepad. "Good idea. And, if I'm chasing this story, I have to skip the trip to fetch Larissa. Do you mind?"

"It's okay. I enjoy peace and quiet as much as I enjoy your company."

"About that," my mom began. "I need to talk to you privately."

I snorted. "Everyone in this world and the next seems to know my business, and I'd hazard a guess that most people in this house have seen me in my birthday suit. There's not much about a dreamwalker that's private. You can speak freely. We're all friends here."

"Elizabeth called first thing this morning." Mom paused when my father moved beside her and took her hand. "I answered the phone."

The tableau of my kitchen froze like a sepia-tinted photograph. The thunder of my heartbeat filled my ears, blotting out all other sound. I searched my mother's face. Her brows were furrowed, and she avoided my direct gaze. The aroma of her delicious stew became cloying and oppressive. I felt hot and cold at the same time.

What wasn't she telling me?

"Larissa?" I managed, rising from my chair on wobbly knees. "Tell me she's okay."

My parents exchanged a worried glance again. Dang. What was this? What could be so terrible? "Please. Say something."

"Elizabeth's decided to file papers for custody of Larissa," Mom said.

My knees gave out. I collapsed in my chair. "I-I-I don't understand."

"No one understands," my father said, coming forward to sit beside me. "That woman is spiteful and mean."

"There's more," my mom managed, her voice hitching.

I blinked back tears, willed my breaking heart to keep beating. There had to be a way out of this disaster. Had to be.

CHAPTER 44

What could be worse than losing my daughter? I'd lost so much already. It wasn't fair. Why had I allowed Larissa to visit the Powells? I'd made a terrible mistake.

I gazed down at the kitchen table, trying to hold it together. My hands. I couldn't keep them still. They shook and trembled and twitched. I yanked them back to me, sat on my fingers, but it wasn't enough. The tremors were deep inside me now, radiating from the chasm that had been my heart.

My regular senses kicked into overdrive.

I heard each breath, each rustle of fabric.

I sensed their pity. An oily, cactus-prickly, wool-sweater-in-July blanket of good intentions filled the air, needling and smothering me at the same time.

My face flamed with heat while my body shivered with cold.

Oh, God. I didn't want anyone's pity.

The enemy had taken my daughter hostage. I needed to bring her home.

Outrage lodged in my throat, along with the need to fling myself around the room like a marauding monster out of control. But that indulgence would solve nothing, would prove nothing. I had to know the whole of it.

I lifted my gaze to my mother's. "Tell me everything."

"Elizabeth's been busy," Mom continued. "She's in the process of filing a restraining order against you. She said you're an unfit parent engaged in dangerous activities, and she'll have you arrested for trespassing if you set foot on her property. You're not to have any contact with the Powells or Larissa."

"I can't believe it," I said, reeling from each blow like a spent prizefighter. "She can't do this, can she?"

"She did it."

Anger flashed through my voice lightning quick. "I have rights. They can't take my child. I'm a good mother."

"With an unconventional job," my mom gently reminded me.

I shrugged. "I can't help my job or who I am. This isn't right. Unless this action stems from Larissa, but I can't believe she's unhappy at home. I'm calling Wayne. I don't care if he's busy with the case. I need his help."

"We called him," my father said. "He's checking into options with Judge Ryals and will be here as soon as he can."

I hugged my arms to myself. I felt so cold. So alone, even though my house was full of people. Their emotions were as raw as mine, and it was too much to take in. I needed to be outside. To have a moment alone to think.

I bolted up from the chair, the wooden legs scraping loudly on the floor. "I need . . . I'm going . . . I can't . . . Air. I need air."

I clomped down the back steps, darted across the drive, and ducked into the greenhouse. Though the racks were mostly empty, there were a few seedlings I'd been nurturing, a few ailing perennials that needed a fresh start, and a few old soldiers that needed to be composted.

But not even the soothing scents of moist earth and foliage calmed the icy-hot fear roiling in my gut. I wanted to scream, but I was too scared to scream. Instead, I pressed my balled fist against my mouth.

This couldn't be. It shouldn't be. I'd done something nice in taking Larissa to visit her grandparents, and this is how they repaid me? By keeping my child? I would not stand for this. No way in hell. As soon as Wayne got here, we were driving down there and getting Larissa. That's what we'd do.

Then the Powells could sue me to their heart's content, but no judge in his right mind would remove a child from the care of a good parent. Of that I was certain. See if I would ever bend over backward for the Powells again. I didn't care that they were Roland's parents. If I had my say about it, they'd never see Larissa again.

Fury fueled my steps, propelling me out of my sanctuary. I needed to do something. I headed into the woods, stomping along the path to make sure the snakes got out of my way. So intent was I on walking off steam that I nearly plowed into my elderly neighbor.

Stepping to the side of the path to allow him to pass, I nodded hello. Good manners surfaced. "Sorry. I was deep in thought. How are you, Mr. Luther?"

"Doing good. What's got smoke shooting out your ears?"

"The Powells. Last time you and I spoke, I was about to take my daughter to visit her grandparents. I shouldn't have done it. They're trying to keep her, and I can't allow that."

"Dear Gussie. That's not right. You need

ammunition against Elizabeth Powell? I'm your man. Lemme bend your ear with stories about her moonshining daddy. Elizabeth wasn't always such a fancy lady. She was Betsy Ripple back in the day, and she spent her teen years delivering her daddy's hooch."

"If you ask me, her name is mud. I allowed Larissa to visit her, and she shafted me. Now she says she'll have me arrested for trespassing if I come to their place. She's using that threat to keep me away from Larissa."

"You call the sheriff?"

"My mom did. He's checking things out. I want to hop in my truck right this second, drive to Jacksonville, and snatch my daughter. I'm not good at waiting."

"Patience is a learned skill, but Betsy's ploy is aggravating no matter how you view it. If Wayne can't come through for you, Morley's pals at Fort Benning could get your gal. All you have to do is say the word."

Despite my anger, the corners of my lips kicked up. I could just imagine a squad of black-faced soldiers storming into the Powells' home in the dead of night. "Fun as that is to consider, I need to try the straightforward approach first."

"Pity. Betsy has it coming to her. Can't

fight karma. She always bites you in the, ah, leg."

"Check. Say, what are you doing out here in the woods?"

"Same thing as you. I like to exercise, and it's safer to walk in the woods than it is to stroll along the highway."

A horn honked in the distance. "Someone's at my house," I said. "I hope it's Wayne with good news for me."

Mr. Luther grinned. "I hope the same thing. Catch you later."

Both of us turned around and headed home. My feet wouldn't go slow. Soon I was running for all I was worth. I couldn't think of anything else but getting Larissa back. And I would get her back. I had to. For her sake and mine.

CHAPTER 45

"Training for a marathon?" Wayne asked as I pulled up short beside his black Jeep. No Saturday casual clothing for him. He wore his standard brown polo with the sheriff's logo and khaki slacks. His badge gleamed on his belt, his gun rested on his hip.

"Nope. But I'm spoiling for a fight." I gulped in big breaths and tried to gather my wits. "Please say you found a legal way for me to kick the Powells in the teeth and get my daughter back."

"Easy. We're going to drive down there and get her."

A blue jay scolded in the distance. "Can we do that?"

His expression hardened. "There'll be trouble if anybody tries to stop me. It's not my jurisdiction, but the Powells have overstepped. Their move to block you from your child won't hold up in court, and they know it. They have no grounds. If they try anything sneaky, I've got sworn affidavits from two judges attesting to your upstanding position in our community. Trust me. I'm itching to put them in their place."

The ruthless look in his eyes took me by surprise, but I was so happy for his help that I hugged him. His arms closed around me, and I allowed myself a moment to savor the comfort before I remembered this was Wayne, the biggest womanizer in the county.

I pushed away and stood my ground. "All right, then. Let's go."

He seemed to be fighting a smile. "Want to say goodbye to your folks or the motley crew infesting your house?"

"Nope. I can send my dad a quick message." Oops. I didn't mean to let Wayne know I could do that. My philosophy to date had been the less he knew about my abilities, the better. But he was helping me, so it was a fair trade.

He stared at me for a long, considering moment. "Thought so. Can you do the same with your kid?"

My jaw tightened. "Why do you want to know?"

"Might come in handy. You can invite her to come outside when we get there. That sort of thing."

I let out a slow breath. "Definitely. I can do that."

Miles and interstate signs rolled by quickly. Wayne wasn't using his lights or sirens, but he wasn't obeying the speed limit either. We'd be at the Powells' house in less than an hour.

"Everything tied up with the case?" I asked.

"Ford Morrison can't stop talking about it. That Cassie is something else. His real name is Felix Daniels. And he really is a he, though he adopted the Cassie Korda persona years ago and went about as a woman."

"Why? Was he hiding from someone?"

"He had a sealed juvie record and some misdemeanor charges as an adult as Daniels. Nothing in the system as Cassie Korda, so if he was hiding, it was hiding in plain sight."

"I don't get it. Why masquerade as something you're not?"

"He wanted to be a female actress. What better way to gain experience than to go about as a woman in daily life?"

Being a female impersonator made sense in that light. "What about her sexuality? I mean his sexuality? Oh, you know what I mean."

"Cassie dated men. Marv didn't sleep

with her, and she never forgave him for that. She found out about Ford's dark side and blackmailed him. She also compromised the financial angel for the movie. That stupid sod slept with her, and Cassie taped them in the act. Ruined his marriage and his wife left him. I'm fairly certain drugs were involved."

"Drugs? Cassie was selling drugs?"

"No. I think she drugged the moneyman. Everything I dug up indicated he's heterosexual. The homosexual charges wrecked his home life, and the money he was spending on the movie was his wife's."

"All because Cassie wanted Marv? Isn't that extreme?"

"Hell hath no fury."

Wayne didn't need to finish that statement. We'd run across angry women in other cases. We had firsthand knowledge of a scorned woman's fury.

A few more miles zoomed by. We crossed the Georgia–Florida line. "Will the case against Cassie hold up in court?"

"The evidence is rock solid. We have the knife Cassie used to gut the victims. There are blood stains by the hilt. We have Ford's recorded confession of being her accomplice. We found blackmail videos in Cassie's possession. She had her claws in Ford and in that assistant guy."

"LA? He was part of this?"

"Yeah, a small part. He rolled over once he heard Ford was in custody and singing. He took part in the woods ritual stuff. Satan worship. We don't want to encourage that around here."

"You arrest him?"

"Couldn't tie LA to the killings, though he certainly had motive and opportunity to kill Marv. Believe it or not, it isn't against the law to worship the devil. LA had no criminal record. Not even a parking ticket. I had to let him walk."

"Bummer."

"But I strongly encouraged him to leave town. Virg said LA caught a plane out of Savannah first thing this morning. The rest of the movie crew are packing up as we speak."

"And Ford? Will he get a deal?"

"He has a deal. I expect he'll get a light sentence, which will be served in a VIP facility. No general population stuff for him."

"Guess his movie career is over."

"I wouldn't count him out. He'll probably make millions off a book deal, then get to play himself in the movie about his life."

I choked out a laugh. Ludicrous as it sounded, several celebrities had parlayed notoriety into commercial success over the last few years. Ford would probably follow in their footsteps.

"Sounds like things will settle down now," I said. "With the film crew gone, the digging up of the county for Blackbeard's treasure should cease."

He shot me an enigmatic glance. "Didn't I tell you?"

"Tell me what?"

"We caught the kids doing that."

I shook my head to clear it. "Kids? What kids?"

"The graduating seniors from the high school. Instead of doing a senior prank this year, they formed a pact to search for gold. None of them wanted to go to college. They wanted to strike it rich and smoke pot on the beach for the rest of their days."

"I'm stunned. No one breathed a word of this."

"And they won't. Both of the judges who vouched for you had kids involved. I cashed in a favor for you, Powell. That means you can't tell Charlotte, ever."

Ever was a long time. But I understood. I could keep a secret, especially if it meant I'd get Larissa back. "Got it."

There were more loose ends we hadn't

discussed. "What about your other suspects?"

"Timmy Ray's a perpetual screw-up, and Barry likes to protest. No surprises there. Reed Tyler now, I did some checking on him. The reason he's been so harried and unavailable is he's been interviewing all over creation. He made the short list of applicants in two other cities. My guess is he'll announce he's leaving soon."

"Smart man. How'd he know the movie deal would sour?"

"Can't say for sure, but some folks have a knack for knowing when the honey pot is running dry."

It was hard for me to think of Sinclair County being anyone's honey pot, but good for Reed Tyler if he landed on his feet. There was no honey pot in sight for Timmy Ray. He'd probably gamble away his inheritance, and Barry would continue to make a stink about stuff he didn't like. Those two had the opportunity to change, but my guess was they wouldn't.

Traffic picked up. We passed the airport. The interstate got wider with more lanes coming and going. We veered toward the beaches and the high-rent district. My anxiety level ramped into overdrive.

Wayne cleared his throat. "We're getting

calls, you know."

My fingers coiled into fists. I willed them to open. "What kinds of calls?"

"Case calls. They're coming in from other jurisdictions in Georgia. The GBI has called twice."

"What do they want?"

"You. They want you to solve cases."

"Oh." Duh. Word was getting out about my abilities. "I don't want to traipse all over the state solving cases. I'm doing this police consulting to keep my head above water."

"I've been deflecting the calls for that reason. Plus, we've got plenty to keep you busy right here, right now, in Sinclair County."

"I need to be a mom first, then a dream-walker, then a police consultant. Somewhere in there, I need to keep my Pets and Plants business going."

Another exit came and went. "You hear anything from the army lately?" he asked.

"No. Roland's alive. I know it. Daddy knows it. But they declared him dead. They must know it's a lie. That's the only explanation I can think of for them to withhold benefits."

"You should get a lawyer. I know several who'd take the case for you."

"I'll think about it."

■ ■ ■ ■

Wayne pulled over once we cleared the gated entrance. The estate homes here had lawns as big as our entire downtown. "Do the woo-woo thing with your kid. Tell her we're here and she's to answer the door. Tell her it's time to go home."

"Will do." I didn't need to turn in the direction of the Powells' home, but I did it anyway. *Larissa. It's Mom. I'm here to take you home. Please open the door in a few minutes when the sheriff knocks. He will escort you out to the Jeep where I'm waiting.*

I faced Wayne. "Did it."

"Just like that?"

"Yep. Now what?"

"Now we hope for easy."

CHAPTER 46

Easy. How did one hope for easy? My nails dug into my clenched fists as Wayne marched up the circular driveway and knocked on the oversized door three times.

I checked with my other senses. There were four people in the house. My guess was the Colonel, Elizabeth, Larissa, and the housekeeper. And it was a minor flood of relief to recognize Larissa's energy signature. At least they hadn't hidden her from me.

Please be easy. Please don't let there be a fuss. Please let Larissa be okay with going home. Please don't let me be wrong about such an important part of my life.

The door eased open. Larissa's shining face seemed so precious and trusting. Oh, how I'd missed seeing her bright eyes, her little button nose, her happy smile, and her long braids. She beamed at Wayne and took his hand without a backward glance. They were halfway down the driveway when Elizabeth appeared in the doorway. Her clarion tones were probably heard all the way in Canada.

"What are you doing with my granddaughter?" Elizabeth demanded. "Stop where you are. Larissa, come here."

Keep coming sweetheart. I opened the Jeep door and waved to my daughter. "Mom!" She broke free of Wayne and ran happily to me. We hugged, and the ice around my heart melted. The ground beneath my feet seemed more solid. Hope surged warm, rosy, and feather light. I welcomed the joyous sensation, though I knew the battle had just begun.

"I'm calling the cops," Elizabeth yelled. "You can't do this. I have rights as a grandparent."

"You're all right?" I managed.

"I'm fine," Larissa said. "Elizabeth said you weren't coming today, that I was to stay with them. Then she said I couldn't use the phone when I wanted to call you. Why is she yelling at us? And why are you shaking, Mom?"

"I'm sorry for putting you in the middle of this. First, know that I always planned to come for you today, that you are beloved and cherished, and I'd do anything in the

389

world for you."

Larissa searched my face. "I don't understand. What's wrong? Why did Elizabeth lie to me?"

"The Powells want you to live with them permanently. I hope you want to come home with me, but I need to ask if that's the case."

"I want to go home. I've been counting the minutes until I could leave. They're fine and all, but this isn't our place." Larissa gestured to the grand, two-story columned home with picture-perfect landscaping. "This isn't me."

"It could be you." My heart wedged in my throat like a chicken bone. "If you lived with them, you would want for nothing."

"I'd want for you, Mom. Let's go home."

I tried to speak. Couldn't. I hugged her again. I glanced over her head at the house where Wayne stood. From the low rumble of his voice and Elizabeth's barred arms, I gathered the conversation wasn't going her way.

"Do you want your stuff?" I asked when Larissa stepped to my side. "I can have the sheriff collect it from your room."

"I'm all packed," Larissa said, gesturing toward the house. "My suitcase is in the foyer."

"Okay. Just a sec." I texted Wayne the information. He glanced at the phone and said something to Elizabeth. She called over her shoulder, and the colonel appeared next. No suitcase.

"What's this all about?" The colonel's angry voice boomed across the lawn.

"Why's the colonel upset?" Larissa asked.

I wanted to shield her from this, but she needed to know what was going on. "They weren't honest with us about this visit. Blocking me from picking you up was their first step in seeking full custody of you. They plan to raise you as their daughter."

Larissa's face paled, then her chin went up. "I don't want to live with them. Not now. Not ever. Come up there with me while I tell them to their faces."

"I can't. She will have me arrested for trespassing, and I'd rather you didn't go up there either. Angry adults say bad things, and you don't need to remember that about your grandparents."

"But why? Don't they like you anymore?"

"They like you better. It's hard for me to say this, but Elizabeth lied to you today because she is certain she can best provide for you. They have no shortage of money."

"There's more to life than money."

Pride swelled in me, threatening to burst

391

out of my chest like a gigantic magnolia blossom. I ruffled her bangs. "When'd you get to be so smart?"

"I'm just me."

Sirens wailed in the distance. "Uh-oh. I'd hoped it wouldn't come to this."

"What do you mean?" Larissa asked.

"It will be her word against ours. But the playing field isn't level since we're on Elizabeth's turf. We need to get back home to Georgia."

"Shouldn't what I want matter?"

"Absolutely, and it may come to that."

But I was wrong about the sirens. The cops coming to the scene knew Wayne, and they allowed us to take Larissa and her suitcase home. From the determined gleams in the Powells' eyes, I knew my victory today was only the first skirmish in the battle. They weren't done yet.

To Larissa's delight, Wayne turned on his lights and sirens for a bit once we hit the county line. At home, Larissa darted inside, and everyone was still there. Her Nesbitt grandparents, Charlotte, Running Bear, Gentle Dove, and Stinger.

"You're welcome to join us for a late lunch," I said to Wayne as we stood beside his Jeep. "It isn't much in the way of a thank you, but I owe you. I couldn't survive if they took my daughter."

"Thanks for the offer, but I can't stay."

"I'm beyond grateful. You gave up your Saturday with your family and everything."

He ran a hand through his thick hair. "I was glad for the distraction."

"Why? Is something the matter at home?"

"My wife decided to return to the living. Dottie's up and out of her bed almost all the time now, huffing and puffing like she's having a heart attack. All she'll put in her mouth is some green liquid she got off the Internet. She won't listen to me. Says I'm lost to her anyway, since I'm married to the job."

"She's right about you being hooked on your job, but for whatever it's worth, you're a damn fine cop."

A speculative look appeared in his eyes. "Coming from you, that means something."

I raised a cautionary hand. "Whoa. Not interested in a personal relationship. We're friends. Work friends, remember?"

"Yeah, but lately, I'm thinking of you in a different light."

"You think of all women in that light. Do us both a favor and focus on someone else."

"Not sure I can do that. I don't seem to be interested in other women."

My head bobbed. "I don't know how to

respond to that."

"Don't respond at all. I'm just putting it out there in the universe. You're a damn fine woman, and I like you."

I scooted around him. "No, you're not. I'm grateful you helped me save Larissa from her grandparents, but you and me? Uh-uh. Your judgment is fogged by today's events. And I do not date married men. Ever."

He studied me. "You always could read me. Even back in the day. You knew when I was sad, you knew how to cheer me up. Why didn't I place more value on that? Why did I let you slip away?"

His honesty struck a chord of respect in me. "We may be compatible, but our goals and priorities have always been different. Working together puts us in close proximity. I need to know you'll respect my wishes to keep our friendship on a professional basis."

"What if I changed?"

"If you want to change an aspect of your life, do it for yourself, not me. But I have to warn you, change is hard. I've been through a lot of changes lately, and it's disorienting. And you don't have only yourself to consider. Your entire family will be affected by any change you make."

"My boys . . ." He swore after glancing at his watch. "I'm late for a ball game. Debrief on the case on Monday morning? I'll provide donuts and coffee."

"Deal."

CHAPTER 47

On Sunday afternoon, Larissa and I found a quiet moment to take a walk in the woods together. My parents had opted to spend Saturday night with us, just in case the Powells rolled in with a battalion of lawyers, but it seemed the Powells had been thwarted for now. Yet I didn't doubt for a minute they'd keep coming.

After all, I had something they wanted.

My daughter took that moment to beam a smile my way. It shot straight through my heart. To think I'd nearly lost her. Tears welled. I blinked them back. Family and friends. Those were the things that mattered. I was blessed with both.

"Thanks for rescuing me," Larissa said. "I didn't know what Elizabeth had done. All I knew was that the air in the house got harder to breathe after she lied to me. Thicker. Like woods smoke, but not as pleasant. I packed my suitcase anyway. You would have sent word directly to me if you weren't coming."

I stepped over a fallen tree trunk in the path and turned to help her over. "Count on it. And I'm sorry you had to go through that. I wanted you to have contact with your father's side of the family, and I nearly broke us."

"They're weird, Mom."

A laugh welled up from deep inside. Ah, how the tables had turned, for a descendant of the whack-job Nesbitts to be disparaging anyone of Powell lineage. "Weird is a matter of perspective, but you have my promise. I won't ask you to visit them again. If they go through channels, they can have supervised visits with you. You and I are family in a way they can never perceive. I thought I'd lose my mind when I heard what Elizabeth planned to do."

Larissa took my hand on a wide part of the path. "Good thing you know a sheriff."

If happiness had a sound, it was the lilt of bird song, the sigh of wind through the pines, the hush of feet on a wooded path. I breathed deeply of my forest, feeling as if my heart might burst from emotion.

"I didn't want to stay," Larissa added out of the blue.

My arm twitched. "What?"

"You thought I'd be dazzled by all the things money can buy, didn't you?"

"I want what's best for you, dear heart. If you'd have come to her door and said you wanted to stay, we wouldn't be having this conversation in the woods."

"They live in a museum. There's no light inside."

"I saw plenty of lights in their house."

"Inside them. They are not like us. They are not nice people."

I stumbled and stopped. "Did they hurt you?"

"No. Nothing like that, but I had to be someone else there. I didn't like that."

Out of the mouths of babes, I thought. "I'm so sorry. I won't put you in that position again. I wanted you to know your grandparents. I tried to do the right thing."

"Elizabeth didn't. She lied. And she hurt you."

As much as I wanted to blast my in-laws, I didn't want to add fuel to this particular fire. It would combust without my help. "She hurt my feelings and made me question my fitness as a mother, but I'm a big girl and I will ensure this never happens again. I'm glad to have you home."

Larissa nodded, filling her eyes with the vibrant forest around us. "I'm glad to be home too. This place. These woods. And Mama Lacey and Pap's place. They're soothing to people like us."

"You got to be pretty smart while you were gone."

"I was always smart. I just didn't know location mattered. I understand now. I'm a Nesbitt, not a Powell."

"You're both, and you will figure that out as you go along. Are you all right with Elvis and Stinger?"

"While I was away, I missed Elvis a bunch. We used to talk at night. I mean, I talked to him. Now I know why he made me feel better. He's a therapy dog. But he needs Stinger as much as Stinger needs him. I wouldn't take him away from Stinger. That would be wrong."

My mind drew the parallels between situations. Did hers? "Stinger and Elvis will stay a part of our lives. I need Elvis at times, too. In fact, Elvis will continue to live with us, and Stinger will come and go, as long as you're okay with that."

"I'm fine, Mom. We'll have more pets. You're a pet magnet."

A dog barked in the woods. A large dog. I cocked my head to the sound.

"See?" Larissa said. "There's one now. She's calling us."

I followed my daughter to where a large, well-groomed black Labrador sat with a trailing pink checked leash. Larissa ran to her and threw her arms around the grinning canine. "This is our new dog. Her name is Maddy."

"Don't get your hopes up, dear. Her coat is glossy, and she's wearing a collar. She's someone's pet. Let me check for a tag." I fumbled around the band of the pink collar. No tag. No identifying anything. Just a dog and a girl who seemed made for each other.

Not wanting Larissa to get her heart broken, I used my senses to scan the area for people. As I ranged outward, I noted a familiar signature nearby. My watcher. He was out there. He was not moving and holding at a very low energy state. If I ever met him, I'd have to ask how he did that. Even someone like me would miss him if they didn't know what they were looking for.

My watcher was a true chameleon. And he seemed to be looking out for us. Was this pet a gift from him? Not knowing if he had extrasensory abilities, I took a chance and pulsed a very soft, very direct *thank you* his way.

"We'll have to see if we can find her owner, but let's take Maddy home with us."

"Thanks, Mom. You're the best."

Larissa and the dog bounded along the path, my daughter talking a mile a minute to her new pet. I had no doubt Maddy was a gift from the universe, a way to soften the blow of nearly being abducted by her grandparents and of having to share her beloved Elvis.

I was halfway home before my senses tingled again. The phrase *you're welcome* whispered through my thoughts. I turned and stared at the wall of pines and palmettos bordering the path. Nothing was out of place. Birds still called. The sun still shone.

What's your name?

The only sound I heard was the thumping of my heart against my ribs. Had I imagined that *you're welcome*? Another woman might have been worried that someone watched her from the woods, but my watcher seemed to have a vested interest in my welfare. I assumed the watcher was human, but what human could vary their energy signature?

I massaged my temples. There were so many things I didn't understand in this world and the next. One thing I knew for certain. There were no answers out here in the woods.

CHAPTER 48

"You doing all right, Powell?" the sheriff asked as I entered his office first thing on Monday. He rose to meet me, still very much the handsome, self-assured jock I'd known in high school. The badge and the gun were as much a part of him now as that ever-present football had been.

"I'm fine. Things at home are great, thanks to you and a stray dog that appeared in the woods yesterday. Larissa is none the worse for wear and thrilled to have a furry companion for the summer. I can't believe no one is looking for such a beautiful and well-mannered dog."

"That's good." Wayne glanced down at his hands. Cleared his throat. "I, um, want to apologize for my speaking my mind the other day. I don't want to make you uncomfortable working around me."

I waved away his comment. "In a weird way, it's okay. You are a professional on the job, and so am I. Let's move on, all right?"

"You don't want to discuss it anymore?"

The tone of his voice implied he didn't believe me. I shrugged. "Nope."

He started to say something. Stopped. Shook his head.

"What?" I asked.

"You're not like most females."

A lifetime of being known as a crazy Nesbitt stiffened my spine. "I thought that was part of the attraction."

"No." Color pinked his cheeks. "I meant I've known a lot of women." He stopped. Shook his head again. "That didn't come out right. Let me try again. Women I've known like to dissect everything a man does, over and over again. You move on to the next thing so easily. It caught me by surprise."

I sighed. "Nothing's to be gained by rehashing what happened, or didn't happen, in this case. I've got a new landscaping client to see in an hour, I have to get Larissa and her new dog to the vet by one, and two people want dreamwalks before sunset. Are you going to tell me about the case wrap-up?"

"I'm going to do you one better. Ford Morrison keeps asking for you."

I owed Ford nothing but contempt. He'd

shot at me with intent to kill. A twinge of
something caused me to clench my teeth. I
massaged the tension from my tight jaw.
"Do you have all the information you need
from him?"

"We have him cold as an accessory to the
murders, but the lawyers cut a deal with
him in order to get Cassie Korda. Ford says
he has more information, but he'll only talk
to you about it. I humored him because I
knew you'd be here this morning to sign
your statement. You curious?"

"I'd rather not see him. An entity from
beyond separated from Cassie after I shot
her, I mean him, I mean, oh, you know what
I mean. This entity is bad news."

"So? You can handle ghosts."

"Says you. Trust me, I can handle a movie
actor. A baddie from beyond is above my
pay grade, and certainly not an issue I want
to tackle first thing on a Monday morning."

"You won't be alone. I'll back you up."

"Bullets and Tasers won't stop this thing."

Wayne rubbed his chin before he answered. "How'd you stop it before?"

"I have, uh, a helper of sorts, in the spirit
world. She's pretty much a baddie herself."

"Give her a ring. I've got time."

I huffed out a disgusted breath. "It doesn't
work that way, and I'd rather leave her out

of it. You don't get something for nothing."

"That's the truth. Look, I'm interviewing the actor with or without you this morning. His lawyer is already here to make sure we play by the rules. You can watch from the next room if you like, and I'll tell him you couldn't make it."

"I'm not hiding from anybody." Oops. That came out stronger than I planned. "I mean, I'll sit in the room with you, but you should be prepared for anything."

"You got chops, Powell. And I'm intrigued. Let's do it."

Even clad in jumpsuit orange and handcuffs, Ford Morrison carried off a larger than life appearance as he entered the interview room. It wouldn't have startled me to see a film crew following him down the hall or if a director had suddenly started orchestrating the lighting.

I deposited the empty paper coffee cup in the observation room's trash. Despite what Wayne thought, I didn't have chops of any kind, but my extrasensory intuition was on high alert. I patted the sack of crystals in my pocket, brushed my hand over the moldavite necklace I wore. Something cold leaned against my legs.

I jolted with recognition. "Oliver? What

are you doing here?" The ghost dog didn't answer of course, but even so, I had backup. Even a nonsensitive would feel Oliver's chilly presence. I gave a light pat in the vicinity of his head.

The door snicked open. "Ready?" Wayne asked.

"Ready."

Ford Morrison gazed at the table when I entered the room. His lawyer, Kurt Boyette, watched us warily.

"My consultant is present as you requested," Wayne said after we were seated. "I've upheld my end of the bargain. What do you have for me, Morrison?"

"I'd like to speak with Ms. Powell alone," Morrison said.

Still no eye contact from him, and I couldn't stop staring at him. Despite his casual posture in the chair, there was a coiled tension in his jaw, a stricture of his neck muscles. My breathing shallowed out as I scoped the room with all my senses for a threat. Four people and one ghost dog were all I detected. I stared at the actor and waited.

"Not happening," the sheriff said. "You got two minutes to tell me what is so all-fired important, or it's back to your cell you go."

"Turn off the recording devices." Morrison nodded at the video camera mounted in the corner of the ceiling. "I'll tell you everything about Hollywood Knights. That's knights like medieval knights."

"You're wasting my time."

The actor glanced up at the flashing red light on the camera. He seemed to shimmer and then he appeared to have increased in charisma and stature. His voice rang with authority. "Hollywood Knights is an invitation-only group of leaders in the film industry. Our mission is to bring Satanism to the masses through the big screen. We make sure symbols and certain décor elements are used on the sets, and we adjust our lines to include key phrases during filming."

"You're trying to brainwash America through film?" Wayne scoffed. "You're not the first and probably won't be the last either. This has no relevance to our case. Give me something useful, or we're done here."

"There's a reason we filmed in Sinclair County. We wanted access to your dreamwalker."

Alarmed, I sat up straighter, exchanged a look with Wayne.

"Go on," the sheriff said.

"We've targeted people around the globe like her. Targeted and tested them." He faced me finally, the center of his eyes filled with crazy. "You think this was about the murder of two innocent victims. Marv and Bee were undergoing rituals to join Hollywood Knights. They acted out that final death scene for your benefit, Dreamwalker."

An icy sensation sleeted through my veins. Crazy as Ford was, he was telling the truth. The visions from Marv and Bee weren't the typical sort I received, and there had been so few of them. Bottom line, I'd been played.

"What do you want from me?" I asked.

"You." He leveled his gaze at me, and I couldn't look away. The full force of his charisma and something else chained me to the chair. I couldn't breathe. The room wavered.

Wayne swore and yelled at me to move. I couldn't budge, couldn't do anything. Wayne grabbed my shoulders and the power Ford focused through me zapped the sheriff. I heard him hit the floor as darkness descended.

I blinked in the murk. Oliver pressed up against my spiritual legs. Good dog, I thought. Where am I, and who has me?

The murk thinned, and I became aware of

a presence of a large host of spirits. Though their faces were mostly obscured, I recognized Marv and Bee nearby. The spirits chanted in a monotone, the sound grating like fingernails on a chalkboard. The noise rose to a deafening roar. Even though it wasn't actual noise, I clamped my hands over my ears.

My tattoos heated. Rose. The scent of fire and brimstone stunk in my nose.

"I didn't call you." I couldn't afford to keep giving this entity hours of my life.

"No charge for this visit." Rose smiled her Gordian smile, the one that made me quake in fear for my life. "I allowed you to be brought here so you'd know what we're up against. The enemy is strong."

"I don't like this."

"No one does. But the fight between good and evil wages across time and space, among the living and the dead. Choose wisely, Dreamwalker."

"I'm not choosing evil. Are you nuts?"

"Then why'd you end up here? This is their power play for your soul. Fight back, or they win."

Easy for her to say.

"I heard that."

"What do I do?"

"Follow your gut."

"I renounce evil," I shouted at the assemblage. "I renounce everything about you."

Rose nodded encouragingly.

I turned to a different compass direction and issued my proclamation again and again. Rose faded. The host faded. The sheriff's office came into view. Ford's lawyer seemed to be doing something to Wayne, who lay prone on the floor.

"Get away from him," I yelled.

Oliver barked at the man, and he scurried away like a crab.

"Who are you people?" the lawyer asked. He gathered up his briefcase and fled the room.

I crawled over to Wayne, relieved that his heartbeat was steady. With a hand on the crystals in my pocket and the other on his arm, I sent a surge of positive energy into the downed sheriff. He stirred immediately.

"What happened?" Wayne asked.

"Not much." I offered him a hand up, which he took.

Wayne glared at Ford, who sat with hunched solders and bowed head. "We are not amused."

Ford said nothing.

Wayne glanced at me. "You all right?"

I touched my moldavite pendant, felt the

410

familiar flush of well-being. "Yeah. I am."

Wayne checked the prisoner's handcuffs then ushered me from the room. When we were alone in his office again, he propped a hip against his desk. "Report, Powell."

My thoughts whirled. Telling Wayne everything was out of the question. "Ford is what he's purported to be. A member of a dangerous group that incites evil and disharmony in the world. With his personal charisma, he draws others into their ranks."

"You learn anything from the dreamwalk we can prosecute him with?"

I shook my head. "Sadly, no. Worse, I now believe Marv and Bee were part of this Hollywood Knights movement, and they sacrificed their lives for the cause. Their dreamwalks were carefully staged throughout our investigation to conceal their involvement. They knew they were going to die. They knew when and where it would happen. They were complicit in their terminations."

"Doesn't matter. In the eyes of the law, it's still murder. Another person ended their lives."

"I need to go."

"When the dust from this case settles, we need to talk about a few of the requests coming in. Law enforcement units from all over are sending information to me on cold and current cases."

"We've been over this. I'm not interested."

"You can't hide from what you are. You read some of these case files, and you'll change your mind. You can do a lot of good in this world."

There was that word again. Good. I called myself an agent for good, but I'd reached my limit of compassion for the day. "Not happening. I can't handle anyone else's problems today. I have work to do and a daughter to raise. I've explained my priorities to you. Helping solve cases isn't first or second on my list. Please do us both a favor and don't mention this again."

"Roger that."

Later that evening, I sat on my back porch, Oliver beside me on the floor. Larissa and her new dog Maddy romped in the yard, laughing and barking and making happy sounds. Stinger was inside watching the news with Elvis, Muffin, Sulay, and little Ziggy.

We'd made it through another day.

The Powells hadn't tried again for Larissa today, so I felt more confident that they weren't invincible. I had family and friends to help me fight them in the real world. I wasn't alone in this battle for my daughter's custody or in the supernatural ones I encountered solving crimes.

I took stock of my life. In the last week, I'd thwarted my in-laws, caught two killers, and rebuked a host of evil spirits. I'd gained a dog ghost companion and struck up a lasting friendship with a medium. Charlotte and I were exploring how to be friends with our conflicting job responsibilities.

My father and I had searched extensively for my husband among the dead. Roland's spirit wasn't there, so I believed Roland was alive. My husband was still out there, on this side of the dirt, somewhere off the grid. Time had dulled the heartache, though I still felt empty. I'd become resigned to Roland's absence and less frantic about his well-being. Wherever he was, I couldn't help him. He'd have to find his own way home.

I sent out a ping into the woods, curious to see if Larissa and I were alone. A life force registered off to my left. A familiar low-energy signature. My watcher.

How many women would feel comfortable knowing someone was out there watching them? I did. My watcher always turned up when I needed him. Whether karma or serendipity was at play in his scheduling, I couldn't say.

A niggling feeling urged me to take a closer look at Mr. Luther. He seemed quite content wandering through my woods. My elderly neighbor wasn't the watcher, of that I was certain, but I was beginning to believe Mr. Luther knew about the watcher. If so, he might know the watcher's identity.

I considered the possibilities. The watcher could be my husband Roland. It might be Mr. Luther's son Morley or one of his Ranger buddies from Fort Benning. It might be a friend or foe who hoped Roland would show his face.

I wanted it to be Roland. But the dampened energy signature. That didn't feel like my husband. Could an energy signature change due to a life event? Could a person purposefully manipulate their life force? Was that the kind of work Roland had done for the army?

It irked me that I couldn't answer any of those questions. I'd learned a lot these past two years of being on my own. I'd learned to question everything. The naive young woman who'd left town with her sweetheart all those years ago was no more. The savvy scrambler who returned to Sinclair County believed in answers. She didn't trust blindly.

She'd also never had a telepathic conversation with her husband. My watcher in the woods was a mystery, which intrigued me. Since becoming a police consultant, my curiosity about people and events that impacted my life seemed limitless. I glanced at the woods again, those ribbons of tree trunks, summer green crowns, and humid shade in between.

Common sense said to leave well enough alone.

But I was flush with the double victory of solving the case and of beating the Powells. I was the dreamwalker, the person unafraid of traveling between worlds. I didn't want to be an ostrich with her head in the sand.

Oliver stirred and sat up, as if he knew what I was thinking. He nodded his head. I shrugged off my concerns and sent the watcher a telepathic message.

I know you're out there.

I'm not the most patient person in the world, but I kept an inner ear attuned just in case the watcher acknowledged my effort. And, just when I'd given up, when Oliver had faded from the porch and Larissa had gone inside for a snack, a faint reply came back.

Leaving soon. Be safe.

I meant to play it cool and wait to respond, but I churned out a quick response. *Who are you?*

Crickets chirped. Squirrels chattered. Birds called their good-nights. Twilight deepened. A car passed on the road in front of my house. Still I strained to listen, hoping and waiting.

The screen door creaked open. Larissa poked her head out. "Mom? You coming in? I made popcorn to go with the TV show."

"Coming." With a last glance at the deeply shadowed woods, I rose and turned to my house. Light spilled out of the kitchen window, welcoming, warm, and wholesome. I may not be a traditional mother, but I was the best mom I knew how to be.

Family and friends came first. Sure, I had a foot planted in the land of the living and the dead, but hands-down, I chose the living every time.

ABOUT THE AUTHOR

Formerly a contract scientist for the U.S. Army and a freelance reporter, mystery and suspense author **Maggie Toussaint** has thirteen published books. Her Five Star mysteries include *Gone and Done It, Bubba Done It, Death, Island Style,* and three titles in her Cleopatra Jones series: *In for a Penny, On the Nickel,* and *Dime If I Know.* Her latest mystery, *Doggone It,* is Book Three in her Dreamwalker series about a psychic sleuth. Maggie won the Silver Falchion Award for Best Cozy/Traditional Mystery. Additionally, she won a National Readers' Choice Award and an EPIC Award for Best Romantic Suspense. She lives in coastal Georgia, where secrets, heritage, and ancient oaks cast long shadows. Visit her at *www.maggietoussaint.com.*

The employees of Thorndike Press hope you have enjoyed this Large Print book. All our Thorndike, Wheeler, and Kennebec Large Print titles are designed for easy reading, and all our books are made to last. Other Thorndike Press Large Print books are available at your library, through selected bookstores, or directly from us.

For information about titles, please call:
  (800) 223-1244

or visit our Web site at:
  http://gale.cengage.com/thorndike

To share your comments, please write:
  Publisher
  Thorndike Press
  10 Water St., Suite 310
  Waterville, ME 04901